Other Books by

Melanie Schuster

Lucky in Love
Until the End of Time
My One and Only Love
Let It Be Me
A Merry Little Christmas
Something to Talk About
A Fool for You
Wait for Love
Chain of Fools
The Closer I Get to You

Before the Storm

Melanie Schuster

ARABESQUE®

Schuster

BEFORE THE STORM

An Arabesque novel

ISBN-13: 978-0-373-83002-2
ISBN-10:   0-373-83002-5

www.kimanipress.com

Printed in U.S.A.

As usual, I have been so richly blessed with angels I have a lot of people to thank. First, Elroy Goffney for taking such good care of my Lolly that she fell in love with you, and for your generosity and understanding in letting me take advantage of your wife's time. You are truly a brother to me. To Betty Dowdell, my sister and friend, for your prayers and your comfort; you're always there for me no matter what hour of the night or day. I could not have made it through this without you. To Mrs. Shirley Bady, who continues to care for me. To my friend Susie Addison as well as her nephews Jeremiah and Simon for their assistance and care.

For her understanding and patience, my editor, Evette Porter. And to Janice Sims for the same. To the members of my book club, you ladies kept me so lifted in prayer I never had to wonder who had my back; you all were amazing in the love and support you sent my way.

To my sister Jennifer for all her support and her understanding and just for being there for me— thanks a billion. And to my nieces, Jilleyin, Amariee and Jasmine, thanks for all the love and concern.

A special thank-you to Dr. Gerald Schell, Steve Leckie and the staff of Fields Neurosurgery Institute for the compassionate care you all gave me.

Thanks to Clint for all your concern and your daily calls to cheer me up, as well as all the good conversations.

And as always, to Jamil. I couldn't ask for a better friend if I had one custom made from scratch. Thanks just for being you.

Prologue

On what seemed to be the hottest day Chicago had ever experienced, Paris Deveraux, soon to be Paris Argonne, made a discovery that would forever change the lives of her entire family. The discovery certainly wasn't the perfect fabric for her wedding dress, although that's why she and her friend Ruth Bennett were shopping like there was no tomorrow. The dress was being made by another friend of Paris's, but time was of the essence since the wedding had been moved up from December to August. Ruth lived in Chicago and knew where all the wholesalers were, so she suggested Paris come up from Atlanta to look for material. Paris agreed at once since she adored Ruth and loved to spend time with her. But the heat was starting to get to both women and something cold to drink seemed like a great idea.

"Ruth, that place looks cute, let's try it," Paris said, gesturing to a small café with an awning and window boxes full of flowers.

Ruth looked where Paris was pointing and agreed. "They have good food, I've been there before. Let's go before we melt right here in the street."

Soon they were seated in the cool dining room sipping iced tea while they looked at the menu. "What looks good, Paris?"

Paris didn't answer, as she was staring across the dining room with a dazed expression on her face. Ruth looked at her and waved her hand in her direction. "Hello, hello, are you in there? What are you looking at? You look like you've seen a ghost."

She still didn't answer; she just picked up her glass of tea and tried to drink it all at once. She put the glass down and blushed as a tiny hiccup escaped. "That's what I get for guzzling that tea, but I couldn't help it. There's someone here I haven't seen in a long time. I didn't even know she was in Chicago," she said distractedly.

Ruth turned in her chair as she tried to see what Paris was seeing. "Well, who is it? Is she visiting royalty or something? You look like Beyoncé or Fantasia just walked in. If it's somebody really important get me an autograph. Ooh, look, they have crab salad," she said.

"It's not anyone like that," Paris said softly. "Her name is Maya and she was married to my brother Julian. She was like a sister to me."

Ruth raised her eyebrows. "I always think of your brothers as bachelors, I forget that one of them was actually married once."

"Yes, Julian is the only one who married. It ended

so abruptly we were all shocked because they seemed so happy together," Paris said sadly. "We all loved Maya and it was hard to accept that she wasn't a part of our family anymore. But now…" Her voice trailed off.

"Now *what,* sweetie?" Ruth's voice was full of concern.

"Now everything is about to change," Paris said with determination in her eyes.

"How are things going to change, sweetie? Just because you saw your brother's ex-wife, something's going to change?"

"No, it's not because I saw *her,* Ruth, but because I saw the person *with* her." Paris put her napkin on the table and pushed back her chair. "Order the chicken salad sandwich on black bread for me and a cup of fruit salad. I'll be back in a few minutes."

Ruth watched her walk across the restaurant and suddenly it became clear where Paris was headed. She dropped her menu as she watched Paris reach her destination. Ruth saw everything and she knew at once that Paris was right. Everything was about to change all right; the Deveraux family was in for a big upheaval.

There's never a dull moment with this family, Ruth thought. And from what she was seeing across the small restaurant, there would be a lot of *not*-dull moments for some time to come. *I just hope they can handle this one.*

Chapter 1

Five months ago...

"Aunt Ruth, you look fabulous. Are you sure this is just for Paris's benefit?"

Ruth Bennett looked at the smiling face of her niece, Benita Cochran Deveraux, and gave her a crooked grin in return. Ruth traveled frequently since her early retirement from her nursing career and one of her favorite stops was her niece's spacious and beautiful Atlanta home. She had just entered the great room of the house where Benita was relaxing with her husband Clay and playing with their five children.

"I admit that I agreed to this meeting with Paris's father just so that I could get her to invite Titus. Yes, it was interfering of me, but everyone knows those two belong together and I thought a little push in the right direction wouldn't hurt anything," she said. "But I have to confess that the prospect of meeting her father is intriguing me for some reason. *Me,* the original I-hate-blind-dates woman," she laughed. "Mark my words, this could be the worst mistake of my life and I have no one to blame but myself. I should have just said no when Paris invited me to dinner to meet her father, but I had to try and get cute by telling her I'd come if she invited Titus Argonne. And she was woman enough to take me on, too! So now I'm stuck," she said ruefully. "But I'm still, oddly enough, intrigued. What could that possibly mean, do you suppose?"

"It means you're going to enjoy yourself tonight," Clay drawled in the deep voice that often startled people hearing it for the first time. "The judge is a great guy. You'll like him, I guarantee it."

Ruth looked at her beloved niece curled up on the oversized sofa with her handsome husband while their children played a noisy board game on the coffee table. Benita was radiant, as always, and it was obvious that her husband was a major part of that joy. Every Deveraux man Ruth had ever met was handsome to a startling degree, possessed of a keen intelligence and completely devoted to his mate. A sudden tremor went down her spine as it hit her that she was about to meet yet another Deveraux man and she wondered if he could possibly be as potent as his nephews.

Benita accurately read her aunt's thoughts and gave her a look of contrived innocence. "It's just dinner, Aunt Ruth. Paris is a good cook and you love her company. And you really will like her daddy, that is, if you like handsome men who also happen to be brilliant and charming," she said teasingly.

If Trey, the oldest son of Benita and Clay, hadn't brought her coat at that very moment, Ruth might have bailed on the whole evening. Instead, she slipped her arms into the cream-colored cashmere coat that Trey held out to her. She patted him on the cheek, thinking that he represented the next generation of gorgeous, engaging men of the Deveraux clan.

"Thank you, darling. You all have a wonderful evening, because that's what I plan to have," she said with her usual aplomb. Trey walked her out to the car she was using that night. He'd been schooled in proper behavior by his parents, but he didn't have to be told to do things like that—it was just part of his nature now. His manners were excellent, even at his young age. He also had a word of advice for his great-aunt.

"You're going to have fun tonight. The judge is the coolest guy I know, outside of my dad and my uncles. And he's *really* going to like you, Aunt Ruth, you're just his type." Making sure she was comfortably seated in the car, Trey kissed her on the cheek and said good-night, then watched as Ruth drove down the long driveway.

Now what does that youngster know about some-body's type? Trey is too wise for his years, she mused as she maneuvered the Jaguar down the long drive. Ruth shivered a little as she drove, and it wasn't just because of the cold winter night. As much as she hated to admit it, she was uncharacteristically anxious about the dinner party. Paris was a wonderful young woman and Ruth was very fond of her even though she knew

Paris to be an enthusiastic and unrepentant matchmaker. Ruth had told herself that the only reason she'd agreed to the dinner was so she could make Paris invite the young man she was in love with. They'd had a spat and it seemed that the only way they were going to get back together was if the issue were forced. In truth, however, Ruth was rather looking forward to meeting a single, age-appropriate man, and Paris's widower father certainly fell into that category. Why she was as giddy as a teenager she couldn't fathom.

Ruth was fifty-four years old and looked ten years younger. She had resigned her commission as an army officer to care for the children of her late sister. After the last one was safely in college, she had resumed her nursing career. She had interesting hobbies, friends all over the globe, a condo in Chicago—which was her home base—and a beachfront home in Hawaii. She was absolutely in her prime and there was no reason whatsoever for her to be having butterflies at the thought of meeting a new man. She laughed out loud at the very notion. "I'm too old for this mess. That's what I get for trying to be cute and getting in Paris's business. And now I'm talking to myself. Whoever said no good deed goes unpunished was right," she murmured as she turned the volume up on the car stereo to hear her Bonnie Raitt CD better.

Paris was busy preparing the salad greens for the meal when her father entered the kitchen. He turned around so she could view him from all sides, smiling as he did so. "Well, do I look to suit you?" he asked dryly. "I can go change if I don't." He struck a pose like

Ben Stiller in *Zoolander* and got the expected laughter from his only daughter.

"You look wonderful. Nice pleated trousers, nice Italian loafers, very nice sweater. Is that the cashmere one I gave you for Christmas?"

Mac Deveraux looked down at the dark green pullover with the polo-styled collar and nodded. "Right on all counts, except the shoes came from Payless."

"They did not," Paris contradicted him. "Can you lend me a hand so I can run and get changed?"

"You're right about the shoes. Kmart was having a sale," he replied, ducking as Paris shook a fist at his silliness. Mac obligingly took over setting the table, although he pointed out that Paris looked perfectly lovely in what she was wearing, which was a pair of flannel drawstring pants and a Tulane sweatshirt.

"Ha-ha. I look like a train wreck and you know it. Give me twenty minutes and you won't know me. I want this dinner to be really nice, and that means I have to look good, too." She looked at her father with contrition in her eyes. "You're sure you don't mind that I invited some people over?"

Mac leaned against the doorway that separated the kitchen from the dining room. "Not at all, cupcake, although I sense that your matchmaking proclivities are coming to the fore again. You're trying to hook your old man up, aren't you? When are you going to give it a rest? You're a terrible matchmaker, baby."

Paris blushed pink as she protested. "That's not true, Daddy. I'm an excellent matchmaker. Look at Marcus and Vera, see how happy they are? That was all due to me, thank you very much. And Maya and

Julian, they were a perfect match," she said with a sad look in her eyes.

She had introduced her oldest brother, Julian, to Maya and they had fallen in love and eloped after a tempestuous and romantic courtship. Unfortunately, the marriage had ended in divorce five years earlier, something that caused a lot of pain not just to Julian but the whole family. Maya was a lovely person and Paris had loved her dearly—in fact, she was much loved by the whole family. Her father sensed her distress and went to her side to put his arm around her shoulders. "Paris, all you did was to introduce them. Everything else they did on their own," he reminded her. "They're the ones who got divorced—you had nothing to do with it."

Paris hugged her father back, reveling in the comforting, familiar smell of his cologne. Her words were slightly muffled in his shoulder as she answered him. "But they were so happy together. And I still miss her, too. I haven't heard a word from her since she left. I don't even know where she is," she mumbled.

The chiming of the doorbell made Paris jump and stare at the clock on the kitchen wall. "Oh, shoot! Leave it to Ruth to be on time, darn it. Daddy, can you get the wine out of the cooler in the garage while I get the door?"

She sped off, leaving her amused parent to go through the pantry to the garage which held a specially designed wine cooler. He selected two bottles that would go well with the roast capon Paris was serving and put them in the refrigerator for a few minutes so they wouldn't lose their chill. He then went into the living room to greet Paris's guest. The two women were engrossed in conversation when Mac entered. He was glad the introductions spared him from speaking for a moment because he couldn't have gotten a word out if someone had paid him. Ruth Bennett was gorgeous. Drop-dead, heart-stopping gorgeous, in point of fact.

She was about five foot nine and had a sleek, athletic figure with long, lissome legs. Her hair was short and sassy and she even had an audacious long lock in the back, a tail that curled around her neck and was tipped with gold. Her jade-green eyes were large and full of laughter, and the green color was highlighted by the dress she wore, a dark green knit that fitted her perfectly and allowed her shapely legs to show to their best advantage. Her smile was warm and genuine and it not only lit up her face, it made everything around her seem to glow.

Paris was wise enough not to gloat; she merely said, "Daddy, this is my dear friend Ruth Bennett. Ruth, this is my daddy, Julian McArthur Deveraux." It was hard for her not to give in to a big silly grin when she saw how they were looking at each other, but she resisted the impulse to shout "See? Told ya so!" Instead she excused herself to get changed, saying she'd be back in a moment.

Ruth had extended her long slender hand when Paris made the introductions and Mac had taken it in his big capable one. Her hand felt warm and soft to his touch and he couldn't think of a reason to let it go, so he didn't. She said "Hello, nice to meet you" in a low, soothing voice and the sound of it was like the mesmerizing scent of sandalwood incense mixed with the seductive sound of jazz—melodic and smoky. He smiled down at her for a long moment before answering. "It's my pleasure to meet you, Ruth. Let's sit down and get to know each other, shall we?" And he led her over to the long, comfortable sofa in the living room to do just that.

Ruth tried to discipline her face as she studied Mac, but it was difficult, even for a woman as worldly and sophisticated as she. Julian Deveraux was an unexpected surprise, and a very pleasant one at that. Of course, with a daughter as stunning as Paris, it was only logical that he would be good-looking, but it wasn't just his classically sculpted features that drew her attention. There was something magnetic about the warmth of his smile and the intensity of his eyes. He looked like what he was, an intelligent, charismatic man who appeared to share her pleasure in their meeting. She settled back against the soft cushions of the sofa and felt her whole body relax. She and Mac were looking at each other with appreciation and frank interest, which should have felt uncomfortable, but for some reason, it didn't. On the contrary, it felt as if they had known each other for some time. The ease with which they were conversing was pleasant and exhilarating at the same time. It was his eyes, she decided. Long-lashed, clear and sexy, they possessed a rakish twinkle that made her pulse jump.

Look at me, she thought. *The next thing you know I'll be giggling like the proverbial schoolgirl. I'm too old for this kind of attraction.*

Ruth tried not to stare at Mac, but with him smiling at her like she was a movie star it wasn't possible to ignore him or even feign indifference to him. So she got even more comfortable and gave him a brilliant smile of her own. There was no point in trying to be coy;

Julian Deveraux was much more than she'd counted on. She was taking his measure in great detail, gradually assessing him, learning to enjoy the warmth in his eyes and his masculine scent, when she was suddenly accosted by a large cat with thick fur in an improbable shade of blue. Laughing in surprise, she allowed the big fluffball to lick her fingers in rapture as he savored her scent.

"You must be Aidan's cat," Ruth told the handsome feline. "I've heard a lot about you."

"This is Merlin and he does indeed belong to Paris's roommate. He apparently approves of you heartily, which is a rare occurrence. Most people don't pass muster with his highness."

Ruth raised an eyebrow when she heard the familiar phrase. "Pass muster? You sound like an ex-military man," she said.

"Absolutely," Mac said with a smile. "My family couldn't afford to send us to college, so I went into the army."

"We have something in common there," Ruth told him. "I was in the army, too."

Mac's expression changed at once. She could tell from his look of avid interest that he was about to begin asking the questions that would normally follow a disclosure like that, but just then Paris entered the living room with a big bowl of roses. She was followed by Titus Argonne, who was looking at her with an unguarded longing in his eyes. Ruth restrained her look of amusement. Young love was such a sweet and tender fruit, something to be handled gently, she thought. After the introductions were made, she left the room with Paris to help her put the finishing touches on the meal.

Paris's irrepressible humor came to the surface as she teased Ruth. "So what do you think? My daddy's something else, isn't he?"

Ruth gave every appearance of disinterest as she put a napkin into a basket for serving the bread. She was going to pretend she hadn't heard a word Paris had said, but she was far too honest for that and it wouldn't have fooled the younger woman in the least.

Ruth had the bread basket in one hand and the smaller basket of parmesan crisps for the salad in the other. Putting one hip against the door between the dining room and the kitchen, she gave Paris a sultry smile.

"Your father is everything you said he was. And a whole lot more."

Chapter 2

The dinner was superb in every way, from the ambience to the conversation to the food. Mac couldn't remember when he'd had such a good time, or when he'd seen his daughter so radiantly charming. Like every doting father, he wanted nothing but the best for his children, especially his only girl. He kept her brothers in check about overprotecting Paris, but he was also guilty of exercising that same trait. Tonight she was the perfect hostess, elegant and sophisticated in every detail but with a down-home warmth that was irresistible. His little girl had grown up, he had to admit it. She was obviously a bright, capable career woman who could take care of herself, but it didn't stop him from interrogating Titus Argonne about the person who was threatening her safety.

Paris hosted her own TV show, a very popular and successful one. In recent weeks she had been the recipient of several threatening—explicitly threatening—letters. Her show was part of the media empire known as the The Deveraux Group, which was owned by her fiercely loving cousins. When they were informed of the letters, they erected a tight circle of investigation and protection around her. At the center of that circle was Titus Argonne, owner of one of the leading investigative firms in the country. Mac had little doubt that the man could do his job, but despite his gut instinct he had to have that man-to-man talk with Titus.

First, however, he had to tear his eyes away from Ruth as she and Paris left the room. Her walk was both self-assured and seductive, deftly reinforcing the first impression he'd had of Ruth Bennett, which was that she was the most appealing woman he'd met in some time. He rubbed the cleft in his chin with his thumb while the two women disappeared into the kitchen through the dining room. Merlin, the big Russian Blue cat, suddenly fled the room when his efforts to unnerve Titus backfired. He'd been staring at Titus while emitting a low growling sound deep in his throat, but it didn't impress Titus at all. All he did was lean forward and say "Boo" to Merlin and it startled him so badly he scampered. Although both men laughed, Mac's expression changed first and he gave the younger man a look devoid of any humor whatsoever.

"You're good at keeping cats at bay, but how are you with humans? Are you sure you can keep my baby girl safe?" Mac paused to observe the subtle shift in the other man's demeanor. His posture became erect and a steely determination replaced his smile. His slightly slanted eyes lost their normal blue gray tint, turning a pale silver color. Oddly enough, Mac was reassured by the change in the man who was supposed to be protecting his daughter. The words Titus spoke were also reassuring; in minutes he was able to convince Mac that under no circumstances would Paris come to harm.

He leaned forward with a look that was as alive with passion as the words he spoke. "Sir, as long as I'm alive no one can put their hands on Paris and live. I have the best trained staff in the free world and even if something should happen to me, their only mandate is to keep her safe and bring whoever is doing this to justice. I can understand your concern about your daughter, but you have to trust me, sir. Nothing is going to happen to her."

Mac was once again impressed by the sincerity he saw blazing from the other man's eyes. The depth of emotion in his eyes was enough to convince him, but he had another question to ask. "So what happened between you and Paris? It's obvious that you have strong feelings for her. I could see that at John and Nina's wedding reception," he said while mentally recalling the passionate kiss he'd witnessed at that happy event.

Titus gained more points by not pretending he didn't know what Mac was talking about. He was about to answer the question in detail but his reply was forestalled by the reappearance of Ruth and Paris with hors d'oeuvres. Both men rose as the women entered the room and Mac gallantly took the tray from his daughter's hands. He looked at the unguarded look of desire on Titus's face as he stared at Paris. It both touched him and amused him because he was pretty sure he was looking at Ruth in a similar fashion. The notion wasn't in any way unpleasant; on the contrary, it was highly stimulating, like everything else about Ruth Bennett.

After the dining room and kitchen had been put to rights and the dessert was served in the living room, Titus complimented Paris again on the delicious meal. "Everything was wonderful, Paris. I had no idea you could cook like that or I'd have been camped out on your doorstep," he admitted.

Paris looked pleased at his comments, but as usual she was disarmingly honest. "Thanks, but I borrowed just about every recipe. The wild rice stuffing is from Ceylon, the spinach and pear salad is from Vera and the sweet potatoes are Bennie's," she said cheerfully.

"Well, it was all good, honey. It doesn't matter where the recipes came from, you prepared them all beautifully," Ruth told her. "Especially the dessert. These are probably the best brownies I've ever eaten in my life and I've had plenty because I'm an ol' chocolate fiend from way back."

Paris blushed even pinker this time. "Guilty again. That isn't my recipe, either. Maya taught me how to make those," she said, glancing at her father.

Soon after dessert and coffee, Ruth announced it was time for her to go. "I need to get back over to Bennie and Clay's while I can still drive. It was a wonderful evening, Paris. The meal and the company were superb and you're an outstanding hostess," she praised.

"I agree wholeheartedly, cupcake. This was a fantastic evening and it's not going to end until I follow Ruth home to make sure she gets there safely. I'll get our coats and we'll be off," Mac said.

Titus said he would stay with Paris until Mac returned, a suggestion that seemed perfectly reasonable to everyone except Paris. Her smile faltered when she realized that she would be alone with the man she was trying to avoid. Her eyes turned to Ruth in a silent plea and Ruth just squeezed her shoulder and gave her a kiss on the cheek. "Talk to you tomorrow, sweetie," was all she said before taking Mac's arm and going out to the waiting Jaguar, which Mac had thoughtfully started for her so it would be nice and warm. Once he had her seated, he waited until she pulled out of the drive before getting into his vehicle to follow her.

There was something comforting in knowing Mac was just a car's length behind her. Despite the fact that she was a totally independent woman who wasn't looking for a serious entanglement, she had to admit she enjoyed the feeling of being cared for even if it was just a little while. *And this is precisely why I should have avoided this man like the plague,* she thought. But even that pragmatic thinking wasn't enough to remove the smile from her face.

She was still beaming when she parked at the top of Clay and Bennie's long driveway and Mac offered her his hand in helping her out of the car. Her ungloved hand enjoyed the heat and strength of his touch and they walked to the door, chatting amiably as they did so. She liked looking at him, liked the way he carried himself and the sound of his voice. And she liked it even more when he took the keys from her hand to open the door for her. But before he performed that little task, he leaned down and kissed her very gently on the lips.

He murmured an apology, saying, "I shouldn't have done that without asking."

By way of an answer, Ruth pulled his head down to her level and kissed him back, softly but firmly. "There," she said. "Now we're even. I didn't ask, either. Would you like to come in for coffee? Then we can talk about our lapse of manners and what we can do about it."

In a short time they were seated in the now-empty family room, drinking the decaf tea they'd opted for instead of coffee. They sat next to each other on a long leather couch and enjoyed the fragrant steam that emanated from the big mugs almost as much as being with each other. Ruth had one leg curled up and the other one was stretched out long and lissome so that anyone who happened to be interested in a glance could get it easily. In this case, it meant that Mac could look with great admiration while they talked. The conversation was easy and varied; they talked about a little of everything. Finally they both put their cups on the coffee table and Mac took her hand.

"What do you think, Ruth?"

Ruth knew what he meant and answered him honestly. "I think this was a wonderful idea and I think I should buy Paris a really nice gift to thank her. A small island or a private bank or something," she told him.

"I agree. I'm thinking of declaring a national holiday in her name," Mac replied, squeezing her hand gently. "I've never enjoyed being matched up with anyone," he admitted. "Blind dates just weren't my thing, the whole idea made me uncomfortable. But I think Paris knew what she was doing this time."

Ruth's only answer was to move a little nearer to Mac at the same time he moved closer to her. They were touching now, the heat of his long, lean body warming hers and the faint aroma of his expensive cologne igniting her senses. She could feel a potent and unexpected response to him, a complex chemistry that lit her up from the inside and she closed her eyes to receive the kiss they were about to share.

"Are they kissin' yet?"

"I can't see, move over!"

Ruth's eyes flew open and she leaned over the back of the sofa to confront the source of the interruption, her great-nephews Marty and Malcolm. They were identical twins, absolutely adorable to behold unless they were up to some mischief, which they usually were. "What are you rascals doing out of bed?" she asked the curly-haired little snoops.

"We wanted to get some water," Malcolm began.

"And we wanted to see if you were gonna kiss," Marty finished. They abandoned their hiding place behind the sofa and came around to the front so they could clamber onto Ruth's lap.

"Why did you need a demonstration? Are you taking lessons or something?" Mac was amused, not embarrassed, which gave him big points in Ruth's book.

Marty assured him they didn't need lessons. "Everybody kisses all the time around here. Mommy and Daddy kiss all day long. All of our aunties and uncles kiss, they kiss a whole lot. Were you getting ready to kiss?" he asked innocently.

Mac reached over and ruffled the little boy's hair. "Yes, we were until you little fiends decided to block. Something tells me you'd better get back in the bed before your parents realize you're running loose."

"Sorry about that, Judge." The new voice was Trey, the oldest Deveraux child. Looking sternly at his little brothers, Trey demanded that they apologize. They did so at once, looking so cute in their cotton pajamas it was hard to believe they'd actually transgressed in some way.

"We're sorry," they chorused. Trey smiled grimly and made a gesture with his thumb that meant "hit it" and the little boys recognized it at once, planting big smacks on Ruth's cheek before dashing up the stairs. Trey followed at a more sedate rate, but not before giving his uncle a huge smile. "You just go back to what you were doing," he said helpfully. "I'll make sure they stay put."

Ruth and Mac looked at each other and burst out laughing, but Mac recovered first. He put his hands around her upper arms and pulled her into a close embrace. "Now where were we before we were so rudely interrupted?"

Chapter 3

The next morning Ruth was seated at the breakfast bar in the sunny kitchen with her niece. Bennie was firm in insisting that Ruth not lift a finger to help prepare breakfast. "I understand the dynamic duo interrupted your date last night, so you just take it easy. My way of apologizing for my curious little ones," she said, shaking her head. As she was stirring the batter for pancakes, she tilted her head to the right and looked at her aunt with open curiosity. "So what exactly were they interrupting, Aunt Ruth? I just need to know, umm, how severely to punish them," she mumbled into the bowl.

Ruth laughed at the disarming expression on Bennie's face. "Now I see where they get it from! I don't remember you being so curious when you were a child, but I think you're making up for it now."

She got up from her seat and went to the refrigerator, taking out two ruby red grapefruit, two huge navel oranges, a bunch of white grapes and a couple of apples. "I'm going to cut up some fruit. I always need to keep busy when I'm being interrogated," she said dryly.

"You don't have to tell me if you don't want to," Bennie said as she preheated the griddle. "But just tell me if you had a good time. Was I right about him being a nice guy or what?"

Ruth smiled a dreamily private smile while she sectioned the grapefruit over a large clear glass bowl. "Nice" didn't even begin to describe Julian Deveraux. Ruth had spent most of the night reliving every single moment of the evening, right down to the moment when he pulled her into his arms for their first real kiss. She dropped the small fruit knife she was using into the bowl and had to fish it out while trying to look nonchalant. The feel of his lips, the taste of him, the nearness of him…she dropped the knife again and the sound of Bennie's laughter brought her back to reality.

"You know what I think Aunt Ruth? I think someone had a very nice time last night, much better than they expected," Bennie teased.

"And what makes you think that? Because I'm drifting off into space and dropping utensils and making a mess of a simple fruit bowl? Or is it because I'm over here grinning like a Friday fool going to a Saturday market?" Ruth laughed and rinsed her hands off at the sink, patting them dry on a paper towel before tackling the fruit again. She was saved from further comment, however, when Braxton, the Deveraux's house manager, entered the back door with a fantastic floral arrangement, which he handed to Ruth.

"I met the florist in the driveway. Whoever sent it has excellent taste, Ms Bennett. It looks like it was custom-made for you."

"I keep telling you to call me Ruth," she murmured as she took the flowers from his outstretched hand. Putting them on the counter, she admired them with her heart in her eyes. She couldn't recall the last time she'd gotten flowers and she'd never received anything like this. These were they most unusual flowers she'd ever seen in her life. They were arranged in a tall rectangular crystal vase in a very pale shade of green. All the flowers were also green. There were cymbidium orchids, hydrangeas, tulips and freesias in various shades of green from palest celadon to delicate jade. Ruth was stupefied. She was about to take the card out of the little Blossoms by Betty envelope and read it when Bennie handed her a cordless phone. She looked at the phone like she'd never seen one before, and then looked at Bennie, who was trying very hard not to laugh.

"It's for you, sweetie. I guess you didn't hear it ring because you were too busy with those beautiful blooms," she said as she went to examine them closer.

Ruth finally collected herself enough to put the phone to her ear. "Hello?" Her voice sounded breathy and girlish and she could have kicked herself. But the person to whom she was speaking didn't seem to notice at all.

"Good morning, Ruth. I hope you slept well."

Her eyes widened as an unexpected shiver went

down her spine at the sound of Mac's deep voice. "Good morning, Mac. I slept wonderfully well and I was greeted by the most beautiful flowers I've ever seen. I have a feeling you know something about them. Am I right?" she asked flirtatiously.

"First of all, I thought you were going to call me Julian," he said reproachfully.

The shiver returned, but this time it was deeper and more tingly. It was true; when Paris introduced Titus to her father he'd told the young man to call him Mac or Judge, that no one called him Julian. Ruth had protested, saying that she loved the name Julian and she thought it suited him. He had turned to her and said, "You can call me Julian if you like. Anything that pleases you." The memory of the sexy look in his eyes when he uttered those words brought a hot blush to her cheeks, but she kept her voice steady as she replied.

"You're right, Julian. I do think the name suits you perfectly. An elegant name for an elegant man," she purred.

"Aw, now you've got me all red in the face and sweaty in the palms. You'd better behave yourself or who knows what I might try with you," he said with a sexy laugh.

"Julian, I've got the feeling you have the potential to be rather dangerous. First you send me these incredible flowers and now you're flirting with me. I may need a chaperone when I'm with you," she laughed.

"I think I can be trusted but we can put that to the test today. How about starting with lunch and seeing where the afternoon takes us? I'll pick you up at about twelve-thirty, is that good for you?"

Ruth looked fondly at the exotic bouquet and let his voice work its magic on her. "It's perfect. I'll see you then, Julian."

Mac ended the call and would have continued to sit in the comfortable chair in Paris's living room with a satisfied smile on his face, but his daughter wouldn't cooperate. She was sitting cross-legged on her chaise longue with most of the day's newspaper spread out around her while she studied the Target sale flyer intently. As soon as she heard him hang up the phone, however, it was on.

"Daddy, did I just hear you making a date?"

Mac looked at her, all disheveled and adorable in her pink cotton sweatsuit, and gave her a smile full of smug satisfaction. "Yes, cupcake, you did. As you are well aware, Ruth Bennett is a charming and very beautiful woman and I saw no reason to waste any time in getting to know her better. You don't have any objection to that, do you?"

"Of course not, Daddy, that's why I introduced the two of you. I think you owe me an apology for doubting my ability to spot a perfect couple. I told you I knew what I was doing," she gloated. "I definitely want an apology. And a present," she added with a gleam in her sparkling eyes.

Mac ignored that part of her speech and looked at her intently. "So how did you meet Ruth?"

"Daddy, she's Bennie's aunt. Her sister is Bennie's mother. In fact, Aunt Ruth resigned from the military to take care of Bennie and her brothers after her sister died. If you guys made it to more of the weddings you're invited to you'd have met her a long time ago," she added pointedly.

Mac made a face; weddings weren't his favorite activity, no matter who was getting married. "Well, I was at John and Nina's wedding and I certainly didn't have the good fortune to meet her," he pointed out.

"That's because you were too busy trying to keep my heathen brothers in line," she mumbled. "If you hadn't been eyeballing them I'm sure you would have met her then."

"You're probably right. So tell me a little about Ruth," he began, only to have Paris cut him off in mid-sentence.

"Daddy, she's wonderful. She's very smart and funny, she's a great conversationalist and an equally good listener. She's intuitive and clever and lots of fun to be around. She's very athletic, just like you. She runs and golfs and goes camping with her friends every year and…" Her voice trailed off as she finally noticed Mac signaling her to stop.

"Those things I can see for myself. She's obviously a woman in great shape and she has a charm about her that's unmistakable. What I meant was why a gorgeous woman like that is single? Is she divorced, widowed, what? Does she have children? Where is her home base? Does she just travel all over the place?" Mac looked serious and intently interested in her answers.

Paris raised an eyebrow and gently teased her father. "Daddy, I believe you're really interested in Ruth. And I think you're asking the wrong person these questions. I can tell you she doesn't have children of her own. Bennie and her brothers were like her children, she gave up a lot to take care of them. She's never been married, unless she has a deep dark secret that no one ever discusses. She's based in Chicago, where she moved after the last of her nephews graduated from college. And she does like to travel. She's on the go all the time, probably because she hasn't got anything to keep her in one place," she told him. "And that's the last time you get to grill me. Anything you want to know about Ruth you'll have to get directly from her."

"I plan to do just that, cupcake." Rising to his impressive height, Mac winked at Paris and left the room singing in his fine baritone voice.

Paris burst into giggles when she realized he was singing the Delfonics' "Ready or Not." *Ooh, I hope Ruth is ready for this. Come to think of it, I hope Daddy is ready for it because it looks like it's gonna get hot up in here,* she mused.

Ruth studied her menu carefully, although what she was really doing was checking out her date. From the time he'd arrived promptly at 12:30 p.m. to pick her up, everything had gone just perfectly and she knew she was in for a delightful afternoon. She raised the menu so she could get a good long look at him without him being aware of her scrutiny, then thought to heck with it and set the paper barrier aside. While he was checking to see what looked good on the lunch menu, she crossed her arms on the table and stared to her heart's content. Julian Deveraux was a darned good-looking man, a man in his absolute prime.

He was tall, like all of his nephews. She wasn't too good at guessing height, but he was several inches over six feet. She loved the way he was dressed, in an expensive looking merino jersey sweater in blue, pleated

slacks and a sinfully soft leather jacket. He had the
same slightly fair Creole coloring as most of his kin, but
his was a deeper shade. He had thick black hair that was
touched with silver at the temples, as was his thick
moustache. His heavy-lidded eyes and long straight
lashes were the perfect foil to his high cheekbones and
firm jaw with the deep cleft in his chin. And then there
was his mouth; so nicely shaped it was almost feminine.
Ruth felt a hot flush wind its way up her chest when she
thought about the way he could kiss. As if he heard her
thoughts, Mac looked up with a smile that acknowledged her scrutiny.

"It's been a long time since a woman looked at me like
that, Ruth. I have to tell you I like it. I like it a lot, as a
matter of fact." As the sound of his voice embraced her,
Ruth had to put her hand to her cheek. Yep, she was
actually blushing, something she hadn't done in years and
years.

She scolded him playfully. "Julian, I had a feeling
you were a dangerous man and I was right. You're going
to have me giggling in a minute if you don't stop it."

Mac was totally unrepentant. He leaned over to get
even closer to her and gave her the devastating
Deveraux smile that had led many a woman down a path
that led to incredible fulfillment. "Giggling? Now that
would actually be cute," he said with amusement. "I'll
bet it sounds sexy. What do I have to do to make it
happen? Should I tell you again how good you look?"

When he arrived to pick her up, his eyes had lit up
and he told her at once that she was stunning. She was
wearing one of her favorite outfits, a violet-colored
wool pantsuit with wide-legged, cuffed trousers and a

short fitted jacket. With it she had on a soft green cashmere sweater and a big Italian wool stole in a purple-and-green paisley print thrown over one shoulder—she looked sophisticated and stylish. She wore big gold hoop earrings in her first holes, accented with tiny purple jade studs in her second hole, and high up on her right ear was a diamond stud that caught the light and drew more attention to her arresting green eyes. Mac had leaned over to capture a breath of her scent and his lips had touched her neck as he did so. "That's an unusual fragrance. Don't think I've smelled it before," he told her.

"It's called K de Krizia. I have a passion for Italian perfume," she admitted.

"I seem to be developing a passion for you, honey. Shall we go?"

She had smiled to herself all the way to Dailey's, the restaurant he'd chosen for their lunch. Now she was trying to find something on which to fix her gaze before she drowned in the essence of the man across the table; he was way too potent for her peace of mind. Luckily their server approached the table and Ruth was so relieved she could have kissed him.

"Have you folks had a chance to decide what you want?" he asked guilelessly.

Yes, I'd like a double serving of that big hunk of man, Ruth thought as she wiped her hands on her slacks. She was able to order the French onion soup and a Caesar salad with shrimp without incident, pleased for some reason when Mac ordered the same. He also said they would share an appetizer of deep-fried olives, something with which Ruth was unfamiliar.

"I've never had them, either, but they looked good for some reason. I hope you like olives. I should have asked before I ordered," he said.

Ruth allowed herself to look into those mesmerizing eyes as she answered. "It just so happens that I adore olives. Black ones, green ones, Kalamata, it doesn't seem to matter. I've been a fool for them since I was a child."

Mac beamed. "Something else we have in common. I'll bet we'll find a lot more things before the day is over."

They ate with good appetite and both of them found the olives to their liking. They passed on dessert for the moment as Mac mentioned something about ice cream later. That was a special delight for Ruth, who had a world-class sweet tooth. So they spent the afternoon at the High Museum of Art, then went shopping, browsing in any little shop or gallery that caught their eye. Ruth found a gorgeous Art Deco teapot for Paris as a thank-you for dinner, and Mac bought the matching teacups. The store offered to gift wrap them, but Ruth refused. She loved wrapping gifts and bought some exotic wrappings so she could customize the gift just for Paris.

They found a Cold Stone Creamery on the way home and shared exotic specially-made ice cream creations like teenagers on a first date. They held hands and Mac even went so far as to lick the corner of her mouth, claiming she had a dab of ice cream there.

"No, I don't," Ruth murmured. "You're just trying to get a kiss on the sly."

Mac looked down at her with a tender expression that made the rest of her ice cream melt. She stared up at him helplessly as he took the remains of her cone and his and tossed them into a nearby receptacle. He tilted her chin up and lowered his mouth to hers. "Okay, no kisses on the sly. From now on I'll just make my intentions obvious, how's that?"

Ruth was vaguely aware of cooing sounds but she didn't have time to discover the source as she gave herself up to the luscious promise of Mac's lips on hers. It was a soft, fleeting kiss but his tongue teased hers enough to make her blood heat and flow into all of her most sensitive spots. She finally pulled away from him with a sigh, only to see the creamery staff smiling at them indulgently and applauding with gusto. She was ready to sink into the floor with embarrassment but Mac wasn't having it. He tightened his arm around her waist and grinned proudly.

One of the younger employees said, "Oh, hey, my mom and dad do that all the time. I think it's sweet."

Her coworker was more pragmatic. "That's why you're a sophomore in college with twin sisters in preschool," he drawled.

The young lady was undaunted. "My parents are just in love and they still know how to show it like that couple. When I'm their age I want to be that hot, that's all I'm saying."

It was one of the few times in her life that Ruth was at a loss for words.

Chapter 4

A couple of weeks passed and Ruth was once again at home in Chicago. She'd spent the last few days getting ready for the monthly meeting of her book club, and she truly welcomed the distraction from her restless thoughts. The distance from Mac was just what she needed. The weekend in Atlanta was wonderful; fun, stimulating and enjoyable in every way, but this was where she needed to be, home in her fabulous loft. She loved living in the loft apartment. It was high-ceilinged and extremely spacious with interior brick walls. Located in a refurbished pasta factory, the outside of the building still possessed the turn-of-the-century charm of the era in which it was built, but the inside was cheerfully modern. The loft was large and open except for the center, which housed the kitchen, bathroom and closets in a cleverly designed addition.

The kitchen was galley-styled with the stove, refrigerator, sink and dishwasher all neatly lined up. Directly across from the galley area was a wonderful work island that doubled as a breakfast bar. It was custom-made of golden oak and was the perfect height and size for serious cooking as well as casual dining. Above the sink were long shelves that displayed her collection of Blue Willow plates inherited from her grandmother. Dark green ivy was festooned along the shelves and lent an air of homey charm to the room. That charm continued through the apartment. Everything from the dining room area to the living area spoke of Ruth; the furnishings were traditional but the accessories were unusual and exotic, just like the owner.

Ruth had a delightful spread ready for the book club. She'd prepared an easy to consume buffet of artichoke dip with crostini, crudités, antipasto, chicken skewers with pesto, stuffed mushrooms and an assortment of lemon, frangipane and raspberry tarts. Beverages were her excellent Hawaiian coffee and a special iced tea made from a blend of white tea flavored with pear and peach essence. The bar looked wonderful with the food arranged on square pottery platters glazed in a pretty shade of green. In addition to the dining room table, there were two round tables set up for easy dining, all of them dressed in soft peach tablecloths with coral napkins that echoed the centerpieces of spring flowers. Ruth always looked forward to hosting the club. She loved to entertain and the ladies of the club were some of her favorite people on earth. She glanced at the kitchen clock just as her buzzer rang. The ladies were arriving and right on time. If she knew her friends,

Kimmi and Capiz would be the first to arrive. Throwing open the door, she smiled widely. "I was right, you two are always the prompt ones," she said happily.

"That's because you have the best food," Kimmi said, licking her lips. Kimmi was the youngest of the group—she wasn't quite thirty. Capiz was closer to Ruth in age, although she was still in her forties. The group members ranged in age from twenty-eight to seventy-two, and in Ruth's opinion it was the disparity of ages, ethnicities and backgrounds that made the group so much fun. Today they were doing the first part of a two-part Brenda Jackson retrospective. They had decided to do it in two parts to encompass her romances in one session and her mainstreams in another. Usually they concentrated on one book at a time, but before tackling a new writer they decided to do an homage to one of their favorite authors.

The discussion was lively and entertaining as always, and when the meeting wound down, the usual friends were left cleaning up and rehashing the funniest parts of the meeting. Kimmi and Capiz remained, of course, as well as Ruth's dear friends Cherelle and Sylvia. Cherelle was in her fabulous fifties and Sylvia was in her sixties. Both ladies were gorgeous, although few could hold a candle to Sylvia. She might have been one of the oldest of the group but she was the raving beauty, with rich brown skin that was smooth and unlined, startlingly platinum-white hair and a figure that many a younger woman envied. She had been a dancer in her youth and she was still a member of a dance troupe that Ruth longed to join, but she was too young.

"I keep telling you, kitten, you have to be at least

sixty to audition. Hang in there, girl, your day is coming," Sylvia teased her.

Ruth pretended to pout while she offered more iced tea. Capiz held up her glass at once. "Ruth, I don't know where you get these teas but they're always wonderful! I was never fond of tea but I think you've converted me. Even my husband is into tea these days," she said in her throaty voice. Capiz was fascinating; her round face combined the best of her Filipino and African-American ancestry and her smiling countenance always made people feel good. She was so funny and charismatic she'd started her own business as a consultant and motivational speaker and she was wildly successful.

In the meantime, the youngster, Kimmi, was staring at Ruth. Kimmi was sporting a daring new hairstyle with dramatic auburn highlights. She'd even had her brows tinted to match, something that amused Cherelle to no end.

Cherelle's own hair was almost jet-black except for one lock of white hair that grew over her left eye. Her caramel skin was smooth and flawless and she was full-figured, but trim and tight because she worked out daily in her capacity as an aerobic instructor. Cherelle loved Kimmi like a daughter and loved to tease her. "Since you got those brows tinted I'm just wondering if the carpet is going to match the curtains anytime soon. I'm just askin'," she drawled.

"Who says it doesn't already?" Kimmi returned saucily. "But check this out, y'all. Something has happened to Ruth. Look at her, she doesn't even look the same," she said accusingly.

Ruth was busy at the refrigerator, getting out a bowl of her special artichoke dip that she had held in reserve, knowing her friends would linger past the meeting and would require sustenance. She took a deep breath and turned to face her inquisitors, each one sitting on one of her comfortable bar chairs with a look of avid curiosity on her face. They resembled eager birds lined up to ambush a freshly filled feeder. She looked at Kimmi, Capiz, Sylvia and Cherelle and the time-honored phrase "resistance is futile" came immediately to mind. She steeled herself to bare her soul and actually had her mouth open to begin when the buzzer rang. *Reprieve!* She raced to the door and made a poignant sound of defeat when the visitor proved to be a handsome delivery person bearing a large box that read Blossoms by Betty in fancy script. Oh, she was busted all right; there was no getting around it now. She handed the box to Kimmi, who was right on her heels, and asked the delivery man to wait until she got her purse.

"No, ma'am, the gratuity has already been handled," the young man said politely. He was tall and lean with smooth pale skin and freckles. His eyes were gray and he had very kinky red hair, cut neat and short. "I'm supposed to unwrap it for you and take the box away," he informed her as he did just that, quickly and neatly. "Now I just need you to sign for this," he added as he held an envelope out to Ruth. "I hope you ladies have a nice afternoon."

Kimmi flirted her long lashes at him and gave him her best smile, the one where all her snowy-white teeth showed and her dimples winked like stars. "You, too, sweetie," she cooed.

As soon as the door closed behind the young man, Ruth looked at the contents of the box and sighed deeply. It was resting on the breakfast bar and was another exquisite arrangement of exotic blooms. These were green, like the last bouquet she'd received from Mac. Lovely green and white calla lilies, more cymbidiums and some other blooms she couldn't identify. She wanted to just wallow in their beauty, but a low *umm-hmmph* was heard behind her. She turned around and was pinned in place by four pairs of curious eyes. "Now I know what a mouse feels like when it's ganged up on by a herd of cats," she said resignedly.

"Don't be melodramatic, woman. Just spill your guts and no one gets hurt," Capiz said merrily. "Let's start with the contents of that envelope, shall we?"

As if she had no control over her fingers, Ruth mutely opened the envelope to reveal a handwritten note in fine calligraphy which read simply "I want you for my Valentine." There was also a first-class round-trip plane ticket to New York City.

Sylvia merely smiled her approval, but Cherelle and Kimmi let out yelps of excitement. Capiz gave a low whistle, and then added her two cents to the rest. "Start from the beginning and talk slow. Just what have you been up to, my dear?"

Ruth leaned against the refrigerator and stared at the card and the ticket. "There's nothing much to tell. I went to Atlanta to visit my niece and I met a man. A really wonderful man. That's not too complicated, is it?"

The silence lasted all of a nanosecond before Sylvia began giving orders.

"Ruth, you go sit down. Capiz, make some more

tea—no, better make something with some kick to it. Cherelle, honey, heat up the dip and Kimmi, get out the fruit salad she has hidden in there and some cheese. This is going to take a while and we're going to need energy."

Mac was talking on the phone when his oldest son, Julian, walked in the back door. From his attire and the fact that he was dripping with sweat, it was obvious that he'd been running. He waved at his father and dove into the refrigerator, emerging with a twenty-four-ounce bottle of icy cold water, which he proceeded to down in about four gulps. He wiped his mouth off with the back of one hand and rubbed the still-wet bottle against his forehead. "That's more like it," he said to no one in particular as he helped himself to another bottle.

Meanwhile, Mac was thanking Betty, a florist, who'd called him to let him know his hand-selected bouquet had been delivered. "The delivery man said she was very pleased and he was pretty sure there were tears in her eyes. He also said some of her friends were there when she got them and they were very impressed with your taste." Betty chuckled softly. "If you keep this up I'm going to be able to take a holiday in Hawaii," she teased him. "I like a man who knows what he wants and you really want this lady, don't you?"

Pleased with her frankness, Mac agreed with her. "I do, indeed. And what I want, I go after."

Julian raised both eyebrows when he heard his father's declaration. As his father ended the call, Julian splashed some of the cold water from the second bottle on his face and let it run down his neck. As soon as Mac was off the phone, Julian looked at him intently. "So what's this I overheard, Judge? Was that a new lady in your life?"

Mac shook his head. "Nope. That was a very nice woman from Atlanta who owns a really special florist shop. She was calling to let me know that the flowers I sent to the new lady in my life had arrived," he said smugly.

Julian pulled out one of the kitchen chairs and straddled it, draining the last of the water as he did so. "You're involved with someone new? So why am I just hearing about this, Judge?"

Mac gave him a look of mock exasperation. "Because I'm a grown man, that's why. I don't need your approval or permission to date, son. Let's not forget who the father is and who the son is," he said tersely.

"Oh, yeah? Remember the retired schoolteacher from Biloxi with the nine daughters? It seems to me that someone in this room warned you about getting involved with her and it also seems to me that that same person had to put out a restraining order on her," Julian reminded him. "And how about that woman from Arkansas who claimed to have all those degrees and own that big house and have all that money? Remember her, Judge?"

Mac tried looking stern and paternal and failed miserably. He was trying to hold in a loud burst of laughter. "Look, I plead the fifth on both those counts. First of all, that nutty heifer from Biloxi was a gift to me from Reverend Ames's wife. She was her play cousin and if you will recall, Sister Ames was the one who set the whole thing up. And Sister Ames was just as surprised as everyone else when we found out that the nine daughters were actually call girls. She had no clue her 'cousin' was a madam," Mac said as the laughter finally escaped.

"And as for that other woman, well, strange things happen on cruise ships. The woman was as crazy as a road lizard, I grant you that. But it wasn't like I picked her out. Your younger brothers introduced me to that nutcase. They had no way of knowing the woman was wanted for questioning in a murder case in Peoria, Illinois, or that she was a compulsive liar and black widow." Mac looked thoughtful for a moment. "Come to think of it she should be coming up for parole pretty soon. Of course, she's the reason I refuse all blind dates and setups. I'm extremely particular about who I get involved with, and not just because I've had some really bad experiences in the past. I've just learned to be very careful over the years."

Julian stood up and put the empty water bottles in the recycling bin near the back door. He washed his hands thoroughly and dried them on paper towels before making another excursion into the refrigerator. "Okay, Judge, I guess you've learned from your misadventures. So how did you meet this one?"

"Blind date," Mac said with a grin, enjoying the look of horror on his son's face. He let him wallow in anguish for a few seconds, before admitting that Paris had introduced them.

"She's Bennie's aunt, the one who raised them after their mother died. She's retired, very comfortable financially, based in Chicago and she travels frequently. She never married, has no children of her own, she's very well-educated, smart, athletic and funny. And get this:

she loves golf, horses and baseball. Great conversationalist and likes to socialize."

Julian was making a massive sandwich of roast beef,
Muenster cheese, arugula, sliced tomatoes and alfalfa
sprouts on pumpernickel. He was nodding as he father
was speaking. "Sounds like there's some potential
there," he acknowledged. "She good-looking?"

Mac assured him that Ruth was more than merely
good-looking, she was stunning. "Don't take my word
for it, here's a picture," he said, taking a photo out of
his well-worn personal planner. It was a snapshot of the
two of them that Paris had taken and it really showed
Ruth at her best, with her winning smile and sparkling
green eyes.

"Wow. Paris has good taste, Judge. She looks like a
real winner, Pop."

"She is, son. As good as she looks on the outside,
believe me, she's twice as nice on the inside. This lady
is a keeper," he said with a dreamy look in his eyes as
he stared at her image.

"Judge, you sound serious. Sounds like you mean to
make this permanent or something." Julian spread a
large quantity of Creole spicy mustard on the bread and
put his masterpiece together. He took a large bite before
giving Mac a piercing look to see if he was kidding
around or what.

Mac looked serenely calm as he returned his son's
look. "Julian, after we lost your mother I was convinced
I'd never find anyone to equal her. The love we shared
was so special I didn't even consider remarrying.
Besides, I had my children to think about. I was more
concerned with raising you properly and, to be honest,

I just closed off that part of my heart. But Ruth isn't like any woman I've ever met before. There's something really different about her, something precious and unique that I'm compelled to explore," he said quietly. "I don't think we were put here to lead solitary lives. I think that love between a man and a woman is a special blessing, one that I've denied myself too long. And, if I might point this out without censure, so have you. It's about time you started filling the hole in your heart that Maya left, son. I think it's time you started looking for a new love, Julian."

Julian almost choked on his sandwich at his father's words. His face turned bright red and an odd look completely changed his appearance. "That's never going to happen, Judge. Never in this world."

Ruth was comfortably seated on what her friends all called "the throne," her oversized armchair that was positioned directly across from the big-screen television in the living area of the loft. There was a wing chair adjacent to it, and a long, comfortable sofa across from the wing chair. The sofa and armchair were both upholstered in a soft suede-like fabric in a warm taupe, and the wing chair was a rich, dark green. There were soft colorful throw pillows on the sofa and chairs, with floor cushions and a couple of roomy ottomans to ensure a high level of comfort for anyone who entered Ruth's domain. The ladies were all seated near enough to Ruth so they could be supportive but not overwhelming. There was no escape to be had now; questions had to be answered.

Cherelle started by asking how she'd met him. "You

know my young friend, Paris…? I know you've heard me talk about her." Everyone nodded and Ruth continued talking. "Well, Paris's father came from New Orleans to visit her in Atlanta and she got the brilliant idea of introducing us. I agreed with the stipulation that she also invite Titus, the young man she's in love with. They had a huge misunderstanding and they've been avoiding each other, so I thought that if I forced her hand…" Ruth stopped speaking when Kimmi waved her hand impatiently.

"Umm, Ruth, honey, I don't mean to be crude, but I could care less about Paris and her boyfriend problems. Let's get back to her daddy. Is he fine?"

Everyone, including Ruth, laughed. It was no secret that Kimmi had a weakness for handsome men, a weakness that had led her into some bad relationships in the past. Ruth assured her that Mac was a good-looking man. "He's quite tall and very distinguished-looking. In fact, I have a picture if you'd like to see him," she said demurely.

Kimmi shrieked, "Woman, you'd better give it up! It's bad enough that you kept this from us for two whole weeks, you've got photographic evidence that you're withholding, too! You owe us big-time for this, get that picture out now or I won't be responsible for my actions."

Ruth was laughing as she excused herself to get the snapshots from that weekend. They were in a small album on the table next to her bed and she gladly showed them off to her friends. "There you go. He's nice, isn't he?"

Capiz was gaping with her mouth wide open. "Nice? Hon, that doesn't begin to describe him! He's gorgeous, you sneaky wench. How long were you planning to keep him a secret?"

Sylvia pressed one hand to her cheek and gave a long whistle. "Girl, he looks like a young Adam Clayton Powell, Jr. So what else is there to know about him other than the fact that he's beautiful?"

Ruth sighed deeply. "He's brilliant, for one thing. He's a justice with the Supreme Court of the state of Louisiana. He's a widower with five children, all adults and all successful. He has a great sense of humor, he's very trim and athletic, likes to work out and he's a golfer. He's kind and intuitive and a good listener. He sends me green flowers because he loves my green eyes. He's a wonderful kisser and he loves to dance. He's too good to be true, actually."

"He's not too good to be true, and he's not too good for you. He sounds just perfect and you sound like you're scared to death," said Cherelle. Her dark, clever eyes explored Ruth's face carefully. "What are you afraid of, Ruthie?"

"Okay, he lives in New Orleans and I live here, so I figured, nothing serious could come out of it and why not a fun weekend, which we did have. But now he seems like he wants to pursue something more and I'm not sure if I can handle it. He calls me every day and he never misses an opportunity to build on that weekend. Look at this," she said, waving the ticket in the air.

Capiz took it from her fingers and made a sound of approval. "I like this. He wants you to be his Valentine, he asks you two weeks ahead, and he set it up on neutral territory. Good move on his part. Too much pressure if he comes here, or you go to him, so you meet in the most romantic city on the east coast on the most romantic holiday. I like him, Ruth. He has class and good sense. Grab him, girl. That's my advice. Get him!"

Instead of looking amused, Ruth looked dismayed. "Look, it's been a long time since I was involved with anyone. A long, *long* time, to be truthful. I don't know if I want a relationship and I don't know if I can handle one. I'm used to being on my own, coming and going as I please and doing what I want *when* I want. I don't know if I have the desire or ability to be involved in something serious. I don't want to screw this up and the possibilities for disaster are numerous," she said sadly.

Kimmi spoke up then, her youth showing in her response. "Well, who says it has to be a serious relationship? You can just have fun with the man and let it go. When you feel like being bothered, you hang, and when you don't you disappear, simple as that."

She suddenly noticed that the other ladies were looking at her as if she were crazy. "What did I say?" she asked plaintively.

Sylvia shook her head. "Kimmi, that may work with the young bloods, but that's not how grown folks handle their business. Ruth is right about this—she needs to make up her mind if she wants to be with him or not because this man is not playing. This man is as serious as a heart attack and Ruth needs to decide if she can handle him or not because he means business."

The other ladies nodded in agreement and Ruth had no smart answer for once. Her green eyes caressed her green blooms and she sank into the depths of her chair with a deep, long and very heartfelt sigh.

Chapter 5

Ruth looked around the baggage claim area of La Guardia while trying to appear nonchalant. The last thing she wanted to do was look like an overeager spinster on her first date, although that's what she felt like. It had taken a lot to convince herself that spending the weekend in New York with Mac was a good idea. The fact that her friends lectured her individually and collectively notwithstanding; for her this was a difficult decision. There was a lot at risk here, but she was convinced it was the right move. Of course, the sound of Mac's rich voice crooning in her ear night after night made the decision a little easier to make. She smiled as she recalled one of their last conversations.

"Listen, honey, we owe it to ourselves to enjoy a romantic weekend in New York. We'll have a suite with two bedrooms so you needn't feel pressured in any way. We'll dine and dance and enjoy each other's company while we get to know one another better. How does that sound?"

"It sounds lovely, Julian. It sounds romantic and intriguing and if I'm to be honest about it, I can't wait to see you again. Shall we meet at the hotel or what?" She closed her eyes as she tried to imagine what their first meeting would be like. Suddenly she was overwhelmed with the desire to see him. Her eyes flew open as his laughing response came across the line.

"Meet me at the hotel? Don't be ridiculous, honey. I'll be at the airport with open arms."

"Oh. Well, okay then. I'll see you soon," she murmured. They talked a little more and when they finally ended the call, she stared at the receiver for a long time. For some reason all she wanted to do was call him back so she could hear his voice again. Thank God for Sylvia, both for being her friend and for pushing her in the right direction.

It was Sylvia, her older and wiser friend, who'd talked some sense into her about the whole situation. The night of the book club after Cherelle, Kimmi and Capiz had all voiced their opinions, tidied up the dishes and left, Sylvia and Ruth had remained seated in the living room, listening to Eva Cassidy on the stereo and having a real heart-to-heart talk.

"Ruth, dear heart, it's time for you to have something in your life besides girlfriends, hobbies and nieces and nephews. You've been running long enough and it's time for you to settle down," she said gently. She paused to peruse the pictures from the weekend in Atlanta and studied Mac's face carefully. It was a picture of Ruth and Mac with Bennie's twin girls sitting on their laps. Ruth was smiling at the children, but Mac was looking at Ruth with a look in his eyes that spoke as loudly as a love song. "This man looks like the one, Ruthie. He looks at you the way my Franco looks at me and that ain't no joke, sister. It took me several years to get that look out of him and you managed it in one weekend. What did you do that weekend besides have dinner with his daughter?"

"We had a ball, Sylvia. We went to lunch at Dailey's, of course, then we went to the museum and window-shopped, but I told you that already. We went to the gym at the complex and worked out, we went to the movies and we had dinner at Lillian and Bump's house. Lillian is Bennie's mother-in-law and she was married to Julian's brother. They've known each other all their lives, you know, and they're very close. Paris used to spend the summers in Atlanta with Lillian when she was a little girl," Ruth told her.

Her eyes fell on the pictures and she was mesmerized by every feature of his face, every expression. When she finally looked at Sylvia again, her face was full of naked emotion.

"Sylvia, I don't have to tell you that I'm scared. Julian is the kind of man most women look for all their lives and here he's just been dropped in my lap like he fell off the good-man tree. He's so smart and funny and sexy and kind…oh damn, Syl, suppose I screw it up? I'm so bossy and set in my ways and contrary, who knows what I'm likely to do? I just don't want to mess this up before it gets started, that's all," she mumbled.

"That's not *all* and we both know it," Sylvia said firmly. "I think we both know what this is really about, Ruth. You're afraid to fall in love because of Jared. It's always been Jared that's kept you from having the love you deserve. It's got to stop, dear heart. You've got to let go of the past once and for all and get your share of the joy you give to everyone else," she said, taking one of Ruth's hands and holding it tightly. On one hand, she hated to see the sheen of tears in the indomitable Ruth's eyes, but on the other, it meant that she was right and she was getting through to Ruth. Sure enough, her friend looked at her with her heart in her eyes.

"You make it sound so easy, Syl. But how do I do that, how do I let go once and for all?"

"You wipe your eyes, you tell this big handsome hunk you'll meet him in New York and you buy some new lingerie. Everything else will fall into place, trust me."

Ruth's expression went from cloudy to sunny and she burst into laughter. Maybe things were really that simple. Or at least they seemed that simple when she got on the plane at O'Hare in Chicago. Now, looking around for some sight of Julian, she wasn't so sure. Suddenly an unmistakable voice called her name. She turned around to find him standing there looking utterly wonderful in a black cashmere overcoat and a fabulous black Borsalino fedora.

"Hello, honey. I told you I'd be here with open arms," he said with a smile.

Ruth beamed up at him. "Well, I see you standing here, but I don't see any open arms, mister."

"Then you're not looking hard enough. Come here, sweetheart," he said as he swept her into his arms.

The kiss he laid on her was enough to stop quite a few observers in their tracks. Ruth couldn't have cared less about the onlookers; all she cared about was the tender passion his touch elicited in her. She felt alive, more exhilarated and excited than she had in years. The slight tickle of his moustache, the softness of his lips and the eager caress of his tongue made her forget everything except the feel of his strong arms around her waist. They pulled away from each other with great reluctance and simply stared at each other for a long moment. Neither one wanted to be the first to break the enchanted silence; they just wanted it to last forever. Forever wasn't very long, however, as they clearly heard the comment of an older woman standing nearby.

"See, Harry? I've told you and told you that married people do *too* kiss like that. You'd better get on the case, buster, or get used to sleeping in the guest room."

The spell was broken, but it dissolved into laughter. "You look incredibly beautiful, honey. As soon as your bags materialize the driver will get them and we'll be on our way, how's that?"

"It's perfect," Ruth told him. "You look quite dashing yourself. I love that hat. Most men don't have the panache to wear one so well."

Mac touched the brim in a rakish gesture and smiled wickedly. "That's because most men don't have my good taste. Besides, I can't take it when my head gets cold," he admitted. "And that's a stylish chapeau you're wearing as well. Doesn't seem possible, but you look even prettier than usual."

Ruth was wearing her cream cashmere coat with stylish wide-legged matching pants. Her cowl-necked sweater was a soft mint-green and her jaunty beret matched it, making her skin vibrantly warm and giving her eyes an extra glow. "Julian, you flatter me way too much," she scolded. "I'll give you exactly sixty minutes to stop it."

He took her arm with a laugh and began to lead her to the baggage carousel. "By then we'll be in the city in our suite. Until then, I get to say anything to you I please."

Ruth stopped walking and turned to face Mac. "Then I get to react any way I like. And it may involve a lot of these," she said demurely as she stood on tiptoe to press her lips to his.

"See, Harry? Take a lesson, why don't you. Those two have probably been married for years and the thrill is still there. Look and learn, you old coot."

Ruth and Mac glanced at the older couple, who were apparently still studying their technique, then looked at each other and burst into affectionate and very pleased laughter.

Mac kept his word and continued to shower Ruth with sweet, teasing compliments as their limousine purred through the traffic. Ruth kept hers, too, and snuggled next to him on the spacious and comfortable seat.

"You have incredible skin, Ruth. It's the color and texture of Tupelo honey, did you know that?"

Ruth looked down at their hands, which were tightly entwined. "Actually, no I didn't know that, Julian. Thank you," she whispered and put a small kiss at the corner of his mouth. It had been years since she was seriously involved with a man, but being with him felt so natural and sweet it was easy for her to allow a little of her natural affection to slip out.

Mac had removed his hat and she ran her hand through his hair, loving the silky feel of it. "There. Now you look even sexier. It's ridiculous that you Deveraux men are all so good-looking. How in the world does one family have so many handsome men in the family tree?"

He laughed heartily and put his arm around her shoulders to bring her even closer to his body. "Please don't let my sons hear you say anything remotely close to that. They're already way too conceited."

"How is that possible? Paris is a true beauty and she's one of the most levelheaded young women I've ever met. She's not conceited in the least," Ruth murmured. The smell of Mac's cologne was intoxicating, mixing with his natural body scent to create a giddy sensation in the pit of her stomach that was most pleasurable. Mac didn't seem to hear her comment; he was too busy angling his head down for another kiss. Ruth sighed with enjoyment and was so busy returning the caress she didn't notice that the limo had stopped in front of the hotel. The driver got out to open her door and as he helped her out of the back seat she got a good look at the place they would be spending the next few days.

"The W Hotel? I've read about these but I've never stayed at one," Ruth admitted.

"Then prepare yourself for an amazing weekend, honey. The sky isn't the limit here, it's just the beginning." Mac took her arm and led her into a lobby that was unlike anything she'd ever imagined.

Warm earth tones, flattering lighting, furniture that looked sinfully comfortable, smiling associates welcomed them and the check-in process went so quickly Ruth wasn't even aware of what was going on. The next thing she knew, they were being shown into a suite that looked like a movie set and the bellman was deftly bringing in their luggage.

"Have a pleasant stay, Mr. and Mrs. Deveraux. If there's anything we can do to make your visit more complete, don't hesitate to let us know," he said with a small bow.

Mac was taking Ruth's coat off while she mulled over the bellman's words. She took off her beret and fluffed her hair by running her fingers through it. "Julian, that's the third time someone has mistaken us for man and wife," she began.

He hung both their overcoats in the spacious closet and turned to her with a smile and four fingers held up. "Actually, that was the fourth time. The staff of the ice cream place in Atlanta, the couple at the airport, the bellman and the limousine driver. While I was giving him a tip he said he hoped we enjoyed our anniversary. He assumed we were in town celebrating," he said with a smug smile.

Ruth could feel her cheeks turn hot. "Ahh. Doesn't that umm, bother you?" she asked timidly.

Mac walked the few steps to Ruth and put his hands around her waist. "*Bother* me? Hell, no, it makes me proud. If people think we're a couple it means they think I'm man enough to have a lovely woman like you in my life. Why in the world would that bother me, honey?"

The giggle she'd been trying to keep at bay escaped

as she put one hand on his cheek. "Most men would run screaming to the hills if it happened to them. Most men value their freedom more than their lives, Julian. I can't think of a single unmarried man who'd actually enjoy being mistaken for a husband."

Suddenly she breathed deeper as Mac tightened his arms around her and held her closer than close. "That's because you haven't met a man like me," he growled softly. "New York is waiting for us, honey. What do you want to do first?"

They did everything, or almost everything they could think of. The maid service unpacked their clothes while they had lunch in one of the hotel's restaurants. Despite the February chill in the air, they did a lot of walking and holding hands. They went ice-skating at Rockefeller Center, they window-shopped and browsed in bookstores and record stores, and at Ruth's insistence they went into one of the hundreds of Duane Reade drugstores that seemed to spring up on every corner.

"I love makeup," she confessed. "Makeup and bubble bath and shampoo and whatnot and I love to buy it at drugstores and discount stores. The selection here is just amazing," she said as she stared at the rows and rows of items just waiting to be purchased.

"Don't overload in here," he cautioned. "Tomorrow we're going to Barney's and Bloomie's and Bergdorf's and I have a feeling you'll want to pick up just a few things here and there."

"Well, you've got me there. But I have to get some of this lotion," she said excitedly. "I get it from my hairdresser in Chicago and it's like ten dollars a bottle!

It's only three-fifty here." She took five bottles of Razac lotion off the shelf but before she could get to the checkout Mac was already in line paying for it. He said he was doing it to save time, but she had her doubts.

"We have tickets to *The Color Purple* and I thought you might like to rest a little before we get ready to leave," he said innocently. His tone didn't fool Ruth for a minute, though. Julian Deveraux was a man who wouldn't let a woman open her purse for as much as a package of gum. She should have recognized that as another Deveraux characteristic. She accepted the inexpensive lotion with a smile, but resolved to not let him spend too much money on her. There was no telling what he might get into in a city like New York.

Chapter 6

Their evening together was as wonderful as the day had been. They went back to the hotel where they spent the afternoon talking until Ruth fell asleep in his arms. They were cuddled up next to each other on the massive sofa with the some wonderful music playing and before she realized what had transpired, Ruth was blinking her eyes and purring with enjoyment as she stretched against Mac's warmth. Her mouth formed an *O* of embarrassment and she got flustered.

"Oh, please tell me I didn't fall asleep on you! Did I snore or snort or do anything else disgusting and unladylike?"

"Ruth, you make me laugh more than any other woman I've ever met," Mac said appreciatively. "Honey, you curled up like a little cat and you looked so sweet and rested I went to sleep with you. I slept very well, too. But now it's time to get ready for the play if we intend to make the curtain."

Taking him at his word, Ruth took a long hot shower in clouds of Goldleaf, one of her favorite fragrances. She used liberal amounts of the lotion and sprayed on a mist of the scent before putting on her silk lingerie. As she put on her bikini briefs and matching bra, she took a good long look in the mirror and even though vanity wasn't an essential part of her nature, she was happy with what she saw. Her body was still firm and tight without even a stretch mark. She frowned a little, reflecting that if things had worked out the way she'd planned she'd bear the marks of having four or five children. *Probably be plump and happy about it*, she mused. Even her breasts didn't have the inevitable sag of a woman her age, but she was never terribly busty. *There are some advantages to being a B-cup, I guess.* She used her travel-sized ceramic curling iron to bump a few curls into her hair before applying her makeup.

Finally she was ready to slip into her ensemble, a simple raw silk dress with a scoop neck and cap sleeves with an empire waist. It stopped just above her knees and it was a buttery shade of ivory that brought out her skin color. She had on a little gold eye shadow and a rich caramel lipstick, to which she added a gold gloss. In her ears she wore a set of diamond studs, a set of big Tahitian pearl drops and she slipped on a matching bracelet consisting of a double row of pearls. She stepped into her pearlized gold sling back pumps and picked up her small gold evening bag with the crystals and faux pearls and decided she was ready to go. She left her bedroom to join Mac in the living room and was touched by his greeting. Not only did he stand up when she entered, he looked at her as though he'd recently arrived on this planet and she was the first specimen of woman he'd ever seen.

"Beautiful. Just beautiful. Now let me get your coat or we won't be leaving here tonight, trust me." He smiled down at her from his towering height and as if he couldn't resist, he kissed her forehead and the tip of her nose. "I wish I hadn't done that," he said with a mock sigh. "You smell so good I could eat you up with a small spoon. Let's get out of here, woman, or I'll prove it to you." And he whisked her out of the suite before she could say a word in protest.

The next morning, Mac didn't think he would ever get out of the shower. The water had been set to its most forceful setting and he'd gradually turned the dial until the water ran as cold as he could stand it. It was either stand in the frigid water like a horny college boy or grab Ruth and pull her into a totally different kind of shower. He could imagine all too well what her body would feel like pressed against his with warm water cascading over them and the tempting fragrance of Ruth's luxurious bath gel arousing his senses even more. He groaned aloud in frustration as this kind of thinking was what got him in the cold shower in the first place. He abruptly turned off the water and stepped out of the stall, wrapped a towel around his waist and stared at his reflection.

He was in good shape for a man of his age. For a man of any age, to tell the truth. When he was growing up he'd been remarkably skinny, filling out gradually as he reached maturity. He was still lean and hard, mostly because of his ingrained habit of working out. It had started in the army when calisthenics were part of his daily routine. He continued to stay in shape after he married, but it was mostly passionate lovemaking and chasing his lively toddlers around that kept him agile. After his wife died, however, running, rowing and long workouts in the gym kept him sane. It was how he sub-liminated his sorrow and rage but it made him look like a much younger man. His chest was still covered with silky hair and his shoulders were broad and muscular. There was very little chance that he would repulse Ruth once he got her where he so desperately wanted her, which was in his arms and his bed. Ruth Bennett was a special treat; like a luscious, rich and totally unex-pected dessert after a decadently delicious dinner. She was everything he'd been looking for in a woman for a lot of long, lonely years and the previous night had only made him even more positive than before that she was the right one.

When Ruth had walked into the living room of the suite dressed for their night on the town, Mac was stunned. Not just because of her poise and elegance, although God knows she looked beyond gorgeous. He was stunned because a sensation he hadn't felt in years overcame him, taking his breath away completely. It was as though she walked out of the bedroom and right into his heart. There was something about Ruth that moved him profoundly, something that touched him in a way that hadn't occurred since his beloved wife had left this world. When he playfully kissed her forehead and her nose and inhaled the feminine fragrance that graced her from head to toe, he felt a rush of desire flow through him like a torrent of summer rain. He wasn't kidding when he said they had to get out of the suite right then and there or he wouldn't be responsible for what happened next. Leaving was the best thing to do, definitely. But spending the evening with her did nothing to lessen the passionate yearning he was feeling.

The musical was as good as it was reputed to be and they enjoyed it thoroughly. After the play they took a hansom carriage ride through Central Park, a time-honored romantic gesture that delighted Ruth to no end. "Julian, how sweet you are! I've always wanted to do this," she'd told him. The pleasure on her face was more than enough thanks for him; he really didn't need to hear the words. The weather cooperated fully, yielding a light snow that made the night seem more magical, besides giving Mac an excuse to wrap his arms around her. They missed most of the sights to be seen because they were too busy kissing and talking to each other in soft whispers. By the time they returned to the hotel, Mac was a mess. He wanted Ruth, not just for a night or a few nights, but for as long as she would give him the pleasure of her company. He looked down at her animated face, alight with enjoyment, and knew he had to go slow or risk losing her forever. It was the going slow part that was going to be difficult.

They decided to have a midnight supper when they returned to the suite. Ruth was totally enthusiastic about the hotel's "whenever, whatever" service. It didn't just apply to room service; anything a guest requested could be obtained through the hotel's staff. Mac had to smile as he remembered the avid interest Ruth showed in the many informational brochures.

"Julian, if I want a milk bath, or a massage, or a mariachi band, we could get it tonight. That's amazing!"

"Would you like a milk bath? Just give me the word and I'll have them get it started for you," Mac offered.

"Nah, I can't stand the thought of wasting all that milk when people are starving to death. I have an idea though—why don't we get out of these clothes and put on something comfortable and order something nice? Do you like strawberries?"

Mac tried to concentrate on shaving while he recalled the rest of the evening. They had gone to their respective bedrooms and changed. He'd taken off his custom-tailored suit and put on his Xavier University warm-up suit, the new one he'd only had for a few weeks. When he emerged from the bedroom, Ruth was curled up on the sofa playing with the remote for the television. "They have those all-music channels," she told him. "What's your favorite kind?"

"Jazz, of course, but I also like R&B and rock. And I have a real passion for the blues," he replied. "How about you?"

"I love jazz, too. And Motown and R& B and blues. But I have a particular love for a certain kind of music," she teased. "You'll never believe me if I tell you and the information may make you despise me," she'd said with a mischievous smile.

"Good Lord," Mac said with mock alarm all over his face. "Is it polka music? Heavy metal? Hip-hop?"

Ruth threw her head back and laughed. "No, no, no,

although I do like hip-hop. My secret vice is doo-wop music. My sister loved it and I guess that's where I got it from. I just adore it and I go out of my way to listen to it, so you might want to reconsider this liaison, Julian. Can you put up with a little doo-wop from time to time?"

By way of answer, Julian sang a few bars of "I Only Have Eyes for You" and laughed when Ruth's jade eyes widened with delight.

Just then room service discreetly knocked at the door and Ruth rose to let them in. She looked over her shoulder at Mac as she went to let the server in. "You really are a dangerous man. Handsome, funny and you sing like Nat King Cole. I'm in trouble, aren't I?"

She'd changed into a lounging outfit that was like a long-sleeved T-shirt with a deep scoop neck. It was made of a silky material in a luscious shade of orchid and it had long slits on both sides so he could see her shapely, sexy legs. As he watched her high, firm butt move with unconscious seduction when she walked across the room, he knew for a fact that he was the one in trouble of the deepest kind. He was falling in love.

Mac finished shaving and washed the lather from his face. He patted his face dry and finished up with an aftershave balm. He leaned into the mirror and trimmed a few stray hairs from his moustache and finally decided he was finished. He went into the adjoining bedroom to get dressed while he thought about the rest of the evening with Ruth. They'd decided to sit on the floor and eat from the coffee table instead of using the table provided for dining. It was intimate and sweet; the two of them feeding each other roast chicken and asparagus spears, followed by big strawberries with a wildly delicious sauce in which to dip them.

They talked for hours, about everything under the sun. Mac asked her about her sister, and she was happy to tell him everything she could remember about her.

"Lillian was the most wonderful person in the world. She was ten years older than me, so I always looked up to her and adored her. When our parents were killed in a boating accident, she took over my care. She became like my mother, Julian. If it wasn't for Lillian I don't think I would have made it through college. And she took care of me in other ways, too. We had a trust fund and she made sure that on her passing her money came to me, not her children. She knew that I'd always take care of her children no matter what, and besides, she knew they would be cared for financially by her husband. She also had a life insurance policy for me, just so I'd have an extra cushion, something to fall back on.

"Lillian taught me everything that counts about being a woman, Julian. How to be a friend, how to keep my word, to be a good steward over my finances and she even taught me how to dress. That's important, too, you know. Through the darkest days of my life, she was always there for me. And through the best ones, too," she said with tears glistening in her eyes. "I always said that when I had a daughter I would name her Lillian, after my beautiful sister."

Mac leaned over and kissed the tears away from the corners of her eyes, then held his arms open so she could rest her head on his shoulder. "This is where I get really nosy, darling. I can't understand why you never had children. Why didn't you ever get married? As beautiful and wonderful as you are, how in the world could you not be someone's wife?"

He was shocked when her response wasn't fast and sassy. He fully expected a quick quip of some kind and he was stunned to see big tears form in her eyes. He rose to his feet and pulled her up with him, sitting down on the sofa and enfolding her in his arms. "Talk to me, honey. Tell me about it," he said softly.

She took refuge in his arms for a while, rubbing her soft hair against his shoulder. Finally she began to talk, in a soft voice very unlike her normal speech. "I was supposed to be someone's wife. I was engaged to a wonderful man named Jared Brandeis. We met in college. I'm from Pennsylvania, you know, and we went to Penn State—Jared was getting his master's degree in education and I was majoring in nursing. I had a work-study job in the library and that's how we met. We were so young and idealistic, we thought true love could conquer all," she said with a shaky sigh.

"Back in the seventies when everyone's ideas were changing about everything, when our generation thought we could make a difference in the world. My friends protested Vietnam, fought for civil rights and stood up for women's rights and we really thought if we challenged the system with passion and purpose the end result would be some kind of utopia," she said with a trace of bitterness. "I was so naive, Julian, and so was Jared. My family was fine with our relationship. Lillian thought he was just right for me and she supported us fully. His parents were artistic and liberal and they loved me, too, despite the fact that they hadn't really planned on having a black daughter-in-law," she said with a sad, wry twist to her mouth. "And yes, Jared was white," she told him before he could ask.

"As a couple on campus we just kind of blended in, I guess, because no one gave us any flack, at least not that I can remember. Maybe I was just so in love I wasn't paying any attention to the signs. Jared never mentioned anything about any racial comments, either. Now that I look back on it, I think we were just blind, just stupidly blind about the whole thing. We had no business being together, none whatsoever."

Max continued to hold her close, stroking her high cheekbone with his thumb and giving her soft kisses on her temple while rubbing his face against her soft, sweet-smelling hair. "Why would you say a thing like that, honey? Why shouldn't two people in love be together, regardless of the color of their skin?"

A choking sound came from Ruth as she struggled to answer him. "Because he was walking me back to the dorm one night and a gang of drunken fraternity boys jumped us. He died a week later from the injuries he sustained in the attack. I was beaten pretty badly, too, but I survived." The pain in her soft voice was hard for Mac to listen to—it was breaking his heart. "If I'd stayed away from him it wouldn't have happened. He was a gentle, kind and very gifted man, and he shouldn't have died like that. It was all my fault, Julian. I'm the one responsible for his death."

Mac's arms tightened around Ruth as he maneu-vered her body closer to his. Kissing her tear-streaked face over and over, he talked to her in soft, reassuring tones. "Honey, you weren't responsible. It wasn't your fault that a bunch of misguided racists went crazy. How can you think that? It wasn't you, honey, it was all them. You couldn't have known it was going to happen."

Ruth couldn't answer for a moment. She wiped the tears from her face and sighed. "I could have stayed away from him," she said slowly. "I could have pretended I didn't know he was flirting with me, I could have ignored the fact that we found each other attractive, I could have done so many things and he wouldn't have died so young. He'd be married and happy and have lots of kids and grandkids if it hadn't been for me," she whispered.

"Honey, you can't know that. He could be miserable, married to some horrible nagging wench with drug-addled, ungrateful kids trying to bleed him dry," Mac said frankly. "You were probably the best thing that ever happened to him. He died tragically, that's true, but he died loving you and protecting you. He died like a man, Ruth, and in the end that's all any of us can ask for."

Ruth rested her head on his shoulder and warned him, "I'm going to cry some more. I try so hard not to think about this or talk about it. It hurts, even after all these years."

"Well, you go ahead and cry if you need to. And when you get through I'll still be here holding you, how's that?"

Ruth gave him a shaky smile and stroked his face. "That will be just perfect, Julian. It'll be just what I need."

Mac held her tenderly, holding his growing passion at bay as he comforted her until she fell asleep in his arms. Finally he stood up, carried her into her bedroom and put her in bed, covering her gently and kissing her lightly before turning off the lamp. He sat in the big chair near the bed and watched her sleep for a long time before going into his own bedroom.

It had been one of the longest nights of his life, but one of the most meaningful. After hearing the story of her lost love, he was even more sure than before that Ruth Bennett was a woman he wanted in his life—permanently.

He finished with his grooming and donned the thick terry robe provided by the hotel. He went into his bedroom and was preparing to get dressed when a knock sounded on the door. With a smile on his face he went to open the door, hoping Ruth had slept as well as he had.

Chapter 7

Ruth awoke in great spirits. She'd slept like a child, snug and secure, even though she had no clear recollection of how she got into bed. She had an idea that Mac had put her under the covers and instead of being embarrassed about it, she felt cherished. After showering and shampooing her hair, she blew it dry, curled and styled it, and dressed casually, in a pair of sleek-fitting jeans, a rose-colored merino wool turtleneck and her favorite walking shoes. They were imported leather slip-ons that cradled her feet and would allow her to walk for hours without discomfort. She added a wisp of makeup, just a basic foundation to protect her skin from the pollutants in the city air, a dab of coppery eye shadow and a little black mascara. A final dab of bronze lipstick, a spritz of Goldleaf and she was good to go.

Her only jewelry was her diamond studs and a pair of gold hoops. She ordered coffee from room service and she had just finished dressing when she heard them at the door of the suite.

After tipping the server, she poured a cup for Mac and took it to him, tapping lightly at his bedroom door. When he opened the door she had to stifle a gasp. He was wearing a bathrobe and she could see the thick, silky hair on his chest. He had no right to look that sexy at this hour of the morning, she decided.

"Good morning. Here's some coffee for you," she said sweetly. "Do you want breakfast in or out?"

He took the cup from her hands and leaned down to give her a quick kiss. "Out, definitely. I was thinking Zabar's, does that suit you?"

Ruth knew about the legendary delicatessen and agreed it sounded perfect. "See you in a few," she said as he turned to finish dressing. She got a good long look at his long, muscular legs that were also covered with silky black hair and almost passed out. She was fanning herself rapidly with one hand as she went to fix her own cup. *Dangerous man, very dangerous,* she thought, but she didn't believe it for a minute. Aside from her sister, Sylvia and Capiz, she'd never talked to anyone about Jared, yet she'd poured her heart out to him as if they'd known each other for years. He was so darned easy to talk to, she mused. There was something comforting about him that made it amazingly easy to confide her innermost thoughts to him. As close-mouthed as Ruth was by nature, that alone made Julian unique and irresistible. That and the fact that he kissed like he had an advanced degree in oscillation; no man, including her beloved Jared, had ever made her knees go weak like he did.

After they were seated in Zabar's eating deliciously decadent chocolate croissants and drinking big caramel lattes, Ruth's face lit up in a smile as she thought about those kisses. She almost spat a mouthful of coffee across the table when Mac casually announced he knew what she was thinking about. "You're thinking about kissing me," he said matter-of-factly. When he saw her cheeks turn the same color as her sweater he took one of her hands in his own. "Aww, honey, don't look like that. I'm thinking the same thing so there's no need for you to be embarrassed. You have the softest lips in the world and they taste just like honey, sweet, warm and spicy. I could kiss those lips all night," he said with those maddeningly seductive eyes caressing her face.

Ruth just sat there with her mouth open slightly, looking like she was ready to be kissed again. She was more than happy to leave the deli, because she needed some fresh air. While they were strolling and holding hands, she took a good look at Mac, who was dressed as casually as she was, in charcoal gray slacks, a gray cable knit sweater and a sinfully soft black lambskin jacket that made his fedora look even more dashing. She stared at him for a moment, and then squeezed his hand. "You don't believe in holding back, do you?"

He smiled down at her and returned the pressure on her hand. "No, darlin', I don't. I don't see the point, do you? We're both way past grown and we pretty much know what we want out of life, so I see no reason to be coy. If you want someone who's going to play games and try to manipulate the relationship, you're going to have to find someone else. Is that acceptable?"

Ruth returned his smile. It was impossible not to, he had a smile of infectious joy and purity. "That's perfectly acceptable, Julian. I'm not much for playing games, either. So are you sure you want to go shopping? There're a lot of other things we can do, you know. Most men don't like to shop," she pointed out.

"I keep telling you, I'm not like most men. I like shopping, mostly because of my children. I used to be totally indifferent to my attire. I liked to fish and hunt and roughhouse with the kids and I couldn't have cared less about clothes. I'd buy my suits from Sears and JC Penney and not think anything about it. Ginger, my wife, was real bohemian and she was not a slave to fashion, so she didn't care, either.

"But some years after she passed I was featured in a local magazine as the worst-dressed lawyer in Louisiana," he admitted. "I'm not kidding, honey. There was a picture of me in a courtroom when I was district attorney, and I was wearing a light blue polyester suit looking like a black Ben Matlock. The boys were so humiliated they refused to go to school," he laughed.

Ruth laughed, too, but hers was one of disbelief. "Julian, I don't believe you! What did Paris say about this?"

By now they had reached their destination, Barney's, that icon of good taste and high prices. Mac laughed even louder. "Ask Paris about the plaid jacket. I had a madras sport coat that I loved for some reason. I used to wear it to church a lot, with tan chinos and a yellow shirt. I think I had a matching plaid belt, too. Paris despised it and begged me over and over to get rid of it, but I never would. It was like an old pal, something comfortable and familiar. After that article, though, I reached for it one Sunday morning and she had cut it to ribbons and hung it back up in the closet with a note attached. The note read 'The seersucker suit is next.'

"I figured if my most obedient child was driven to those lengths it was time for me to clean up my act and ever since then, I've paid a lot more attention to how I look. Paris swears the change in my appearance was one of the reasons I was appointed to the Supreme Court. I don't know if that's true or not, but I do like to shop now."

"So what are we looking for?" Ruth asked curiously. "Anything in particular?"

"Not really. Just meandering around until we find something we can't live without. Like those earrings," he murmured. "Those would look perfect on you," he said as he indicated a stupendous pair of tourmaline teardrops dangling from a diamond bow.

Before Ruth could utter a protest, a chic-looking salesperson slithered up out of nowhere. "Your husband has exquisite taste, madame," she cooed.

Ruth was wearing an angora beret and leather gloves that matched her sweater, so her ring finger wasn't visible. "We're not married," she said hastily, only to be interrupted by Mac.

"Oh, sweetheart, please stop saying that. We agreed to a trial separation but you know I can't live without you. When are you going to take me back, my love?"

Ruth's laughter started in her toes and worked its way through her entire body until it burst out merrily in the relative quiet of the jewelry department. She was laughing so hard he finally had to take her out of there. They spent the rest of the morning going from store to store, enjoying each other's company; they even relished the brisk February weather. Suddenly it occurred to Ruth that she hadn't brought anything especially dressy with her. "Julian, are we doing anything special tonight? I don't think I have anything really fancy with me," she said thoughtfully.

"Ever hear of the Rainbow Room? I thought dinner and dancing there would be a nice evening," he said innocently.

"Oh, shoot! I have to do some power shopping right now," Ruth said with a frown. "How could you not tell me we were going there, of all places?"

Mac grinned with no remorse whatsoever. "It's called a surprise, honey. If I told you about it in advance, how could you be overcome with joy later?"

Ruth made a face at Mac and looked at her watch. "Your turn is coming, mister. In the meantime, I'll meet you back here in an hour," she said sternly. They were standing in front of Bloomingdale's and Mac was still chuckling over the look of consternation on her beloved face. She got him back, though, giving him a sudden swat on his firm backside, saying, "Don't be late, cowboy, or I won't be waiting."

A few hours later she was still tickled by the look of shock and desire on Mac's face when she gave his hard buttock a good squeeze. *Serves him right, pulling a fast one on me,* she thought. In the end, though, she felt she had the upper hand right now. She'd taken off to the after-five department of Bloomie's at the speed of light, looking for something stunning to wear. There were any number of dresses from which to choose, but she wanted to knock his socks off. She wanted to make him look at her as if she were the most beautiful woman he'd ever seen in his life, audacious as that notion was. It wasn't ego that spurred her on; it was a deep-seated yearning to please him, to make him as happy as he was making her. She didn't even want to think about how much the weekend spree was costing him, but she knew he was dropping a bundle, just to make sure she was having a wonderful time. Now it was time for her to turn the tables on him, and she was pretty sure this delicious confection of a dress would do it.

A little sales associate had attached herself to Ruth as soon as she entered the department and although Ruth had done her best to shake her off civilly, the young woman clung to her like a limpet. She brought her frock after frock, all of which Ruth deemed unsuitable. Too frilly, too ingénue, too daring, they were all too *something*. The young Asian woman, who was named Alison, kept bringing her outfits, and kept her bright smile beaming during the whole ordeal. She had one number she wanted Ruth to try on, something that just didn't seem right for Ruth. It was sheer and black, that's about all Ruth could discern as she kept waving it away. Finally, after trying on number twelve in an unending series of fancy dresses, Ruth had to acknowledge that Alison was the most patient and good-natured associate she'd ever encountered. "Okay, Alison, let's try it," she said with a sigh of resignation. "It can't be any worse than any of these," she added, waving her hand at the piles of discarded finery.

Now, as she gazed in the bedroom mirror, she thanked her guardian angel for bringing Alison to her. The dress, besides being the most expensive Ruth had ever purchased, was the most flattering. It was strapless and the snug bodice fit like it was made for her, lifting her small bosom into a stratosphere of tempting cleavage. It was made of a heavy matte satin and basically unadorned. The skirt was magnificently bouffant and made of silk organdy with a light sprinkling of black brilliants that gave it a subtle sparkle. It was matinee length, which revealed enough of her legs to entice, yet would make her look graceful and sexy while dancing. There was a diaphanous wrap made of the same fabric of the skirt, and while Ruth had goggled at her reflection in the dressing room mirrors, the intrepid Alison had scooted off to find a bag and shoes. The shoes were basically evening sandals in black *peau de soie* with a sparkling black ornament on the toe of each shoe, and the bag was a dainty sequined number just big enough for a lipstick, handkerchief and a compact. It was by far the most amazing outfit Ruth had ever worn in her life and she couldn't wait to show it off for Mac.

Before she left Bloomie's however, she had done two things. First, she'd asked to speak to the store manager so she could impress on him what a jewel he had in an employee like Alison. After the man had thanked her effusively and assured her that Alison would be amply recognized for her professionalism, Ruth had asked one more question of the young woman. "Where's the lingerie department?"

Now it was time for the show to begin. Sure enough, a sexy voice called her from the living room of the suite.

"Are you ready, honey?"

Ruth touched the pearl drop in her earlobe and smiled like a wise and contented cat before answering. "Yes, I am. Are you?" She turned out the light in her bedroom and walked into the living room where her escort awaited. Suddenly the light in the room seemed brighter when his eyes caressed her from head to toe. She returned his smile with one of her own, made even more feminine than usual with the sheer red shimmer of her lip gloss. For once the usually voluble Mac was totally silent, as though he couldn't find the right words to say to her. She turned around in a slow circle, trying to hide her elation at his response.

"Will I do, Julian?" she said in a sultry purr.

"Ruth. Honey, you're...*damn,*" he whispered. "I can't remember enough words to tell you how you look tonight."

He held out his hand and she walked toward him, giving him her small hand in return. "Well, I can tell you that you look magnificent. You're the handsomest man I've ever seen in my life, Julian. You've come a long way from being the worst-dressed lawyer in Louisiana," she teased him.

He was wearing a custom-tailored black suit that emphasized his height and his lean physique. His crisp white shirt was set off by a handmade silk tie in an African-looking print and he looked so good Ruth could feel her heartbeat pulsing in every part of her body. Now it was her turn to tell him that they needed to leave right now if they intended to step a foot out of the suite that night.

"Your wish is always my command," he assured her and in minutes they were on their way.

* * *

It was an enchanted evening from beginning to end. Mac hired a limousine to transport them and it gave the night a Cinderella-like air. The Rainbow Room was everything Ruth could have desired. The ambience was perfect for a romantic rendezvous. To heighten the atmosphere, they were lucky enough to be entertained by the incomparable Jane Monheit, a young jazz singer whose melodic voice drenched the air with an invitation to love. There was a rotating dance floor and they took full advantage of it, dancing the night away when they weren't partaking of their sumptuous three-course meal. It was particularly gratifying to Ruth that Mac never took his eyes off her. Jane Monheit was a true beauty with huge hazel eyes, long, wavy brown hair and a curvy body that could stop traffic, but Mac, unlike the majority of the men in the room, ignored her completely. All his attention was fixed on Ruth and she loved every minute of it. The only time he turned away from her all night was when the maitre d' brought them a bottle of very expensive champagne.

"It's from the gentleman over there," the man said with a discreet nod to a table across the room. "He hopes you and your wife will accept it with his compliments.

There was no mistaking the smiling face of the former President of the United States and his lovely wife. They both waved a greeting to Mac and Ruth, who were duly impressed. "My goodness, somebody's been stepping in some high cotton," she laughed. "Dare I ask how you know them?"

Mac waited until the champagne was opened and

poured, then lifted his glass to hers. "Let's just say we were fighting the same fights. I'll tell you about it some other time. Right now I want to sip a little of this and then take you back out on the dance floor so I can show you off some more. You're one hell of a partner, honey. In fact, you're one hell of a woman. Come on, darlin', let's show them how it's done," he said as he rose and held out his hand.

Ruth really could have danced all night, just like the words from the old musical, but there were better things in store for her. When the limousine arrived to pick them up and transport them back to the hotel, she was more than ready to go. She had excused herself earlier to go to the ladies room and she'd also used her cell phone to test the "whatever, whenever" service of the hotel. She explained what she needed to the concierge, who assured her that all would be in readiness when they returned. A thrill of anticipation ran down her spine as they drove through the streets of Manhattan, partly because she could hardly wait to get there and also because Mac was playing with the long curl that graced the nape of her neck.

The feel of his fingers on the sensitive skin of her throat was thrilling. It was sending little frissons of anticipation all over her, reducing her to a sensual mush. He was also kissing her, caressing her ear with his tongue while he whispered endearments to her, some in French and some other language she couldn't understand. His intentions were plain and needed no interpretation at all. By the time the limousine stopped in front of the W, Ruth was weak from his tender, loving assault on her willing flesh. She was vaguely aware that they were getting out of the luxurious car, only slightly more aware of entering the elevator. As soon as the doors closed, Mac enfolded her in his arms and kissed her, long and sweet. His lips seemed to burn into her soul, his breath became her breath and every beat of his heart was echoed by her own. She had no recollection at all of getting to the suite, but when he opened the door her wits came back to her as she could see that everything was just the way she'd specified.

"My turn," she murmured in a soft, dreamy voice. "This is *your* surprise. I'll bet I can get changed before you," she added, allowing her new black satin evening coat to slide down to the floor. She draped her organza wrap around his neck and used it to pull his head down to hers for one last kiss before she disappeared into her bedroom.

She lost the bet, though, because Mac was ready before she was, although in fairness, she had more to do. She had to remove her gown and put it away, then don the items she'd purchased in the lingerie department at Bloomingdale's. It didn't take too long, but the results were well worth it. This time when she entered the living room, she looked like a Vargas pinup girl come to life. Mac was waiting for her, looking pretty much like a *Playgirl* centerfold himself. Ruth had bought him a Valentine's gift at Bloomie's and had it laid out on his bed. It was a lounging robe of rich silk jacquard with satin lapels and it was the deep red color of Merlot, which made him look even more ruggedly handsome. And it went beautifully with her outfit, too.

She was wearing a short lace gown with a matching floor-length peignoir in sheer flaming red. She debated about the red satin mules with the marabou feathers, but thought *what the hell* and put them on, too. When she strolled into the room, the sight of Mac in the candle-light took her breath away. The "whatever, whenever" service had accomplished everything she asked and the living room was filled with lit candles and long-stemmed red roses. The incredible voice of Jane Monheit filled the room from the stereo system. There was a tray of fruit and a box of Godiva chocolates, as well as a bottle of champagne, which Mac was pouring into crystal flutes. A slight mishap occurred as he over-filled one of the flutes while he stared at her, but he re-covered at once.

They didn't speak at first; they merely looked at each other. It was hard to say who moved first, but they ended up in each other's arms, holding on for dear life. One tiny kiss followed another and another until there just wasn't anything else in the world but the feel of his lips on hers, the taste of his tongue, and the smell of his cologne. When they finally broke the last kiss, Ruth couldn't resist teasing him. "How do you like your surprise, darling?"

"I love it," he answered as he picked her up and carried her to the sofa. "You're going to fill my life with surprises, aren't you?"

Ruth didn't answer him right away; she was stroking his chest with one hand and nibbling his ear at the same time. Finally she answered him as her head found the perfect position on his shoulder. "If that's what you'd like. Anything you want," she whispered.

"I want you, honey. And right now I want to see those legs of yours. Stand up, just for a second," he en-treated. Ruth did so, but slowly as she was reluctant to

leave the warmth of his arms. She rose gracefully and
did a model turn for him, playfully letting the sheer robe
slide down her arms so she could remove it and toss it
into his lap. She stood before him clad only in the short
lace gown and the stiletto-heeled mules, letting him
devour her with his heated gaze before modeling the
ensemble, allowing him to get his first good look at her
long, shapely legs. When he could stand no more he
reached out for her and pulled her into his lap. She
cupped his face in her hands and teased his lips with the
tip of her tongue, tasting them gently and insistently
until he opened for her, returning her gentle touches
with masterful strokes of his own. They explored each
other's lips while his hand explored the bare expanse
of her leg, caressing her calf and rubbing her silken
thigh until he reached the most feminine part of her.

Ruth was shaking with need, wanting him so much
she felt she was melting into him. Her hands had found
their way under his robe and she felt the hard muscles
under the thick, silky hair she'd wanted to touch ever
since she'd glimpsed it that morning. "Julian," she whispered. "Julian, touch me."

He was kissing her neck, her collarbone and making
his way down to her breasts. Her scent intensified as he
continued his passionate discovery of her body, moving
his hand from her thigh to her breasts. They filled his
hands just perfectly and her nipples began to bloom,
engorged with the heated desire he was creating. The
strap of the delicate gown slipped off easily and allowed
him to access her pliant flesh. When his mouth touched
her sensitive tip for the first time, a hot explosion which
she had no control over began in her. His tongue traced

her nipple and it grew larger and harder as he took it in his mouth and sucked, gently at first. The motions of his mouth grew stronger and the sensations rippled through her until she began to move in his arms, desperately needing release from the fire building inside her. She cried out, saying his name over and over again and he responded the way she needed him to, putting his hand back on her thigh, but going higher this time, touching her where she wanted to feel him most, stroking the juicy tender jewel between her legs until the gush of sweet liquid signaled her completion.

She clung to Mac's neck, tasting him with little licks of her tongue as she murmured his name. He returned the caresses, holding her tighter and uttering her name with such tenderness it made big tears roll from her eyes. She gasped softly as he stood up suddenly and carried her into her bedroom. There were candles in there, too, and the bed was already turned down to reveal the rose petals with which the bed was covered. He gently placed her on the bed and lay down next to her, kissing her softly before he licked the fingers he'd used to pleasure her. "That's why I call you *honey*," he murmured. "You're so sweet, Ruth. Sweet to look at, to be with and to taste. And I want to taste you again, but I need something from you first."

"Anything, Julian. Anything you desire is yours," she said breathlessly.

"I need your love," he told her as he lowered his head to hers.

Chapter 8

A week later, Ruth was back in Chicago, but anyone could see she wasn't herself. She looked the same, albeit with the radiance of a newlywed. She acted the same, attending the book club meeting that was held at Sylvia's spacious home in the suburbs. But there was an air of distraction about her that Kimmi discerned at once. If there was anything Kimmi was good at, it was ferreting out personal information about other people. Her coworkers were well aware of this proclivity and had learned to keep their mouths shut at their peril. Ruth knew this, too, and tried her level best to act as normally as possible but her veneer of poise was wearing thin, especially after the meeting ended. She was helping tidy up after the ladies left and she could feel Kimmi's inquisitive eyes following her every movement. Ruth wasn't aware that she had touched her neck several times during the meeting or she'd have been better prepared for what came next.

She had just closed the door of Sylvia's dishwasher when Kimmi leaned over and adroitly turned down the neck of Ruth's sweater. Kimmi and Ruth shrieked at the same time, making Sylvia come out of the dining room with a look of alarm on her face.

"What happened?" she asked anxiously.

Kimmi pointed dramatically at Ruth's neck. "Hickey! I knew it—I knew that's why you had on that sweater!"

Ruth straightened the neck of her peach-colored turtleneck and rolled her eyes in exasperation. "You ol' hoochie. It's called a passion mark, if you must know, and this is why nobody tells you anything, you nosy little girl," she said fondly as she snapped a dishtowel at Kimmi.

Sylvia's eyes lit up with amusement as she looked at the two of them. "Kimmi, you know grown folks are entitled to some privacy. If Ruth wanted us to know she had an exciting weekend in New York, I'm sure she'd tell us," she said pointedly.

"Oh, I know that, Sylvia. I really wasn't trying to be all up in her business," she said earnestly before correcting herself. "Well, maybe I sorta kinda was, but I didn't know people your age could get hickies," she said with wonder in her voice.

Sylvia and Ruth both started laughing. "You need a keeper, Kim Patrice. I don't know which is worse, your total irreverence or your complete ignorance! You make me sound like Methuselah's mama," Ruth said. "For your information I'm only fifty-four and women a lot older than me continue to have very fulfilled and exciting sex lives," she scolded.

Kimmi looked innocently repentant. "I didn't mean you were all dried up or anything. You're one of the hottest ladies I know, you keep yourself together and that's for *real,* for real. But my mother doesn't do anything like that," she said. "I just thought it was what older ladies did, 'cause my mama has no interest in those, umm, *activities.* She's just all into church and stuff and she and my daddy never, you know, get busy like that."

Without even looking at each other, Sylvia and Ruth spoke in perfect unison. "That's because she was scared she'd get another one like *you.*"

Kimmi blithely ignored the insult and made a suggestion. "You should put some Vaseline on that, Ruthie. It'll go away much faster."

"In that case, maybe I should put some Vaseline on you," Ruth mumbled.

Luckily, Kimmi had to leave. She never missed choir rehearsal and she freely admitted that she needed the practice. "I'm living proof that all black women can't sing," she said ruefully. "But that doesn't keep me from making a joyful noise." She kissed Ruth on the cheek before leaving and apologized for the passion mark episode. "That was my bad, Ruth. I was just excited for you. And you know I'm going to try to pry the details out of you, so just be ready," she warned as she left to go to rehearsal.

Sylvia's laughter joined Ruth's as they left the kitchen and went into the family room. Sylvia's house was beautiful, a one-story gem with all kinds of custom-

made details that expressed the personalities of the oc-
cupants. Sylvia's husband, Franco Cardinelli, was a
very successful land developer as well as being a very
devoted husband. There was nothing on earth he
wouldn't do for his wife and their four children. And
his doting behavior also included nine grandchildren,
now that the younger Cardinellis were all grown,
married and reproducing. He joined them in the family
room for a moment on his way to his weekly poker
game with his sons. Ruth laughed when he poked his
head in the room and looked around like a secret agent
on assignment.

"Are they all gone?" he asked in a stage whisper.

"Yes, darling, all the ladies have departed except for
Ruth. You're safe for the moment," Sylvia said as she
held out a graceful hand to him.

Franco liked the members of his wife's club, but he
liked being out of the house when the meetings took
place. All the chatter and merriment was wonderful, but
they often tried to include him in the discussions and he
always felt completely ignorant when they did so. He
was a native of Italy whose suave good looks still drew
attention wherever he went, but the only woman he had
any interest in was his much-adored wife. He came over
to claim a kiss from her sexy lips and smiled when Ruth
told him what a hit the mini calzones and the gelato had
been.

"The pastries were wonderful, too, Franco. I've had
a cannoli before but the others were to die for," she said,
licking her lips.

"They're called *sfogliatelle*," he said, still stroking
Sylvia's neck. "I love to cook, but only for my sweet-

heart." He kissed her hand and then said something in Italian that made her giggle madly.

Ruth watched them wistfully as Sylvia rose gracefully and walked with him to the door. She was still wearing a faraway, goofy look on her face when Sylvia returned and sat next to her on the big cushy couch. Sylvia gave her all of thirty seconds to snap out of her reverie, then got down to business.

"Passion marks and daydreaming. You've been back from New York for a week and you've been avoiding me like I'm a door-to-door religious zealot. Are you going to give it up gracefully or am I going to have to bribe it out of you with a cappuccino and another pastry or two?"

Ruth's reaction wasn't what Sylvia expected at all. Her face went from relaxed to tense and her expression was bleak at best. "Syl, I don't even know where to start. It was the best weekend I've ever had in my entire life. Julian Deveraux is amazing," she said glumly. "He took me to a W hotel," she began.

"I know the ones you mean. Franco and I have spent several weekends in total luxury, so I know your accommodations were wonderful. Was he not good company?" Sylvia probed gently.

"He's amazing, just like I said. We went to see *The Color Purple,* which is fantastic, by the way. We had a hansom cab ride and there was snow falling just like a scene from a movie and we necked like crazy. We went to that wonderful deli, Zabar's for breakfast, and we went shopping. Shopping, Syl! Other than Franco, I don't know any men who enjoy that, but we had a ball. He took me to the Rainbow Room on Saturday night and it was just magical. Jane Monheit was performing, we danced all night and get this, our former president sent us a bottle of champagne. He and his wife even exchanged partners with us on the dance floor, can you believe it?"

"Girl, quit! You danced with Bill himself? Is he a good dancer?"

Ruth gave her a real smile this time. "Yes, he is and a very personable fellow, too. Julian and he go way back and we had lunch with him on Sunday. We went to church at Abyssinian Baptist Church in Harlem, and then we went to Sylvia's restaurant and had the best chicken and waffles I've ever had in my life. We stayed in Harlem most of the day and just had a ball. I've never been with anyone so intelligent and charming in my life. He has a ridiculous sense of humor and we laughed so much my sides actually ached. He's…he's just everything, Syl."

"Then why do you look so forlorn, honey?" Sylvia's eyes grew enormous when she saw Ruth trying not to cry.

"Don't pay me any attention," Ruth said hastily. "It's just that Julian calls me *honey*. That's his special name for me because he says I'm so sweet. He's the one that's sweet, Sylvia. He's just wonderful," she said sadly.

"Well, *I'm* just confused. If he's so swell, why do you look so miserable? It sounds like you had a perfect weekend and you're looking like somebody stole your car! What the hell happened to you in New York?" Sylvia demanded.

"It's very simple," Ruth said in a small quiet voice. "I fell in love. And that's the last thing I ever wanted to do."

When Julian made his shocking request, Ruth had been stunned into momentary silence. He repeated the

*words in an even firmer and more persuasive tone as
he continued to hold her, caressing her with infinite
tenderness. "I want you, Ruth. I've only felt like this
about one other person in my life, and I don't expect to
feel like this again. Everything about you excites me.
Your wit, your spirit—" he paused as he quickly
divested her of the scanty lace gown "—and your incredible beauty," he said as he devoured her with his
passion-filled eyes. "Damn, you're fine," he groaned as
he stroked her soft skin that was heated with her desire
for him. "Honey, I could make love to you for days and
days and still not have enough of you. That's how bad
I want you, Ruth."*

*Ruth had untied the belt of his robe and was helping
him out of it. She was delighted with what she saw; his
broad shoulders, the thick black hair that covered his
broad, muscular chest, his flat stomach and the look of
adoration on his face. "I want you too, Julian. I didn't
think I could feel like this again," she whispered. "I
want you more than you know," she confessed. Their
arms entwined as they reached for each other, drawn
into another long kiss. The feel of his mouth on hers was
wonderful, but it wasn't enough. Gently pulling away
from his lips, Ruth put her mouth on his neck, nibbling
the tender skin gently as she breathed in his scent. Her
hands clung to his shoulders as her lips worked down
his throat to his chest. She was angling her body under
his when he suddenly stopped. Taking her hands in his,
he pinned her gently to the bed.*

*"Honey, you're driving me crazy with that," he
moaned. "I meant what I said, darlin'. I want you, Ruth.
I'm falling in love with you and I want your love in*

return. We're past the age of playing around and dating, we need to know this is the real thing. At least I need to know that," he said, kissing her again and again, soft little kisses that punctuated every few words. "Can you tell me what I need to hear? Am I the man you want for the rest of your life?"

Ruth stared at Mac, totally taken with the gentle, penetrating look of tenderness in his eyes. She tried to answer him honestly, but the words wouldn't come. She touched his strong jaw with the tips of her fingers, stroking him softly as her lips rose to his in another kiss, this time a long, languorous one that made time seem to stop forever.

Sylvia's eyes narrowed and she pursed her lips before speaking. "Come on in the kitchen. We need something a little stronger than cappuccino. Ruth, sugar, unless you mean to commit to this man I suggest you run like hell," she said frankly.

"Run? But Julian would never hurt me," Ruth said in confusion. They reached Sylvia's big kitchen and Ruth took a seat at the work station in the middle of the room. Franco was an amateur chef who took his work quite seriously and there was every kind of cooking implement imaginable. A sleek stainless steel rack over the work island held a variety of high-end pots and pans, while the cupboards beneath housed all manner of serving dishes and other equipment. Ruth watched while Sylvia skillfully measured coffee and started the complex-looking espresso maker. "Why are you telling me to run, Syl? You just told me the man sounded fabulous and now you're saying head to high ground. I don't get it," Ruth said fretfully.

Sylvia was busy getting a bottle of sambuca and fetching cups and saucers as well as the plate of pastries filled with cream and candied fruit. "Look, sugar, I'm not saying that Julian Deveraux isn't everything you said he is. I'm sure he's every bit the magnificent man you've described. But—" she paused in her tasks to look Ruth deeply in the eyes "—this man is completely serious. He's fallen in love with you, Ruth, and he has no intention of letting you go. If you can't handle that kind of commitment, you need to step and fast because ol' boy ain't playing. I ought to know, Franco is that same kind of man and he put me through hell, hear me? Pure, unadulterated torture," she said, but she was smiling when she uttered the words.

Before Ruth could demand an explanation, Sylvia gave her one. "I was just starting out as a professional dancer while I met Franco. I was with a dance troupe in Milan and Franco attended the opening night performance and the reception afterward. We were taken with each other right away and we spent as much time as we could together during the two weeks I was performing in Italy. Well, I didn't have a lot of experience with men. Make that *no* experience, okay? And if you think my baby is fine now you should have seen him back in the day. Mmm-mmm, what a man! So I was more than willing to make him a gift of my virginity but he politely told me 'no, thank you,'" she chuckled.

Ruth was fascinated by the story as she sipped a tasty espresso drink laced with the coffee liqueur. Sylvia didn't disappoint her as she continued talking. "He told me in no uncertain terms that he wanted to be the first man and the last one to touch my body the way a husband should and that if I couldn't handle it we couldn't see each other anymore. Of course, he used to kiss me until I couldn't remember my name, where I lived, the day of the week…ooh, my baby can *kiss,* you hear me? Anyway, he treated me like a princess and he confessed his love every day until I realized I would be the biggest fool in the world if I let him go. So we got married and the rest is history.

"He left Italy and the start of a brilliant career to come to America with me. This was back when inter-racial marriages weren't cute, either," she said with a glint in her eye. "We had a lot to handle but we dealt with everything together. We've always been a team and we've always worked everything out because there was no way we were going to lose each other," she said with a soft sigh. "I've had more love in this lifetime from Franco than you could possibly imagine. There's nothing he wouldn't do for me and vice versa. But," she said, her voice turning stern, "your Julian is cut from that same cloth and if you aren't ready to commit to him mind, body and soul, you need to break it off now."

Ruth took a final sip and held out her cup for more. "You might have to drive me home because I think I need to get good and tipsy tonight. I don't know what I'm going to do, Syl. I'm not going to pretend that I don't care about Julian. He's everything I've ever wanted in a man. I've never felt this way, not since Jared." Nodding her thanks as Sylvia filled her cup again, she thought of something. "I told him about Jared."

Her friend looked up in shock and Ruth nodded her head with a resigned look on her face. "I did. Told him everything, even about what happened after I got out of the hospital, and I've never told anyone but you about that."

Ruth had been enjoying breakfast with Mac on Sunday morning when he suddenly asked her an unexpected question. "Honey, you mentioned that you were also hurt in Jared's attack. I should have asked you this before, but frankly, I wasn't thinking clearly. How badly did those animals hurt you, darlin'?"

She'd had to take a long drink of water before she could answer him. "I was beaten pretty badly, Julian. I wasn't even able to attend Jared's funeral, something that bothers me to this very day. But it wasn't until a few years later that I knew the extent of the damage done to me. I found out I wasn't going to be able to have children as a result of the injuries. That hurt almost as much as losing Jared," she'd admitted.

She was surprised at the dark crimson rage that washed across his face when he heard the story. He used a word she knew he'd never say in front of a woman without deep provocation, and then he apologized. He took her hand and held it tightly, letting his strength flow into her. "Honey, how did you stand it? Losing your fiancé and then finding out you were rendered barren, how did you handle it all? You're a strong woman, Ruth. Exceptionally strong."

Ruth squeezed his hand tightly and assured him she wasn't nearly as strong as he imagined. "After Jared died I went to pieces. I was so distraught I was ready to drop out of college and I only had one semester to go. Once I finished my clinicals I was done with my nursing degree but I was so heartbroken I couldn't face it. So that's when I went into the army. They said I could finish my clinicals in the service and go in as an officer and I thought why not. I needed to get away, far away from all the ugliness and the pain and this seemed like the perfect plan. My sister Lillian about flipped when I told her because it was a done deal. I didn't tell her until I was already enlisted. But her husband was okay with it—he'd gone into the army after a huge personal disappointment and he said it made a man out of him," she told him.

"Everything you see here is the result of my sister, Lillian Bennett Cochran, and the United States Army. They made me the woman I am today," she'd said in a joking manner, but she was serious. "That's why I didn't go over the deep end when I found out I couldn't have children. I was about to be deployed to Vietnam and it just didn't seem to matter to me that much. I had no intentions of getting married and having children so it was like the last chapter in a book. Over, done, complete."

Sylvia was impressed. She knew for a fact that Ruth didn't confide much of anything to anyone unless she knew them very, very well and for her to have shared that much of herself with Julian was unprecedented. "Wow. You really did fall in love, didn't you? Did you tell him about Big Benny and what he did to the punks that beat you up?"

Ruth made a face. "Well, no, I didn't. I saw no point in telling him that my brother-in-law had been a racketeer back in the day and used some old connections to have each one of those miserable little racists beat bloody. That may come out at some point in the future, but why scare the man to death now?" She gave a weak laugh.

"Okay, point taken. But you just seem so torn, Ruth, and I don't understand why. This man sounds perfect for you. Tough, tender, smart, principled and romantic. Not to mention age-appropriate, intelligent and sexy. What's not to like? Why are you so freaked out about this? Love is a gift, sugar, it's not a booby prize," she said sagely. When Ruth held out her cup again, Sylvia raised an eyebrow. "Yes, I'm definitely driving you home. Now why is this man turning you into a lush?"

Ruth took a defiant swallow of her drink and a big bite of the meltingly wonderful pastry. She moaned out loud, only partly because of the delicious tastes mingling in her mouth. "I'm not ready for this, Sylvia. I'm fifty-four years old. Since Jared I've never had a relationship that lasted more than a month, and I don't know if I can. There are so many ways I can screw this up I can't even begin to count them. I don't know the first thing about living with another person, much less a man. I haven't lived with anyone since I raised my sister's children and that was a zillion years ago. And besides, he lives in New Orleans. I live here in Chicago and I love it. I have no desire to move to Louisiana, none whatsoever. I'm too set in my ways, too selfish and stubborn to be that involved with a man. This could never, ever work," she said with a hiccup. "Never."

Sylvia was shaking her head in disagreement even before Ruth finished her diatribe. "Girl, stop. Just stop this. So you live in Chicago, so what? You're here about one week out of the month because you travel so much. Chicago is your home *base,* not your home. And as far as you being selfish, you just need to quit. You're one of the most selfless and generous people I've ever met in my life. Look at what you did when your sister passed away. You resigned your commission and raised her children. Now is that the act of a selfish person?

"You do more volunteer work than anyone I know and you have friends of all ages who flock to your side because they know they can count on you for anything at anytime. You're not selfish, or stuck in your ways or cranky, you're just afraid. Okay, so the man of your dreams, the man you *stopped* dreaming about years ago, was just handed to you on a silver platter. That doesn't mean that you're going to mess up the relationship or anything dire like that. Love is the most wonderful gift you can get in this lifetime and guess what? His *daughter* gave it to you. She's the one who brought you two together and if that's not a good sign I don't know what is. Give yourself a chance, Ruth. Let this man love you, and you love him back with everything you've got," she said emphatically.

Ruth had gone from morose to anxious to elated as Sylvia talked; now her face wore a dreamy expression. "Maybe you're right, Syl. I have to say, I've never met anyone like him. He's such a gentleman, the way he held back from me…" Her voice trailed off as Sylvia shook her head.

"He's not a gentleman, sugar—he's possessive, just like my Franco. You think because he held back he was being refined and genteel? Sister, he was putting you on lockdown, just like Franco did me. He wants you so bad he's probably in pain but he's going to hold out until you tell him yes, that he's the only man you'll ever want. Gentleman, my foot. Tell him yes and see how much of a *gentleman* he is," Sylvia laughed.

Ruth joined in the laughter. She was still laughing

when she answered her cell phone. Her eyes widened and her face tensed as she listened. "I'll meet you in Atlanta. Don't worry about anything, darling, she'll be fine. I love you."

She snapped the phone shut and turned to Sylvia. "I need to get to Atlanta right away. Paris has been in an accident."

Chapter 9

From the moment that his nephew Clay Deveraux called Mac to inform him that his daughter had been in an accident, everything around him felt like the fast-forward setting on a DVD. Clay was a lot like Mac; he was a cool head in a crisis, he was calm and resourceful, and nothing meant more to him than family.

"Judge, Paris's car was forced off the road in an accident tonight. Paris is fine, they think it's just a concussion, but they're keeping her in the hospital overnight for observation," Clay told him. "There's an ice storm going on here, but we don't think that the weather caused the accident. Titus thinks, and we agree, that it has something to do with the threats she's been getting. As soon as we can get cleared for takeoff, we'll have our plane there to get you and the boys, if you think it's time for them to be let in on this. According to Charlie Brown, it should be about an hour before they can clear a takeoff, so be at the airport in about ninety minutes."

Charlie Brown Airport, named after a county commissioner, was one of the two airports to which most private jets were diverted to cut down on the traffic at the heavily traveled Hartsfield International.

"Somebody will be there to pick you up, Judge. I don't know if it'll be me or someone else, but you don't have to worry about getting a ride in. We'll take care of her until you get here, don't worry about a thing."

Clay's efficiency and his assurances were most welcome, but it didn't stop the sudden lurch in Mac's stomach. He loved all his children devotedly, but Paris was his baby girl, his heart. He fought off his anxiety and pressed the speed dial on his cell phone to reach the one voice that could bring him some comfort. "Ruth, darlin', Paris has been in a car accident. Clay says they're just keeping her in the hospital for observation, but he also thinks the accident was a deliberate attempt on her life. I'm leaving for Atlanta tonight, but I had to hear your voice before I went to the airport."

He was gratified beyond measure when her reply came, quickly and emphatically. "I'll meet you in Atlanta. Don't worry about anything, darling, she'll be fine. I love you."

Mac was actually smiling when he made his next call. Out of habit, he called his oldest son first, telling him to get his brothers and get to his house within thirty minutes. And less than twenty minutes later, all four men arrived at Mac's home in New Orleans's historic Garden District. There was a comforting semblance of normalcy as he could hear his sons arguing loudly over some inconsequential thing or another. His high-spirited, hot-tempered sons rarely missed an opportunity to blow off steam, even when the topic was of no importance whatsoever. Tonight, it seemed that Philippe and Lucien were of the opinion that the comedienne and actress Mo'nique was finer than Jill Scott, something that Wade heartily disagreed with.

"Man, you just stupid. You have no taste at all," Lucien said hotly. "Just look at those shoes you're wearing, that tells me all I need to know about your ability to judge what looks good and what doesn't. Mo'nique is *foine*, man. Her skin, her eyes, those lips," he argued.

Philippe backed his twin up enthusiastically. "That hair, those curves and that beautiful smile, man, how can you say Jill Scott is finer than that sister?"

"Jill has beauty, sophistication, depth and soul, besides having a remarkable singing voice, how does *that* compare to Mo'nique?" Wade said angrily.

"Seeing as how none of you has any possible chance of meeting either lady, much less attracting her attention, why don't you all shut up," Julian said with dry amusement. "Judge must have something important to say or we wouldn't all be here. And besides that, you're all wrong. Queen Latifah has them all beat."

The uproar was about to ensue in earnest when Mac entered the living room. "Sit down and pay attention. I have something to tell you and I don't want any histrionics. We have a crisis on our hands and it's time you were made aware of it. Before I go any further I must insist on your full cooperation because we don't have time for foolishness. Got it?"

The men were already seated and watching their father with the respect he was due. In short, clipped sentences he explained about the threatening letters Paris had been getting and the steps her cousins had taken to protect her. He also explained what had transpired that evening. "I suppose I owe you an apology for not bringing you into the loop earlier, but we can debate that some other time. Right now I need to get to the airport. Clay is sending the corporate jet to pick me up and I'll be in Atlanta shortly to see about our girl." He looked at each of his sons in turn. "I know how much you care about your sister and perhaps I should have told you about the situation when it first arose. I thought I was doing the right thing because I was hoping it would die down. I was wrong."

"Look, Judge, don't worry about it. You were right not to tell us, those monkeys would have gone to Atlanta and clowned, so you did the right thing," said Julian. The fact that his brothers didn't try to pound him for the monkey remark was indicative of the gravity of the situation. "I'm going to go home a get a few things. I'm going with you," Julian added.

"See, you should keep a bag in the car the way I do. I'm always ready to go at a moment's notice. I'm going too, Judge," Lucien said.

"You keep a bag in the car because you're a *hound*," Philippe said with a short laugh. "You need extra clothes because you sleep around so much. It won't take me long to pack, Pop, I'm coming, too."

Wade, the quietest of the group, had little more to add, other than to say he'd be back in thirty minutes. "I just hope whoever did this knows what's in store for him," he said in a stony voice.

Mac wouldn't have believed it possible, but the presence of his sons and Ruth's reassurance actually made him relax a little, although that wouldn't be accomplished until he saw his daughter with his own eyes. And short of knowing that Paris was safe from harm, nothing could make Mac feel better than seeing Ruth again. Despite his anxiety, he could actually smile at the thought.

Sylvia was a friend to Ruth in so many ways she couldn't begin to imagine her life without her. After she took Ruth back to her loft, she got busy. It was Sylvia who called her son Carmine, who was an executive at O'Hare International Airport and expedited getting her a seat on the next thing smoking to Atlanta. Sylvia also packed for Ruth while Ruth took a shower and put on fresh makeup. She smiled when she saw that Sylvia had laid out clothes for her to put on, an outfit that included another turtleneck, this one purple angora.

"Syl, I can't thank you enough for this. If you weren't here I'd still be trying to figure out what to take with me. If anything has happened to my girl, I don't know what I'll do. I don't know what Julian will do, either. That young woman is a huge part of his life. He adores her, Syl, he really does. He just dotes on her," Ruth said in a muffled voice as she put on her silk camisole and her sweater. She added a spectacular pair of earrings, a pair so beautiful Sylvia had to come investigate.

"Woo-hoo, those are something else! What kind of stone is that?" she asked.

Ruth blushed. The earrings were cushion cut ovals of chrysolite with an eighteen-carat gold bezel, with smaller ovals of tanzanite dangling from the base of the bigger stone. The chrysolite was a unique shade of pale yellow-green that contrasted beautifully with the purplish-blue tanzanite and also made her eyes look even more gorgeous than usual. "They're my Valentine's Day gift from Julian. He has good taste, doesn't he?"

Sylvia's devilish sense of humor came to the fore as she responded. "Yeah, he has good taste all right. Real good taste. But does *he* taste good? That's what really matters, sugar."

Both women were still laughing as they went into the living room. The buzzer rang and it was Franco, who had come to take them to the airport. He looked at the laughing pair as he picked up Ruth's bag. "You girls need to shake a foot if you plan to make that flight," he cautioned.

Sylvia kissed him on the cheek. "It's shake a *leg,* sweetheart. Shake a leg means to hurry, not shake a foot."

Franco kissed her back. "Shake anything you like, just get going, *cara.*"

Ruth loved her niece's husband for any number of reasons, but tonight it was his sheer efficiency that endeared him to her. Not only were he and Titus Argonne waiting when she got off the plane, but Clay had a car at her disposal, too.

"Aunt Ruth, Judge and the boys will be coming in at Charlie Brown Airport on the family plane. Titus wanted to meet with him to explain what's been going on, but I figured you'd want to see him as soon as possible. So he'll take you out to the airport and Marcus and I will follow you out there so you'll have your own transportation. And before you ask, she really is fine. She's resting comfortably and they're going to discharge her in the morning and you and Bennie can fuss over her all you like. She really is fine," he promised her.

Ruth hugged him tightly, thinking once again that Deveraux men were a breed unto themselves. Her niece had certainly gotten a wonderful husband in Clay Deveraux. And for the moment the thought that she, too, had a devastating Deveraux man hot on her trail didn't cause her stomach to knot up. Instead a comforting warmth spread through her like the glow of her own private sun.

The flight into Atlanta was quick and comfortable, two things for which Mac was profoundly grateful. He was even more grateful that his sons went to sleep so they couldn't think up something else to banter about. It was just Mac and Julian, quietly conversing in the rear of the luxurious plane.

"Judge, if Clay says Paris is going to be fine, she is. That's the end of it. Clay isn't going to give you his word on something that he doesn't believe to be true," Julian said comfortingly. "I don't know if that Titus person is on the job or not, but we'll find out about that in just a little while," he added with a lethally feral grimace.

"Julian, I'm only going to say this once. Don't start any mess with Titus, okay? The man is a consummate professional, extremely capable and, more to the point, he has some very, very strong feelings for your sister. He knows what he's doing and we need to let him do what he does without any interference."

Julian gave his father a skeptical look. "You act like you know this man or something."

"I wouldn't claim to know him, but when Paris informed me about the threats, I came to Atlanta to make sure she was okay. She made dinner for me and Bennie's aunt, Ruth Bennett, and Titus was there. I had an opportunity to talk with the young man at length and I'm convinced he has a vested interest in Paris's safety. He cares about her very much, son, and whoever tries to hurt her better be long gone before Titus finds him. It's that serious," Mac said as Julian continued to look doubtful.

"Love is an amazing emotion, son. Aside from your mother there's been no one on this earth I love as much as my children. Your safety, your well-being and your happiness have always been paramount with me, I hope you know that," he said quietly.

"Of course we know that, Pop. As a matter of fact, you may have spent a little *too* much time with us. You haven't had a serious relationship since Mom died and that's a long time. There should've been something more in your life than your kids and the law."

"What I had was more than enough," Mac said with a quiet finality. "When you become a father, you'll understand what it's like to have that kind of love. From the time you hold that little baby in your hands for the first time, your life becomes totally different. Ask Clay, ask any of your cousins about how it feels to have that kind of love in the palm of your hand. You have to remember, son, I loved your mother beyond measure. I didn't really want to be involved with anyone after she died, not on a permanent basis. What I wanted was to make sure my children were clothed, fed, comforted, loved and grew up to be productive and successful adults. I hate to say it, but I was really concerned about Paris the most because she was my baby girl," Mac admitted sheepishly.

"Men are always proud of their sons, they love their sons, but those little girls just wrap their fingers around your heart and don't let go. Just wait until you have one of your own, you'll know what I'm talking about."

Julian looked out the window at the impenetrable night sky before answering his father. "Pop, the chances of that are slim to none. After the Maya debacle I have no interest in that kind of involvement. Your marriage may have been idyllic, Clay and them may have all found fabulous wives, but that doesn't mean that marriage is for everyone. It's not for me," he said firmly. "Pop, I don't have to tell you how torn up I was after Maya left me. You know, probably better than anyone, what I was like after she was gone. If you think I'm putting myself through that kind of hell again, you're crazy," he said fiercely. "No disrespect intended, sir, but I think I'm just like you. I'm a one-woman man and when that woman is no longer attainable, the game is over. Period."

"Look, son, I don't want you to think I've been pining away from a broken heart for all these years. Your mother was a unique and vibrant person. She was an exciting, unconventional and totally remarkable woman. And if she thought I was sitting around whining because she was gone she'd come back and kick my butt six ways to Sunday." Mac laughed softly. "I've dated my share of women since I stopped grieving for your mother. I just never met anyone I wanted to make a permanent part of our lives. I had my children to consider, Julian. I couldn't risk getting too involved with someone who couldn't deal with a houseful of hooligans and my Paris. But I haven't been a monk, either," he said defensively.

Julian grinned at his father. "Well, Judge, since we're all grown now you don't have us as an excuse anymore. So when are you going to start looking for someone special?"

"What makes you think I haven't found her?" Mac enjoyed the stupefied look on his oldest son's face before he relented.

"I'm still seeing Ruth," he said smugly. "She's a beautiful woman with a personality to match and we've been enjoying ourselves tremendously," he said with a smile.

For the rest of the short flight to Atlanta Julian deftly questioned his father about Ruth, and Mac just as deftly sidestepped any question he didn't want to answer. By the time they had safely landed and were getting ready to head into the airport, Julian was ready to concede that his father's reputation as a wily and formidable attorney was well-earned; he had gotten very little information out of the older man. But he did get answers to some of his questions in a most unexpected manner. As they entered the airport, a sultry voice said "Julian," which made both father and son turn to the source of the sound.

It was Ruth, looking elegant, enigmatic and fascinating—at least the younger Deveraux men thought so. It was quite obvious that Mac was thinking something else entirely as he went to her at once, bending his head for a long, welcoming kiss.

Chapter 10

After capturing her eager lips in a kiss, Mac had very little time to actually talk to Ruth. First, he had to introduce her to his sons, who wasted no time in surrounding the couple. Ruth didn't seem uncomfortable in the least; she just leaned against him with a smile while she greeted each man in turn. Mac's arm tightened around her waist as he did the honors.

"This is Julian, my oldest son. This is Wade, the next oldest. The youngest are Philippe and Lucien, as you can see they're twins. This is Ruth Bennett," he said, unaware that he was revealing his heart as he looked down at her. He fixed his sons with a steely glare and warned them, in the voice they all recognized meant business, to behave themselves.

Ruth was smiling and shaking hands with all of the

men when Titus cleared his throat and made a subtle gesture to indicate he needed to talk to Mac alone. While his sons all fawned over Ruth, Mac, Clay and Titus moved to the side to confer.

"Mr. Deveraux, I can't tell you how sorry I am this happened. I was hoping that the letters would be the end of this, but on the chance I was wrong, I kept Paris under surveillance," he began.

Mac waved his hand impatiently. "I understand that, son. And please, call me Mac or Judge. I told you, nobody calls me Mr. Deveraux. How is Paris doing?"

Titus's face gave it all away as he reported that Paris was sleeping soundly when he left the hospital. His usually stoic face softened into a sweet expression Mac would have wagered that no one had seen in years. "They gave her something to help her sleep. She got a pretty good bump on the head and she'll probably be bruised and sore tomorrow, but she's tough, sir. She'll be fine. I know you want to see her tonight, but I think it would be a good idea if you and I talked tomorrow. And her brothers, if you think they'll listen to anything I have to say." His eyes turned a stony gray as he looked at the four Deveraux men approaching with uniformly unfriendly expressions on their handsome faces. Apparently they were finished charming Ruth and decided to go on the attack.

"Mac, I'm going to take you and Ruth to the hospital," Clay said tactfully. "I'm ninety percent sure there won't be any trouble here tonight, right?" He looked at his cousins, who were still focused on Titus, the man they considered to be responsible for their sister's condition.

Mac put his arm around Ruth again as he shook Titus's hand. "We'll talk tomorrow, son." He turned to his sons and gave them his usual farewell. "Don't call me if you get locked up. I'm not posting any bail for grown men. And if you're smart you'll leave Titus alone because he looks like he can take you."

Clay escorted them to a waiting Chrysler 300 and, as promised, got in his Jaguar to lead them to Piedmont Hospital, where Paris had been admitted. There wasn't a lot of conversation in the car between Mac and Ruth, but words weren't needed to express what Mac was feeling. Instead there was a comfortable quiet as they held hands and just relished being together. When they arrived at the hospital they were allowed to see Paris for a few minutes. Ruth went to the bed and Mac was stunned to see tears gathering in her luminous eyes as she leaned over to kiss Paris's slightly swollen cheek. "Sleep well, baby, we're here," Ruth murmured.

Mac looked down at Paris and for a moment it was like being in the nursery looking at her innocent slumber. She really hadn't changed too much from the time she was a little girl; to him she often looked exactly the same. Right now he was just glad to see her looking rested, albeit a little bruised. Ruth took his hand and held it tightly, seeming to sense what he was feeling. He kissed her brow and brushed her long hair away from her face. "We'll be back in the morning, cupcake."

As they were leaving the room, the nurse assured them they would take excellent care of her. "Don't worry about a thing, Mr. and Mrs. Deveraux, she's in good hands." Ruth looked helplessly at Mac when she heard her referred to them, once again, as a married couple, but it didn't seem to faze Mac at all.

"Thank you for saying that," he said graciously. "We'll be back in the morning to get her. And I warn you, her brothers may be here later. If they cause any trouble, well, do what you have to do," he said dryly.

The hospital wasn't very far from Paris's home, so in a very short time Mac and Ruth were there; alone at last. Conversation was still at a minimum as Mac busied himself bringing in the luggage and Ruth hung up her coat and went into the kitchen to make a pot of tea. Mac followed suit, hanging his overcoat in the closet next to Ruth's and then joining her in the kitchen. He washed his hands as he watched her removing two large mugs from the glass-fronted cupboard that lined the kitchen wall.

"Tea? Can you add a drop of bourbon to mine? This has turned out to be one hell of a day," Mac commented as he slid down onto one of the tall stools next to the work space in the center of the room. Ruth stopped what she was doing and turned to face him. Smiling sympathetically, she said, "Yes, it has. You must be exhausted."

He looked at her, his face completely serious as he took in every aspect of her appearance. Her hair was in its usual chic style, with the long curl at the nape beckoning him like a coquettish finger. Her trim figure was delightful to behold in her purple sweater and sleekly tailored black slacks. She was wearing a different pair of flats, a ballerina style that managed to look sinfully comfortable and stylish at the same time. The faint scent of her fragrance enchanted him and he was tickled to see that she was wearing the earrings he'd given her for Valentine's Day. He shook his wrist so she could see that he was wearing the thick gold link bracelet she'd given him. He liked the way it looked on his strong wrist and hadn't taken it off once since she gave it to him. He could have looked at her forever, but he had other plans in mind.

"You love me," he said quietly. There was no teasing in his tone, he was utterly serious. Ruth looked him straight in the eyes, and there was no laughter in her gaze, just a clear, passionate acknowledgment of the truth.

"You know I love you, Julian. And you love me, too." The words lingered in the air poignantly, like the fading notes of a distant melody.

Mac held out his hand and she took it, walking to him without haste or trepidation, her steps deliberate and sure. She stopped when she was in his arms, sighing as he rose to hold her as closely as possible.

"I do love you, honey, more than you know. And I want to show you how that love makes me feel," he whispered as he licked her ear.

"What are you waiting for?" she murmured.

Without another word they left the kitchen to go upstairs.

If someone had told Ruth what the evening would bring, she would've broken out in hives from sheer nerves. Instead, she was as comfortable as though she and Mac had been a couple for years. When they reached the top of the stairs, she allowed him to lead her into the guest bedroom, where they calmly began getting ready for bed. Paris lived in a brick carriage house in the Ansley Park area of Atlanta. It had been Vera Deveraux's home before she married Marcus, and Paris rented it from her. It was a cozy, nicely decorated place with which Ruth was very familiar, and so was Mac. He'd already put both their bags in the room he used when he was visiting, and the sight of their suitcases sitting side by side at the foot of the king-sized bed seemed perfectly right to Ruth.

"How about if I unpack for us while you take a shower? I think you need to relax a little after the day you've had."

Mac put both his hands around her waist and pulled her against him. "How about if we unpack really fast and take a shower together? That sounds like a much better use of our time," he said in his low, sexy voice. "You didn't happen to bring that little red nightgown with you, did you?" He gently palmed her behind and flexed his fingers over its firm curves.

Ruth blinked because Mac's touch was arousing her to a point where she couldn't think straight, and also because she suddenly realized she had no clue what Sylvia had put in the bag. "Julian, I haven't the faintest idea what's in there. Let's find out what Sylvia decided was appropriate nightwear for the weekend," she said with amused curiosity.

In a short time they were in the shower, locked in each other's soapy arms, laughing like mad. It turned out that Sylvia hadn't packed a single item of sleepwear; instead there was a note that read, "If you play your cards right you won't need a nightie. Good luck and good loving." They were still cracking up over her bold move, but the amusement was beginning to give way to something else entirely as the heady scent of the imported Mango bath gel they had used wrapped itself around them. Ruth loved the way Mac was caressing her body almost as much as she loved looking at him.

"Julian, you're in such good shape," she began, but before she could elaborate she gasped as her knees went weak from the way he was caressing her body with his lather-slicked hands. He used his hands to cup her small, taut breasts, rubbing them in circles while his thumbs teased her nipples into firm peaks that begged for his tongue. Sliding his hands down around her waist, he anchored her against his massive erection and groaned as she moved against him. She purred out loud, the soft sound becoming keener and louder as he picked her up. Wrapping her legs around his waist she rubbed her already sensitive breasts against the mat of soapy hair on his broad chest.

"This feels better than I imagined," Mac admitted.

Ruth was finding it more and more difficult to speak. "You thought about this before?" she gasped out.

He was rubbing her behind over and over, the heat from his hands bringing her dangerously close to a much-needed release. "Of course I did. I fantasize about you, honey. I dream about you and I think about you day and night. But nothing compares to this. You're incredible," he moaned as their bodies began to writhe against each other in a dance of desire that was almost painful. By mutual consent they rinsed each other off with the handheld showerhead and Mac gallantly offered a warm towel out to Ruth to wrap around her. He put one around his waist and picked her up to carry her into the bedroom, where they dried each other off and kissed madly before Ruth forced him onto the bed.

"I'm going to give you a massage," she said with a smile. "Unless you have some objection to having my hands all over you," she teased.

Mac surprised her by turning her over on her back. "I do have a problem with that. I want you, honey. I want to kiss you all over starting with that hot, sweet mouth of yours and ending with those sexy toes and everything in between. The massage can wait, but this can't," he growled. He knelt over her trembling body and kissed her, taking her lips in a deep, penetrating mating that explored every bit of her mouth while she returned the favor. While they were kissing, his hands were gently kneading her breasts, his clever thumbs circling her nipples until she thought they might erupt from the sensation. When he finally took her right one in his mouth, he began sucking feverishly, his tongue making the nerve endings in the sensitive tip dance. His hands moved down her taut rib cage, as he licked his way down the middle of her chest, stopping to pay tribute to her navel.

"Honey, this is as cute as the rest of you," he said with delight. It was a perfect round little outtie that nestled like a sweet little treat for his tongue and when he licked it and pulled it into the warm recess of his mouth, Ruth clenched her hands on the linens and moaned aloud. She was trying to tell him how good it felt, but all she could manage was a primal, throaty sound. By now her entire body was moist and glistening from his touch and the best was yet to come. Her thighs were tensed, twisting and rubbing against each other, until Mac gently urged them apart. "Open wider, honey, so I can taste how sweet you really are," he crooned. Ruth's head rolled restlessly on the pillow and she brought the back of her hand to her mouth as she felt Julian take full advantage of her new position.

He slipped another pillow under her hips, parted her weak but willing thighs even wider and allowed his warm breath to heat her waiting apex of love. He buried his face in her femininity and kissed it the way he had kissed her mouth, but with more intensity. He explored every bit of her soft sweetness, over and over as she bit the back of her hand to still the cries that were rising in her throat. He ended the sweet torture by finding her jewel, licking it like candy, then sucking it gently. When the sucking turned into a tender nibbling, Ruth became his willing supplicant, screaming and calling his name, crying out with a passion she had no idea she possessed. He relented gradually while still sucking and licking her until he was sure she'd climaxed at least three times. He finally began to kiss his way back up her torso, licking off the slick sheen of perspiration he'd made appear on her body. When he finally got to her face, she placed trembling hands on his cheeks and tried her best to kiss him, but she was too spent from his loving.

He kissed her gently and put his arms around her as she draped herself over his chest and lay there trying to breathe. "Still love me?" he teased.

Ruth's hand was stroking his chest and she was still trembling as she tried to speak. It took her almost a minute before she could murmur a response. "You know I do. I said you were dangerous, didn't I?"

"You might have mentioned it a few times."

"I think I forgot to mention that I'm a dangerous woman, too," she cooed as her hand found his long, thick manhood that was waiting for her touch. "And," she promised, "I'm about to show you just how dangerous I can be."

"I'm ready whenever you are, honey, but I think I need to leave you for just a moment," he told her.

He was back in a few minutes with a small tray holding a carafe of iced water, a goblet full of crushed ice, a bowl of strawberries and grapes and a box of condoms. "They were in my briefcase," he said sheepishly. "But I also thought you might be thirsty." He poured some water into the goblet and handed it to her, watching as she took a few deep swallows. He was touched to see that she had straightened the bed and finger-combed her curly, still-damp hair while he was gone. "You're beautiful, honey. You're the most beautiful thing I've ever seen in my life, and I've done some traveling," he said with a smile.

Ruth took another swallow of water before handing the goblet back to him. She picked up a strawberry and bit into it, smiling at him like Eve in the garden. "I've been all over the world, Julian, and I can't remember ever seeing a man as fine as you. Now before you get conceited, come on over here. You're going to work for this, sweetheart."

Before she could say another word, he had dropped his towel and they were kissing wildly, sharing the sweet, juicy berry with gusto. Now it was Ruth who was in control, forcing him onto his back as she knelt beside him, exploring his body with her hands and her mouth. She gave his nipples the same treatment she'd received, but she kept one hand on his manhood the whole time, squeezing it gently as she learned every inch of its turgid strength. The parts of his chest that weren't adorned with silky hair were smooth and muscular, and his flat, hard stomach boasted a navel that was a definite innie, a place her tongue adored while Mac moaned with pleasure. She had kissed and licked her way down to his most vulnerable spot and when he would have denied her that pleasure, she pushed him down again. She stopped her exploration of his hot flesh long enough to take another sip of the iced water before placing the glass on the nightstand. Without warning, she took him in her mouth and the twin sensations of her cold lips and her hot tongue were almost his undoing.

It was Mac's turn to call her name in a voice made rough with pure sexual excitement. His fingers tangled in her hair, tightening as she made a meticulous exploration of his penis with her questing tongue. Somehow she'd slipped a tiny chip of ice in her mouth and the mixture of fire and ice had him writhing and roaring with sensual joy. He had to sit up to pull her off his body, but only long enough for her to straddle him. She looked at him with half-closed eyes and smiled. "What's the matter, darling? Wasn't I doing it right?"

She was stroking his hips with her soft hands and her back was arched slightly so that her breasts with their still engorged nipples were on full display. Mac put his hands on her buttocks and flexed his long fingers, looking at her with a bemused expression while he recovered his breath. "Okay, so it's like that, is it?"

Ruth didn't answer; she just moved her hips sensuously so he could feel the moist treasure that was waiting for him. He reached for the box of condoms and tried to take one out, but Ruth took it from him. "Let me do that, Julian. I love touching you," she said with an innocent air. She proved it, too, applying the condom in the most sensual manner possible. As soon as she was finished, Mac showed her that he was now in control, flipping her over on her back and opening her thighs so he could join their bodies. When Ruth felt the force of him entering her she put her hands on his shoulders and a long shuddering cry emerged from her throat. He thrust into her repeatedly as she clenched her vaginal walls around the magnificent strength of his erection.

Her hands tightened on his broad back and she abandoned herself totally to Mac. She could only whisper his name and the whisper suddenly became a scream as he brought her to a convulsive climax that made her world go black for a moment. They lay entwined, both of them damp and fragrant with the exquisite scent of their love. Ruth tried to choke back a tiny sob, until Mac kissed her eyelids and made her look into his eyes. "I love you, honey. You're mine now, and I belong to you."

The tears she had been trying to hold back started pouring out of her eyes but they didn't last long because Mac's body started moving in hers again.

"Don't cry, honey, I've got you. You're mine now, I've got you. I love you, Ruth," he whispered, and the moan became a chant as they continued to make love until the night sky turned into dawn.

Chapter 11

Mac had to laugh at the expression on Ruth's face the next morning. She was in the guest bathroom curling her hair when Mac appeared in the doorway with his shirt undone so she could see the magnificent chest that had brought her so much pleasure the night before. She stopped what she was doing and looked at him suspiciously. "Julian, don't come any closer. We have to get dressed so we can go get Paris and if you do that again we won't leave the house," she said in a voice that sounded slightly breathless.

"If I do what, honey?" he asked, full of feigned innocence. "What did I do?"

Ruth put one last curl in the top of her head before using the small ceramic iron to make her sassy tail behave again. As she pulled the long lock through the heated iron she made a noise of disgust. "You know what you did," she said grumpily. "It was bad enough that you kept me up until dawn, but when you woke me up this morning…" Her voice trailed off and she smiled at her reflection in the mirror. After quickly styling her newly curled hair she licked her lips and tried to glare at him.

"Didn't you like it, darlin'? If it didn't please you I won't do it again, but you seemed to enjoy it as much as I did," Mac said offhandedly.

By now Ruth had joined him in the bathroom doorway and had her arms around his waist while she rubbed her cheek against his chest. "You know I liked it. Almost as much as I like you," she said as she teased his nipple with her tongue. "But we don't have time to play right now, we have to see about our girl."

It always made Mac's heart turn to mush when Ruth referred to Paris like that. For one thing, he knew she wasn't aware that she was doing it, and for another, he knew she meant it. Ruth loved his daughter dearly and it only made him love her all the more. If they weren't trying to leave the house he'd have thrown her across the bed and treated her to a repeat of the morning's frolic. He'd awakened Ruth in the most intimate way possible, by putting her long legs over his shoulders and pleasuring her until she screamed his name. He loved hearing his name torn from her silken throat in total abandon. When he met her he thought she was a sexy woman, but the wild passion she turned loose on him was more than any man could hope for. He wanted to tell her so right then and there, but he knew better. They'd be back in the bed in about two seconds if he had his way and while Ruth would love it, they really did need to get to the hospital.

"I'll try to behave, honey, but you bring the beast out in me. You're too damned sexy, that's your problem." He put his hands around her waist and was tickled to hear her stomach growl. "How about I make you breakfast, something healthy and low-carb?"

She made a little face but agreed. "I love breakfast, but I'll be honest, I'm too hungry for healthy. I want a fried egg sandwich and a cup of really strong coffee," she sighed. "I wonder if there's a diner around here."

Mac raised an eyebrow and winked at her. "You change the sheets and meet me in the kitchen in ten minutes, how about that?"

True to his word, when Ruth entered the kitchen carrying the sheets she'd removed from the bed, Mac was putting the finishing touches on her breakfast and it looked fabulous. There was rich-smelling coffee in a big mug, just the way she liked it. A V8 juice in a pretty green juice glass sat next to a pink glass bowl of sliced strawberries, kiwifruit and big green grapes. And holding down center stage was the most perfect looking fried egg sandwich Ruth had ever seen. It was on golden brown toast and she could see a lacy dark brown edge on the egg, just the way she liked it. "Oh, my, Julian, that looks heavenly. Let me put these in the washer and I'll be right back."

She reappeared in a couple of minutes and they sat on the tall stools of the work island, facing each other with smiles of utter content on their faces. They held hands and said grace. They'd no sooner finished saying Amen when Mac started teasing her. "I said change the sheets, not bury them. Are you trying to hide evidence of our night of passion, honey?"

Ruth took a tiny sip of coffee and made a little noise of approval. "I certainly am. You know how nosy Paris is and she'll be home in a few hours. It's not like we can keep this a secret from her for long."

Mac laughed as he watched Ruth take her first bite of the sandwich, which she had cut neatly in half on the diagonal. "This is perfect, Julian, just what I wanted. You can cook, too. I may have to take you home with me," she said blithely.

"I get around in the kitchen," Mac admitted. "I can do basic stuff like meat loaf, spaghetti, casseroles, things that kids will eat. I have a few specialties like what you're eating," he said with a grin. "And I make a mean fried bologna sandwich, too."

"It just so happens that's one of my weaknesses. There were times in 'Nam when I'd have sold a body part for a good fried bologna sandwich or some barbeque. I eat healthy now with only occasional trips to the dark side where the Häagen-Daz's and the Ben and Jerry's live. I don't overdo, but," she said with a sigh, "I truly can't resist good barbecue. Especially a grilled sausage on a bun with grilled onions…ooh, I go crazy. How good are you with a grill, Julian?"

"As good as I am at making love," he said with a straight face.

"I'm going to be big as a house," Ruth said sadly.

Mac's laughter echoed through the kitchen. He watched Ruth finish her meal, thinking that once again she'd revealed herself to him in a very sincere and un-selfconscious way. She looked happy and sated as she daintily ate the fruit while she sipped her coffee. Suddenly she put her cup down and looked at him, her eyes soft and serious at the same time. And she did it again; with one simple question she drew him into her enchanted aura without even trying.

"Julian, you don't really talk about your wife. Can you tell me about her?" she asked sweetly.

If Mac was surprised by her question, he didn't let it show, Ruth thought as they finally drove to the hospital to see about Paris. She'd insisted on tidying up the kitchen while he told her about his wife, Genevieve. "She was a Louisiana girl, she and her sister Gertrude. They were from Shreveport and they were both named after great-aunts or something, which is why they had such old-fashioned names. Everybody used the French pronunciation of her name, though, so it suited her better. Most people called her ViVi, which really got on her sister's nerves because no matter how hard she tried she couldn't get anyone to call her Trudie. It just didn't suit her, probably because she was so uptight. She was always Gertrude to everybody, Gert, if they wanted to piss her off." Mac chuckled.

"But not Genevieve—she was like her name, exotic and exciting. I called her Ginger, though, because she was sweet, spicy and hot like ginger. In a lot of ways, Paris is just like her. She was tall and plump, a good-sized girl. She had this pretty long black hair and these flashing black eyes and she was curious about everything. People, places, events, everything—I think she was probably the best-read person I've ever met. I think that's where Paris gets that curiosity from, although her mother channeled hers into the law. She was bright and funny like Paris, but much more intense. She was a true intellectual and she loved to study, to learn.

"We met young, married young and started a family young, which is probably how we did it all. If we'd waited until we were older, we'd have had more sense than to start a family in the army and try to go to school at the same time, but we did it. We were a team, we worked everything out. We took turns watching the kids, we made friends on base so we could spend time together without them, we studied together and we managed to accomplish most of our dreams, although she didn't live to see them all," he said with a hint of sadness.

"Paris is a lot like her physically, although she pays a lot more attention to her attire and her makeup than her mother ever did. Ginger was a real gypsy sort, as long as it was clean and decent, it could be red plaid and purple paisley, she didn't care. But she always had a certain charm about her that made her the most captivating woman in the room. She drew men to her like flies. Women, too, come to think of it. Even though she was light years away from some of the wives we met on base in terms of her attitudes and her ambitions, she still managed to have lots of friends. She didn't preach at people, I guess that was her secret. You didn't have to believe what she believed, you just had to be a good person and she was fine with you."

Ruth was now finished with the kitchen and was leaning on the counter, watching him with fascination. "You said she went into law, too?"

"Yep. She went into environmental law before anyone really knew what it was. She had a passion for ecology and she loved her state. She loved Louisiana and she hated what the oil companies had done to it, them and the other big businesses that were buying up the land and destroying it and the people they were shoving aside in their greed. That was her passion and she was a true tigress. When it came to her family and her law, you'd better not cross her or there was hell to pay. She was so full of life and so tough. It was just unbelievable that she could die. I honestly thought she'd live forever, Ruth."

Ruth moved to his side of the work counter and stood close to him, placing one hand on top of his and her arm around his shoulder. "What happened, Julian?"

"She'd had a headache off and on for some weeks. She wasn't one to complain, but I could tell and she did admit to having some discomfort a few times. I kept trying to get her to go to the doctor, and she promised me she would, but she was working on a big case and the kids were getting over the measles or something. She was just too busy to make an appointment and I was too stupid to make her go. And one day she just dropped dead. She passed out at the office and was dead before she hit the floor. It was an aneurysm," he said quietly, not bothering to wipe away the tears that appeared in his eyes.

Ruth couldn't help herself; she put both arms around his big shoulders and held him while she kissed the tears away. "She sounds like a wonderful woman, Julian. I think I would have liked her very much."

Mac turned on the stool so he could return her embrace, holding her tightly and letting her comfort him. He rubbed his face on her soft hair and kissed it.

Then he kissed her forehead and tipped her chin up so he could look in her eyes. "She would have liked you, too. She would have called you a woman with a good head on her shoulders. She would have loved having you for a friend, honey."

Ruth buried her head in his neck and squeezed her eyelids together tightly so the torrent of sentimental tears wouldn't gush out. "Me, too, Julian," was all she could say.

By late afternoon, Paris was home from the hospital and her family was gathered around her making sure she was comfortable. She had protested several times that she was fine, she didn't need to be waited on, but it didn't do a bit of good. Mac watched the scene with amusement as Lillian, Bennie and Ruth fussed over her.

"I'm fine, I really am," she protested. "The boys brought me ice cream and candy and magazines, none of which I need, but all of which I appreciate," she said as she smiled at her brothers, who were lounging about on the floor and the chairs like big jungle cats. "I'm just fine. Aunt Ruth, I'm still surprised to see you. I had no idea you were here. I was so out of it from whatever they gave me last night I didn't know what was going on. Where did you spend the night?" she asked innocently.

Ruth's face turned bright pink and for once in her life she had nothing to say. If Paris had looked at her father she'd have noticed a definite redness along his ears, too, but her attention was all on Ruth. "Were you at Bennie's house? I know the boys were there and they didn't mention you being there," she mused.

Ruth looked like a doe in the crossfire of an AK-47.

Suddenly Bennie thrust a plate in the younger woman's face. "Have some pie," she said.

Paris looked tempted, but shook her head. "I can't use this as an excuse to eat like a horse. So, Aunt Ruth, were you in the guesthouse at Clay and Bennie's?"

Bennie practically shoved the plate up Paris's nose. "Have some pie," she repeated firmly. "I made it just for you—it's Key Lime from Ceylon's recipe. Want a bite?"

"Oh. Okay, it looks delicious," she said as she took the plate from Bennie's hands.

Mac wanted to laugh at the scene but he knew Ruth would have his head if he did. He was getting ready to go back to New Orleans, as were his sons. They all had court appearances the next day and as long as Paris was healthy and cared for, their concerns were allayed. Besides, Mac wanted to get them out of there before it became too obvious that he and Ruth had spent the night in Paris's guest room. Some things were too private and precious to be shared with the world and this was one of them.

He managed to get a few minutes alone with Ruth before he left, though. "I'll see you next weekend. I'm looking forward to seeing you, honey. To be perfectly honest, I'm going to begrudge every minute that we're apart," he said while kissing her neck.

He loved hearing the soft sigh that escaped her lips. "I am, too. Are you sure you want to come next weekend? I told you all my friends will be there for our customary Academy Awards party. They can be rather...*intense,*" she said dryly.

"This is a must, darlin'. We both want to see Paris walking the red carpet and what better way to meet your friends than all at once? It'll be fun, you'll see," he crooned as he continued to kiss her. They were in the pantry, of all places, but it was the only place they could be alone. It was sweet, in a way, hiding from the family and necking like teenagers. Ruth gasped as Mac demonstrated his agility by putting his hand under her sweater and her bra, massaging her breast while he kissed the daylights out of her.

"Judge, let's get going, we don't want to hold up takeoff."

Ruth sprang away from Mac, adjusting her top and giving him a glazed smile. "You're a hot mess, Julian. You should be ashamed of yourself," she fussed, but it was obvious she was teasing.

"Ashamed of myself for what, darlin', falling in love and wanting to show it? I don't think so." He treated himself to one more quick kiss and whispered that he'd call her that night.

Ruth wandered back into the living room in time to see all the men leaving. She waved her hand and added her goodbyes to everyone else's but she forgot to school her face into its normal demeanor. She was still looking all gaga over her little tryst in the pantry and eagle-eyed Paris was all over it in a nanosecond. "Okay, Aunt Ruth, the jig is up," she said with a glint in her eye. "And no, Bennie, I don't want any more pie, thank you very much. I want to know what's going on with Aunt Ruth and Daddy. I've seen that look before so don't try and lie. You two are in love, aren't you?"

Ruth looked around the room, trying to find a quick exit. She had no allies, either. All Bennie could do was hold out a plate and start laughing as she did so. "Have some pie?"

Ruth sat on a flowered ottoman next to Paris and all but snatched the plate from her niece's hand. "If I'm going to be interrogated the least you could do is give me some coffee to go with this bribe," she grumbled.

Lillian was ready for her, handing her a coffee that was hot and black, the way she liked it. "Here you go, Ruth. Now start at the beginning and talk slow. We don't want to miss anything," she said with a huge smile.

Chapter 12

"You're on the run—you know that, don't you?" Sylvia's voice was gentle but the words still sounded like a rebuke to Ruth. The fact that she was packing her bags to go to Hawaii notwithstanding, she didn't feel like hearing the truth. She looked around for something else to put in the bag.

"Syl, can you hand me those sandals? The green ones?"

Sylvia sighed deeply and picked up the little thong sandals. She held them out to Ruth and then snatched them back. Holding them against her chest, she looked at her friend with exasperation. "You're ignoring me and you know how that drives me crazy. You're running away from Julian and we both know it. What's the matter, sugar, has he done something to make you angry?"

Ruth gave up her frantic packing and sat cross-legged on her huge four-poster bed. She scooted over to make room for Sylvia, who joined her at once. Brushing a loose strand of hair off her forehead, she went for a nonchalant look as she faced Sylvia's questions.

"I'm just going to Hawaii for a week. I go there several times a year, as you well know. I have a cottage there, or did you forget that? How does that qualify as running away?" She defiantly bit a tiny snag of cuticle off her thumbnail and refused to look at Sylvia directly, something that her friend pointed out.

"You're hiding something from me," she said doggedly. "You won't look me in the eyes and your toes are wiggling and the only time you do that is when you're trying to lie about something. You're the worst liar in the known world, so you may as well give it up. And you never go to Hawaii in April, so you must be running away. What's up, chick?"

Ruth looked utterly crestfallen. "Syl, I'm so confused I don't know what else to do but get the hell out of Dodge. I need some time to think. I'm just totally overwhelmed at this point," she admitted.

"Has Julian done something? Are you not getting along? I know I've said this a hundred times, but when he was here last month you two seem so well-suited. I've never seen you so happy and relaxed in my life. You looked like you were having a ball," Sylvia said gently. "What's been going on?"

Sylvia was referring to the weekend of the Academy Awards, when Julian had come to visit Ruth in Chicago. It had been a wonderful weekend, full of laughter and lovemaking and fun. Despite his assertion that he could get a car, Ruth had insisted on picking him up from the airport, and from the moment his tall frame came into her view she'd been filled with a joy she hadn't felt in years. Every time he kissed her it set her heart dancing with excitement and they kissed long and often, so she was giddy with happiness the whole time he was there.

He'd admired her loft greatly, particularly the bedroom with the skylight and the massive bed, and the bathroom, which was custom-fitted. Ruth could remember his exclamation when he saw the huge tub and shower enclosure.

"Honey, this thing is gigantic! I don't think I've ever seen a bathtub this big in a private home. This looks like something from a spa or an exercise club. This thing is big enough for six people," he said in wonder.

"Maybe not six people, but definitely big enough for two," she said demurely. "This place belonged to a former Chicago Bulls player. He got traded to Miami and put the place up for sale. He had to have the floor reinforced to hold it, but if you ask me, it was worth the expense."

Mac had agreed heartily and tried his best to persuade her into it right then and there. She almost gave in to him, but they had tickets for a concert that night and there was no way they'd get out of the bath in time. But after a great evening out that concluded with drinks at the Green Mill, where they were lucky enough to catch a performance by Kurt Elling, they came home and took full advantage of the tub.

Ruth had filled it with hot water, lacing it with bath salts with a fresh pine fragrance and adding an expensive German bubble bath with the same scent. While she was preparing the tub, Mac was busy making a delicious concoction of crushed ice, fruit juice and seltzer that was as pretty to look at as it was refreshing to drink. When he was finished with the drinks he brought them into the bathroom, where Ruth was waiting for him, already up to her neck in bubbles with lit candles all around the room. He joined her in about ten seconds, laughing as he did so. "I've never taken my clothes off so fast in my life," he told her.

They changed positions, so that Mac was leaning back with Ruth between his legs, reclining against his chest. They stayed that way for a while, both of them relearning the other's touch, the feel of their bodies close together. Ruth's hands were stroking his long legs under the bubbling hot water, and he was massaging her breasts while he kissed her nape and her shoulders. "I missed you, honey," he murmured.

"I missed you too, Julian. I'm so glad you're here," she returned. Her soft tone turned to a gasp of surprise, and then a low hum of contentment as Julian's hand found her most sensitive spot, causing her to arch her back and move her hips sinuously against his hand. She could feel his sex, long, hard and eager against her back, and she tried to turn around to explore him in the same way he was pleasuring her. He was too determined to bring her to ecstasy, however, and he continued to massage her, one hand on her breast and the other one deep in her womanhood, touching her just the right way, coaxing her closer and closer to the brink until her cries echoed in the scented room. When her body's trembling and throbbing began to subside, she was finally able to turn around and straddle him. She took him in her hands and leaned forward to kiss him, rubbing her breasts against his chest as she did so. Then she leaned back with a sweet smile. "Your turn."

Sylvia had to bring Ruth back into the here and now by poking her in the arm. "Earth to Ruth, come in, Ruth. I know what *that* look means and I'm too young to be exposed to such things, so let's stay on target. The party was a lot of fun and everyone loved Julian, so what's the problem?"

Ruth had to smile when she thought about her annual Academy Awards soiree. It was something she did every year for all her movie-mad friends, but this year it was very different. She'd made the main course, as usual; her friends would bring the salads and desserts. She'd prepared her stuffed eggplant, a delicious mixture of tomatoes, scallions, mushrooms, ground turkey, season-ed breadcrumbs and feta cheese that was stuffed into the hollowed-out halves of the eggplant, sprinkled with mozzarella and baked. Mac had tasted the mixture and declared it amazing. "I use a lot of basil and a little oregano, and I also use turkey Italian sausage to give it more oomph. I'm glad you like it," she said modestly.

Mac had made an appetizer, claiming he wanted to make sure her friends approved of him. When Ruth tasted the big mushroom caps stuffed with spinach and crabmeat with a hint of Pernod, she sighed with delight. "These are beyond delicious, Julian. They were going to love you anyway, now they'll just be trying to steal you away," she teased him.

The party was a huge success. Everyone was abso-lutely charmed by Mac, especially when his sense of humor was displayed. Ruth started laughing out loud when she remembered the sight of him sitting on the big chair in the living area. He was surrounded by her unabashedly curious friends, especially the extra-nosy Kimmi, who had no shame in asking personal questions. Mac had whipped out a folder, saying, "I thought this might make it a little easier to get the ball rolling. I prepared a resume for your perusal," he'd said in his deep voice. Everyone had collapsed in laughter except Kimmi, who read hers as if it were the lost books of the Bible.

"You're laughing about Kimmi, aren't you?" Sylvia asked.

"Yes, I am. That girl is a mess, asking him point-blank if he were financially able to care for me in the way I was accustomed! Ooh, that child is something else," Ruth said fondly. "But the best part was watching Paris on the red carpet. Wasn't she gorgeous?"

She and Mac had shared the big chair and everyone else was comfortably seated as the pre-award festivities were aired. Ruth was afraid that Paris would get lost in the shuffle, but there was no chance of that. "Oh, Julian, look at her! Look at our baby, isn't she beautiful?" Ruth had screamed in her excitement but no one paid that any attention, even Mac. Paris did indeed look radiantly lovely on the arm of her college friend, Billy Watanabe. Billy had been nominated for best score and best original song and he and Paris looked elegant and sexy as they strolled into the Kodak Theatre with all the other participants. But people kept stopping them to interview Billy and basically to gawk at Paris, who was wearing a custom-made gown that made her look like the brightest star in the Hollywood constellation that night.

"Yes, sugar, she's a beauty all right. And you and Julian looked like proud parents while you were watching her. In fact, that little idiot Kimmi kept hunching me with her elbow and pointing at the two of you, all teary-eyed and sentimental. It was hard to believe you two haven't been together forever. Is that why you're running away? Does that make you uncomfortable?" Sylvia's face was warm with concern for her friend.

"No, that's not it, exactly. I think it was New Orleans that did it," she said dolefully.

Sylvia's look went from concerned to calculating. "That's right, you went to visit him. Did something bad happen? Did he show a side of himself none of us knew existed? Did one of his old girlfriends come to the house…?"

Ruth unfolded her legs and slid off the bed. "Syl, are you still watching those soap operas? How do you have time for that mess, busy as you are? Come in the kitchen, I need some tea or something."

"I only watch *Days* and I TiVo it. So what happened when you went down there? Was it terrible?"

"Sylvia, it was absolutely wonderful. Just perfect. And that's the problem."

Mac lived in a Greek-revival-style house typical of the Garden District in New Orleans. It was relatively small, which meant there were only five bedrooms. The two-story house with the big pillars in the front enchanted Ruth right away, as did the beautifully landscaped lawn and the garden in the back of the house. The highlight of the house, for Ruth, was the dining room, which led into a solarium that opened directly onto the patio. The ceilings of both rooms were paned glass that made the area irresistibly sunny and inviting. The sunroom was full of thriving green plants and the garden beyond was just coming into its spring growth and Ruth could imagine having a late breakfast out there, drinking in the sunlight and the enticing smell of the greenery. She couldn't help herself, she sat down on a big wicker chair cushioned with overstuffed pillows and stared out the window with a sigh of enjoyment. Bojangles, Mac's cat, joined her, leaping into her lap and settling down for a nice nap.

She smiled at the memory as she shared it with Sylvia. "Julian said that meant he approved of me. He said Bojangles normally avoided all visitors, but he'd taken a liking to me. He and Bojangles gave me a tour of the whole house and it's just lovely, Syl. It looks like something out of *Architectural Digest*. And just when I was thinking that his late wife has exceptional taste, it was like he could read my mind. He told me that he and Ginger lived in Lafayette, Louisiana. She'd passed away before he moved the family to New Orleans. But he had pictures of her on display and she really was a beauty. Paris looks just like her," she said thoughtfully.

Sylvia gave her a fake grin and drummed her fingers on the counter. "You're dragging this out on purpose. If you're going to keep me in suspense you've got to feed me. Do you have any veggies in there?" she asked, pointed to the refrigerator.

As she prepared cherry tomatoes, cucumbers, celery and baby carrots and a low-fat blue cheese dip to go with the iced tea they were drinking, Ruth hastened to get the rest of the story out. "We had a fabulous time that weekend—New Orleans is a beautiful city, Syl.

We went sightseeing, we had dinner at Emeril's and Antoine's, his sons came over one night and Julian grilled chicken and fish for us, we went dancing at Tipitina's, and of course we went to the French Quarter. I met his friends, we went to church on Sunday and the only person I met who could qualify as an old girl-friend was a family friend named Charmaine some-thing or other. She seemed a little bit too interested in my presence, if you know what I mean, but you know how old family friends are," she said carelessly.

"As far as I'm concerned the weekend was perfectly lovely. I adore Julian and the feeling only gets stronger every time we're together.'

Sylvia was stunned into silence for a moment. "So he doesn't feel the same way, sugar? He certainly looked like he's crazy about you. Were we just assuming too much?"

Ruth's green eyes got a faraway look and the sigh that came from her chest seemed to start from the deepest recesses of her soul. "Not at all. Julian loves me very much, Sylvia. In fact, he asked me to marry him."

Sylvia was so stunned she forgot to swallow, allowing iced tea to roll down her chin onto her soft pink shirt. Ruth quickly handed her paper towels to stem the tide while she finished telling her the news.

It was late morning, the day that Ruth was sche-duled to depart. Mac had risen before her, mainly because she was so deeply asleep he didn't want to disturb her slumber. She eventually came awake with Bojangles's help. The big black-and-white cat had leaped onto the bed and was patting her face with his paw while issuing a musical little purring sound. She blinked her way to consciousness and smiled. "Good morning, Bojangles. I hope I wasn't snoring," she cooed as he nuzzled her cheek. She didn't know where Julian was but she decided she'd better get showered and pretty before he came back into the massive master bedroom suite.

She brushed her teeth thoroughly, took a long hot shower with copious amounts of her K de Krizia bath gel and managed to dry off, lotion her entire body with the matching lotion and finish off with the eau de cologne, and still no Julian. This gave her enough time to fix her hair, apply a little makeup and change the sheets. She had just finished putting the bed back together with the crisp blue-and-white striped linens when Julian appeared in the doorway. "Good morning, honey. You look adorable. Are you hungry?"

"You look pretty cute yourself," she said. He did, too, in a pair of chino slacks, a navy T-shirt and a pinstriped cotton shirt with the sleeves rolled up. His feet were bare and he looked casual but delectable. "Of course I'm hungry. I'm always hungry in the morning."

"Well, do you feel like being pampered?" He put a long finger under her chin and tipped her head back for a kiss as he did so.

Ruth savored his kiss and gave him one of her own before answering. "Actually, I do feel like being pampered a little. What do you have in mind?"

"I thought I'd make brunch for you and serve it to you in the solarium and then give you a massage. Is that agreeable?"

"Only if I can return the massage," she said with a smile. "I give a very good one. And why didn't you

wake me up this morning? If Bojangles hadn't come to get me I'd probably still be asleep."

"I thought you might need some extra rest. We didn't do a lot of sleeping last night," he said, pulling her into his arms.

Ruth could feel heat all over, and not just in her erogenous zones. He was completely correct; they did very little sleeping the previous night. What they did was make love from the time the door closed behind them until the very early dawn. They'd spent the evening in the Quarter, laughing and talking and enjoying the jazz and honky-tonk music that poured out of the many bars and restaurants that lined the fabled streets. They started kissing the minute they hit the back door of the house and each kiss got more arousing until they started a mutual striptease that began in the kitchen. First her sandals landed in a corner, startling Bojangles, who promptly left the room. Then Mac's shoes left his feet to join hers.

His sport coat was tossed into the solarium, and his belt went into the dining room, then Ruth's raw silk bolero jacket went flying. They continued to kiss each other with growing fervor as each item of clothing was discarded. By the time they reached the living room Ruth had shimmied out of her strapless sun dress and stood before her man in pink lace bikini panties and a matching strapless bra. She almost made it to the foot of the stairs before Mac grabbed her around the waist. He'd been delayed by removing his slacks and shirt, and he was clad only in his silk boxers. "Where're you goin', honey? You're not trying to run away from me, are you?"

She turned around and smiled mischievously as she unhooked the front fastener of her bra. They kissed again, this time with Mac's hands caressing her breasts. They were walking up the stairs when Mac realized that in addition to walking backward, Ruth had deftly removed her panties and she was now totally nude. In seconds she found herself lifted into his arms with her legs wrapped around his waist. He placed her on the bed and stripped off his shorts before reaching for the condoms on the bedside table. As he put one on he looked down at Ruth with true adoration mixed with pure lust in his eyes. "Honey, I can't wait until we're married so I can do away with these things. I want to feel every bit of your hot, wet, sweetness all over me," he growled.

Sylvia raised her finely arched eyebrows as she considered what Ruth had just told her. "I'm sure that was the edited version," she said, grinning, "but I don't know if that constitutes a proposal, sugar. Men say a lot of things in the heat of the moment."

"Too true, Syl, but it's not like that's the first time he brought it up. When he was here he said something about remodeling the master bath in his house *after we're married.* He asked me if there were a lot of things I wanted to change about the house in New Orleans *after we're married.* He hasn't gone down on one knee or given me a ring, but for someone who's not serious he sure brings it up a lot." She had finished mopping up the counter, picked up the glasses, refilled them with tea and found a luscious pair of mocha brownies in the freezer where she'd hidden them from herself. She whipped them out with a flourish and nuked them while Sylvia considered her words.

"Well, if I was a betting woman, I'd give you odds that ol' boy is serious as a heart attack. Seeing as how you two are old enough and mature enough to know your own minds and emotions, he's just taking it to the next level without a whole lot of foolish debate. He wants you, you want him, y'all are sho' nuff in love, so to him it's a done deal. And this is why you're running to Hawaii with the speed of a thousand people. I say sit your butt down and talk to the man, that's what I say. Don't scamper off like some insecure soap opera diva—stand your ground and get some things cleared up," Sylvia said firmly. Her eyes brightened as Ruth put a brownie in front of her, with a fresh linen napkin.

"Syl, I know it sounds ridiculous, but I don't know what to say to him. I love him to death, but *marriage?* There's a reason I've reached this ripe age without benefit of clergy. I don't think I have what it takes to be a wife, especially not now. It's too late for me," she began, only to have Sylvia cut her off with a roll of her eyes and an especially loud and unladylike suck of her teeth.

"Let me ask you something. Did you feel like screaming at any time you were together? Did it annoy you to be in the same room with him? Were you looking for places to hide, places to be alone? Where you trying vainly to find things to talk about? Did you hate his friends?"

"Of course not, Syl! Whenever we're together I feel happy and peaceful. I'm relaxed in his company and he's totally comfortable in mine. We have great conversations about any and everything and his friends are charming," she said emphatically. She thought a moment and added, "Well, I could do without that Charmaine but everyone else was wonderful. I love being with him and all I want is more time with him and his family. His sons are hilarious and you know that Paris is my girl," she said with a spirited assurance.

"And yet you want to scuttle off to Hawaii like a hermit crab. Does this make sense? Any sense at all?" Sylvia chided her.

Ruth was saved by the bell as her cell phone went off. Her face paled and she clutched the counter. "I'm on my way, darling. I love you."

"Sylvia, I have to get to Atlanta right now. They got that sick bastard who was after Paris."

Chapter 13

Mac looked over at Ruth, who was sleeping soundly in the passenger seat of his Cadillac Escalade. She was curled up comfortably with the seat reclined and her head was resting on a soft velour pillow he'd procured just for her. It was two days before the first weekend in May and they were heading to his friend Lincoln's horse farm in Louisville, Kentucky. To horse breeders all over the world the first weekend in May meant one thing; the running of the Kentucky Derby. To him it meant something else, though; it meant that he and Ruth had been seeing each other for three months. Three of the most pleasurable months he'd ever had in his life, actually. He was ready to pledge his life to the woman beside him, an act that most people would call extremely foolish, but Mac knew it was right.

It wasn't her beauty, her intelligence or her vivacious personality; although the good Lord knew they all played a part in her appeal. It was her heart that had drawn Mac in and held him captive. They had talked on the phone at least once a day since the day they met, sometimes two or three times a day. They had spent time together in New York, Atlanta, Chicago and New Orleans and now they were taking the ultimate "couple test," a road trip to Kentucky. But during all that time what had impressed Mac the most about Ruth was her unlimited capacity for love. She doted on his daughter and loved her like she was her own. She loved her nieces and nephews and her multitude of friends and treated them like they were the most important people in the world. And she had opened her heart to Mac and loved him unreservedly with the fervor of a young girl combined with the sultry confidence of a mature woman. When she smiled at him, when she touched him or he just heard her voice, he knew, deep in his heart, that she was the one.

When she raced to be with him after Paris's accident, he knew. When she dropped everything to come to him when the man who'd been after Paris was captured, he knew. It might seem like the ultimate folly to fall so deeply in love after such a short time, but at fifty-seven he was experienced enough and lucky enough to know the real thing when it was handed to him so sweetly by his own daughter, of all people. And if things proceeded according to plan, this was the weekend he was going to make it official. The ring he'd had made for her delicate finger was burning a hole in his pocket; he couldn't wait to put it on her. Even Julian, the son with the bitter taste in his mouth regarding love, acknowledged that this was the real deal. Mac still got a smile out of remembering the look on Julian's face when he came over the morning that Ruth was due to depart for Chicago.

To his credit, Mac thought he'd done a thorough job of removing all traces of the activities of the night before, but he'd missed a couple of things. Julian had come in the back door and was surprised to see his father preparing what looked like a feast in the large modernized kitchen. "Dang, Judge, you're throwing down in here. Coffee, beignets from the Quarter, cheese grits, grillades, fresh fruit, scrambled eggs, biscuits…is it somebody's birthday and I just forgot?" He'd licked his lips with gusto and was reaching for a plate when Mac warned him off.

"This is a special meal for a special person, so I suggest you take yourself on down the road and find a Sonic or a Mickey D's," he said sternly.

Before Julian could protest, Bojangles had come strolling into the kitchen dragging something lacy and pink in his mouth. Julian took it out of the cat's mouth and dropped it at once when he realized it was a strapless bra. "Uhh, okay Pop, I gotta run. Talk to you later, I'm sure," he muttered as he made a dash for the same door he'd entered. He'd paused for a minute and looked his father in the eye. "You did good, Pop. Ruth is a wonderful woman and she's just what you've needed for a long time. I call best man," he added as he slipped out quietly.

Mac had laughed out loud as he retrieved the bra while scolding Bojangles. "I was looking for that. Get your own woman, you little pervert." Bojangles just rolled over and purred loudly.

Now they were taking a road trip, a tradition that was supposed to sound the death knell for couples. Especially new couples like him and Ruth. So far though, it had been nothing but fun. She was perfectly happy to let him drive, although she would take over the wheel from time to time. They didn't quibble over which music to play because they were so busy talking they didn't care what was on. At one point she turned to him and confessed that they could be going anywhere and it wouldn't make her a bit of difference. "But," she added hastily, "I'm really glad we're going to the Derby. I still can't believe that I'm actually going to see it in person after all those years of wanting to go."

Mac had a friend named Lincoln Alexander who'd been a trainer for years before starting his own breeding farm. Mac had partnered with him in the purchase of a thoroughbred named, appropriately, Kentucky Rain. The colt was now a three-year-old and an odds-on favorite in the Derby. Mac was happy to be able to have Ruth come with him to watch the race, something she eagerly agreed to do. She had an avid interest in horses, yet another thing they had in common. She flew to New Orleans to drive up to Kentucky wi him, and then would go to Atlanta with him for Paris's birthday.

Long car rides were supposed to be torture for couples, but so far the ten-hour trip from Louisiana was proving to be a lot of fun. Ruth didn't question his directional skills, partially because the SUV was equipped with OnStar, and she didn't require an excessive amount of bathroom breaks. She had packed them a gourmet lunch to be consumed on the road, she loved telling jokes and she smelled lovely, as always. As far as Mac was concerned, she was the perfect companion. She stirred slightly in the seat, and then yawned daintily and her eyes popped open. She always woke quickly and she always seemed to be in a good mood. Mac had known his share of women who went to sleep as sweet as baby bunnies and wakened like Stegosauruses, so this was a pleasant change.

She sat up, raised her seat and smiled. Popping an Altoid in her mouth, she took a long swallow of the bottle of spring water in the cup holder and asked where they were.

"About an hour from Louisville, honey. The traffic is getting to be heavy, so bear with me. This is one of the best-attended events in this part of the country, so folks flock here every year."

Ruth nodded agreeably. "I've always seen those huge crowds, even when the weather is dreadful. I hope we have a nice sunny weekend. I'm always terrified for the horses when the track is muddy. Some horses like a muddy track, but it's so dangerous for them! When something happens to a horse I just die a little inside because it's so awful for them," she added. "I'd make a terrible trainer because I'd be so scared my jockey would get hurt I'd pull the horse from the race or something. I'm just a big ol' chicken, I guess."

There it was again, her loving, giving nature. If bad weather arose at a horse race most women would complain about getting wet or ruining their outfit, but Ruth's concern was all for the horse and rider. He reached over and took her hand, loving the feel of her soft, moist skin. She squeezed it gently and won his heart all over again by bringing it to her lips to plant a kiss on the back. Then she surprised him totally by saying, "Sometimes I don't think I deserve to be this happy, Julian. You're like a beautiful gift that was delivered to the wrong house," she said in a small voice.

Just ahead of him traffic came to a complete halt and he had to extricate his hand and maneuver carefully to avoid rear-ending the poor sap in front of him. From then on it was stop-start-curse-stop-start, so he didn't have a chance to ask her why in the world she felt like that. He made a mental note to ask her at his earliest opportunity, though. But sooner than he imagined, they were pulling into Falling Water Farms, the large and very well-kept horse farm that was their destination. His questions would have to wait as they were greeted by their hosts Lincoln Alexander and his sister Marilyn.

They were attractive and friendly people in their early fifties. Neither of them had ever married; they were orphaned at an early age and devoted themselves to raising their younger siblings. Without betraying any confidences, Mac had hinted at the truly difficult time they'd had keeping the family together. "Most people would have given up and let social services take over, but Linc and Marilyn aren't like most people. They made some tremendous sacrifices to keep their younger brothers and sisters together. Maybe one day you'll hear the whole story. You won't believe it, honey. Even now I can't completely comprehend what they went through," he told her as they made themselves comfortable in one of the guest cottages on the premises.

Whatever problems they'd overcome didn't show on their faces, however. Lincoln and Marilyn were both tall, with deep permanent tans from working outdoors so much and lean, muscular frames that spoke of daily physical exertion. They were warm and friendly people, but modest and quiet by nature. Whenever Ruth complimented Marilyn on the beauty of the ranch and the main house, she accepted the accolade with a shy smile.

"Thank you. It's a combination of Lincoln's vision, our hard work and God's goodness to our family," she said quietly. "Would you like a tour? We can walk or ride, whatever you prefer."

Mac was impressed when Ruth eagerly said she'd ride. She did so like she did everything else, with a natural grace. "You seem totally at home up there," he teased her when she was astride her mount, a pretty black filly with a lot of spunk.

"I dated a horse trainer for a while. He taught me everything I know," she said, patting her mount, Ebony, on the neck. It was a good thing she wasn't looking at Mac or she'd have seen a totally new expression; a flash of anger blazed across his face so quickly that no one saw it except Linc, who wasted no time in getting on Mac's case. The two men were ahead of the women and as they trotted the paths around the ranch, Linc let him have it.

"Man, I've known you for a long time and I've never seen you like this. I didn't think you had it in you but you're jealous! Admit it, you want to go find that horse trainer and beat him senseless, don't you?" Linc's warm gray eyes were full of merriment.

"Aww, here *you* go," Mac grumbled. The deeply possessive streak that had been an integral part of every Deveraux man for generations was indeed coming to the fore. Mac couldn't have said why the idea that some other man had taught his honey how to ride was galling him, but Linc was dead right, Mac was as jealous as a schoolboy over what amounted to nothing. "Just you wait, old man. Your turn is coming. You're going to find yourself head over heels with some woman one day and then it won't be so hilarious," he groused. "You might have escaped matrimony up until now, but that doesn't mean your day isn't coming."

Lincoln laughed self-consciously, his light brown skin taking on a reddish hue. His gray eyes crinkled in amusement as he shook his head. "I don't think so, partner. I'm way too old for that stuff. No woman in her right mind would put up with me," he assured his friend.

"Don't say 'never,' Linc. You're just setting yourself up for some woman to pounce on you. Look at me, I was sitting around minding my own business when my daughter, of all people, introduces me to this incredible woman. And now—" he said, only to be cut off by Ruth.

"Now it's time for lunch," she informed him as she cantered up next to him. "I'm going to help Marilyn." She leaned over to kiss him lightly. "Don't forget who loves you," she whispered.

Mac watched the two women ride off with a smile on his face. "See what I'm telling you? Never say never, my friend, it's a big bold word but it really doesn't mean that much."

Marilyn seemed genuinely happy to have Ruth's company, especially since Falling Water Farms was hosting a big party that night. "We're not big party people. We don't go to a lot of them and we sure as heck don't *give* them. This is a working ranch and we just don't have a lot of time for a social life. But since Rainy is doing so well, we kind of felt we needed to do something festive," she said wanly.

Ruth's heart went out to the woman. She was obviously uncomfortable with her new role as hostess to a multitude of friends, neighbors and strangers, and fortunately, entertaining ran in Ruth's blood. She patted Marilyn on the shoulder and assured her it would be a great evening. "I'm going to tell you a secret," she said in a conspiratorial tone. "All you really need for a great outdoor party is a lot of good food and some good loud music. If the weather cooperates, you've got it made."

Marilyn brightened at once. "We did get the best caterer in the county. From what I understand she and her staff are like magicians. She was on the Food Network and she's been in *Gourmet* magazine and *Bon Appétit*," she recited, and then reddened along her cheekbones. "I have no idea what that means," she confessed. "I read it in her brochure. I don't spend a lot of time watching television and when I do, I'm so old-school it's pitiful. I watch *Columbo* and *Matlock* reruns, stuff like that. And the only magazines I ever read are about horse breeding and training." She blushed again. "I'm pretty hopeless, huh?"

Ruth wanted to hug her, but sensed it would just embarrass her to tears. Marilyn was tall and naturally slim with the muscle tone that came from years of hard work. Her wavy brown hair with natural blond highlights was pulled back in a long sensible braid and she had piercing gray eyes that were just like her brother's. She had a strong profile and beautifully chiseled

IMANI™
ROMANCE

An Important Message from the Publisher

Dear Reader,

Because you've chosen to read one of our fine novels, I'd like to say "thank you"! And, as a special way to say thank you, I'm offering to send you two more Kimani Romance novels and two surprise gifts – absolutely FREE! These books will keep it real with true-to-life African American characters that turn up the heat and sizzle with passion.

Please enjoy the free books and gifts with our compliments...

Linda Gill

Publisher, Kimani Press

Peel off Seal and Place Inside...

PUBLISHERS
FREE GIFT
SEAL
THANK YOU

THE EDITOR'S "THANK YOU" FREE GIFTS INCLUDE:

▶ Two NEW Kimani Romance™ Novels

▶ Two exciting surprise gifts

PLACE
FREE GIFTS
SEAL
HERE

▼ DETACH AND MAIL CARD TODAY! ▼

168 XDL EF22   368 XDL EF23

FIRST NAME

LAST NAME

ADDRESS

APT.#

CITY

STATE/PROV.

ZIP/POSTAL CODE

Thank You!

The Reader Service — Here's How It Works:

If offer card is missing write to: The Reader Service, 3010 Walden Ave., P.O. Box 1867, Buffalo, NY 14240-1867

BUSINESS REPLY MAIL
FIRST-CLASS MAIL   PERMIT NO. 717-003   BUFFALO, NY

POSTAGE WILL BE PAID BY ADDRESSEE

**THE READER SERVICE
3010 WALDEN AVE
PO BOX 1867
BUFFALO NY 14240-9952**

NO POSTAGE
NECESSARY
IF MAILED
IN THE
UNITED STATES

features, the kind of aristocratic beauty that couldn't be bought or painted on, yet she seemed as shy as one of her foals. All she needed was a little dose of self-confidence, something Ruth had in abundance and was more than happy to share.

"You're hardly hopeless. I admit to an addiction to *Charmed* and *Murder, She Wrote,* so we're even. Marilyn, relax. The caterers are taking care of the setting up, the decorations and the serving, right? The music is covered because your neighbor's son has a jazz band that's playing and you hired a DJ to alternate with the live music," she said as she ticked off points on her fingers. "The only thing you need to do is get yourself ready to have a good time tonight because this is going to be the party everyone's talking about tomorrow. Trust me," she said, linking her arm through Marilyn's. "All you need is a long bubble bath and a great dress and you're good to go."

"Then we have a problem," Marilyn said dolefully. "A great dress is not something you'll find in my wardrobe."

"Well, let's go look in mine," Ruth said. "I like shopping way too much," she confided. "We're about the same size and I know there's something that will fit you. Come with me and we'll work some magic."

Magic was a good word for the party that night. The caterer was every bit as good as Marilyn said she was; she and her efficient staff provided ribs, grilled chicken, steak and Brunswick stew, all done to perfection. The side dishes were equally delicious and included grilled corn on the cob, cole slaw, potato salad, green salad and fruit salad, potatoes baked on the grill, cornbread, garlic bread and cheese biscuits. There were too many desserts to count, and an array of nonalcoholic beverages in addition to a well-stocked open bar. The decorations were in the Falling Water Farms colors of emerald-green and royal purple and everything was festive and beautiful, including Marilyn, who'd bowed to Ruth's insistence that she accept the loan of a dress. It was a simple sleeveless dress with a bell skirt and a low-cut back and there were low-heeled sandals in the same color to go with it. Marilyn looked like a different person, regally elegant, but also happy and approachable. Everyone at the party was stunned by her appearance, except Mac, who knew the identity of Marilyn's fairy godmother.

To him it was just one more example of the kind of woman Ruth was. He knew that the dress and shoes were new, he'd seen the tags. He couldn't think of another woman, except maybe Paris, who'd have gone out of her way to do something so kind for a near-stranger. Ruth had just finished dressing in a different ensemble, a formfitting ivory dress. It would have been totally plain but it had a halter neck with wide straps set far apart to allow her beautiful collarbones to show. It also had a sweetheart neckline that emphasized her bosom. Her breasts might have been small by some standards but as far as he was concerned they were perfect. Ruth was adding a rose-gold lip gloss to her luscious lips when she saw Mac staring at her.

"Is something hanging out that shouldn't be?" she asked as she tried to look over her shoulder in the mirror.

Mac laughed before he pulled her into his arms. "Nothing's wrong, darlin'. You look beautiful, as always. I was just thinking what a special person you are. How did you persuade Marilyn to borrow that dress from you? She looks great in it, but I'm surprised she took it. She and Linc are very proud people," he said thoughtfully.

Ruth rubbed her nose in Mac's thick moustache. "I really want a kiss. A big juicy one, but I just put on my makeup and I'll mess it up," she murmured. "You'd better make sure I get my fair share after this shindig. And what's wrong with borrowing a dress from a girl-friend? Marilyn needs more girlfriends in her life, I can tell. She's worked too hard for too long and she needs some fun. That dress is a gift, by the way. She'll figure it out by the time we're halfway to Atlanta," she added with a smug grin.

Mac held her tighter. "I love you. I love the smell of you," he murmured as he buried his nose in the crook of her neck. "I love the taste of you, the feel of you and the heart of you. Your big, loving heart that opens to everyone like a rose in the sunshine."

Without warning he led her into the sitting room of the guesthouse and sat her on the floral settee. Going down on one knee, he pulled a box out of his pocket and opened it, showing her the ring it contained. "Marry me, Ruth. I love you with all my heart and I'll do anything in this world to make you happy. Marry me, please, so we can live the rest of our lives together in happiness."

As he spoke he took the ring out of the box and slid it onto her ring finger, a finger that was trembling like the rest of her body. She glanced at the big oval ring for a moment, but her eyes went to his and she couldn't look away. "Are you serious, Julian?" she whispered.

Mac broke into laughter. "Of course I'm serious, woman. Would I be down here on one knee if I was playing around? You have to know how I feel about you, honey. Other than my children there's no one in the world who's as precious to me as you are. And you can't convince me you don't feel the same way about me. I can see it every time you look at me, I can feel it every time you touch me, and I can hear it every time you call my name."

By now tears were running freely down Ruth's face and it was like a knife in his heart. He stood long enough to scoop her up in his arms and sit down on the settee with her in his lap. "Honey, you can't cry like that. Even if you're happy, seeing those tears just does something to me. Stop crying and talk to me, darlin'. Tell me what's in your heart," he crooned.

"I love you," she whispered. "I've never loved anyone like this, not even Jared and I loved him with all my heart. I go to sleep thinking about you and I wake up smiling because I know I'm going to hear your voice. When I'm with you I feel something way beyond happiness—I feel like a real woman. Not just because you're the sexiest thing I've ever met in my life, but because I feel your respect, your admiration, your love and protection. I'm so glad we met, Julian. I feel like buying Paris a small island or a diamond mine or something to show my gratitude," she said with a shaky attempt at a smile. "When you look at me sometimes I wonder what I ever did to deserve this happiness," she said as yet another tear trickled down her cheek.

Mac kissed her tears away and pulled her even closer. "Honey, you make it sound like I'm some kind of superman. Believe me, I'm not. I'll be happy to prepare a list of all my shortcomings for you and my house-keeper will gladly attest to the fact that I'm lucky to be able to afford household help or I'd be living in squalor," he teased her. "All I am is what you see, a hardworking man who loves you more than air. Marry me and let me prove it to you."

"But it's only been three months," she began, only to have his lips cover hers.

"Marry me."

"I'm selfish and demanding," she whispered.

"Liar. Marry me," he answered as he licked her neck.

"I'm bossy and uncooperative," she murmured.

"Are you going to marry me or are we going to miss the whole party while I sit here and beg you?" Mac asked sternly.

"Yes."

"Yes, *what?* I want to hear the words," he whispered as he kissed her again.

"Yes, Julian MacArthur Deveraux, I, Ruth Theresa Bennett, will marry you, because I adore you and I can't begin to imagine living without you. I love you, Julian. I'm sure I'll give you a hard time sooner or later, but I love you with all my heart."

Mac roared with laughter. "I'd rather have a hard time with you than a good time with twenty other women. I like making up so we can fight anytime you like. As a matter of fact, can we make love right now?" he asked in a seductive voice. "I haven't made love to you as my official fiancée."

Ruth scrambled off the settee. "No, we can't because the word *quickie* means two hours to you. It's a good thing this dress is silk faille and doesn't wrinkle," she said, smoothing the front of it down. "We're going to the party and acting like civilized people for three hours. And then we're going to come back here and I'm going to give you a bath."

Mac raised an eyebrow. It sounded nice, but not earth-shattering—they'd done that many times.

"With my tongue," she cooed.

Mac groaned and leaned over while he tried to clear that image from his brain. "Say, aren't you going to look at your ring? You may hate it," he cautioned.

Ruth's fingers splayed out in front of her and she stared at the most gorgeous ring she'd ever seen. It was a five-carat oval green stone with fiery purple flashes and it had three smaller stones on either side in a paler shade of green that flashed gold. Set in eighteen-carat gold, it was feminine, yet bold and modern. She covered her mouth with her other hand while the tears started again.

"It's incredible, Julian, what in the world is it?"

"It's called a bicolor tourmaline, honey. I wanted something to go with those fascinating eyes of yours. The smaller stones are chrysoberyl. If you don't like it, you can keep it for a regular ring and we'll go get you some diamonds or something. I had this one made for you because of those beautiful eyes of yours. Those beautiful leaky eyes," he added fondly as he used his linen handkerchief to dab them away.

"Julian, I'm never taking this ring off again, are you crazy? I love it and I love you for giving it to me. I have to fix my face and we have to leave here now or we'll never make it to the party. But," she cautioned him, "we're not staying long. Not long at all," she said in a dreamy voice while she stared at her ring again.

The only thing that could have made the weekend any better was a victory for Kentucky Rain and Falling Water Farms. A sumptuous brunch was prepared by the catering staff, who had been hired for two days, but everyone was too keyed up to eat much. Everyone except Mac and Ruth, that is. They both ate with great appetites because they'd made love with such intensity and passion they were both starving. No one seemed to notice the amount of food they were putting away and it was just as well. Scrambled eggs, sausage, grits, cinnamon coffee cake, raisin toast and fresh pineapple disappeared from their plates in a very short time and they were sipping tea and making goo-goo eyes at each other while everyone else was preparing to leave for Churchill Downs where the race was held.

In keeping with the tradition of the race, Ruth had a special outfit to wear. Women always dressed in their most exquisite spring finery and wore fabulous hats to the Kentucky Derby; that is, those who were sitting in the boxes and the stands. The loud and happy crowds that thronged the infield wore anything and everything and it was a huge party. Mac and Ruth would be sitting with the Alexanders in the owner's box. Mac was looking dashing in a cream-colored suit with a cream shirt and a tie that bore the Falling Waters colors. He also indulged his fondness for hats by wearing a Panama hat styled like a riverboat gambler's. He looked handsome, rakish and charming and he was a perfect foil for Ruth. When she emerged from the bedroom of the guesthouse, fully dressed, Mac had to take a deep breath.

"Honey, let's blow off the race and find a justice of the peace. You're going to outshine every woman there, Ruth," he said warmly.

She blushed a little and modeled her outfit for him, basking in his praise. She was wearing a pale green silk Valentino dress with a deep *V* neckline and sheer long sleeves. It had a raised waist and a flowing skirt that was just the right length to show off her legs. Her taupe heels made her legs look even longer and sexier than usual. Her hat was delightful, a pale green organza trimmed with horsehair braid to give it body. The brim was huge, dipping gracefully in the back and turned back in the front so her face was displayed. The brim was laden with pale green silk flowers so that she looked like the very essence of spring, a walking bouquet. Mac was beginning to learn her scents; she alternated between Goldleaf, K de Krizia and Flower by Kenzo. Today was a Goldleaf day and it was the perfect accent for her ethereal look.

Everyone else seemed to think she was looking pretty hot, too, as a number of photographers took her picture. As usual, Ruth wasn't aware of the attention she was getting; she was focused completely on the prerace festivities and soaking up the atmosphere around her. Even when Mac pointed out various celebrities like Star Jones-Reynolds, Kanye West, Jack Nicholson and other Hollywood luminaries, Ruth wasn't that impressed.

"I want him to win, Julian. Linc and Marilyn have worked so hard, they deserve this win," she said with an intense edge to her voice. "He's going to win, I can feel it."

Finally the crowd stood to sing "My Old Kentucky Home," the traditional lead-in to the call to post. They watched the jockeys being led into the gates, and the crowd roared as the horses took off. Ruth held Mac's hand tightly as the field of horses vied for space. Even the fastest horse could lose a race if it got squeezed out of position before the real running began. Suddenly, after the second turn, the distinctive green-and-purple harlequin silks of Falling Water Farms came into view as Kentucky Rain started to pull away from the field. One length, then two, then three; it was obvious that Kentucky Rain meant to win this race and by an incredible five lengths, he did. He crossed the finish line well before any of his competitors, prancing and tossing his head as if to say "Ha! How ya like me now?"

The box in which they sat went wild, erupting with laughter, tears, congratulations and sheer joy. Incredibly, Mac and Ruth were included in the winner's circle because as an investor, Mac was part owner of the magnificent stallion. Ruth turned to Mac with a brilliant smile on her face and said, "He won, Julian! He really won!"

Julian smiled down at the woman he would love for the rest of his life and kissed the hand that wore his ring, thinking that he was the real winner; he'd won her heart.

Chapter 14

"I know what I want, Mommy. I want ice cream with peaches."

Maya's eyes crinkled up in a smile as she looked at the light of her life, her daughter Corey. "Ice cream is dessert, sweetie. You have to have lunch before you have dessert. You're going to have a nice grilled cheese sandwich and a cup of soup and then you can have some dessert."

Corey's thick eyebrows met in the middle as she knit her brow in thought. "What kind of soup?" she asked suspiciously.

"What kind would you like? They have tomato, chicken noodle, gazpacho and vichyssoise."

Corey was clearly tempted by the array of unfamiliar choices but she wasn't giving in without a fight. "It's too hot for soup," she pointed out. "I want something cold so I don't get sick from the heat. Something like ice cream," she said innocently.

Maya had to hide her smile. Corey had gotten her again with her unerring logic. It was unseasonably hot for June; there was not question about it. But Maya wasn't going to cave in just because her four-year-old was capable of arguing her into the ground. Now it was her turn for a logical argument.

"Well, how about gazpacho? It's a Spanish soup that's made with tomatoes and vegetables and it's served very cold." Maya always took the time to explain things to Corey in detail because the child usually understood every word and also because it was easier to gain her cooperation if she had all the facts.

The ploy worked because Corey looked quite interested in her description of the soup. "What does it taste like?"

Maya rested her chin in her upraised hand. By now most mothers would have told their child to sit up, shut up and eat what was put in front of her, but Maya wasn't like most mothers. "It tastes like V8 juice with crunchy vegetables in it, like cucumber and celery. Would you like to try it?"

"Yes. But I need a cold sandwich, too. Can I have tuna instead of grilled cheese?"

"Absolutely, sweetie. And then you can have ice cream for dessert."

They both sat back in their chairs, each satisfied that they had won the negotiation. Maya stroked her little girl's cheek with the back of her hand. With her busy schedule, they didn't often get to spend a whole day together and they were making the most of it, having a girl's day out. On the few occasions she had downtime with Corey she could forget how hectic her life was. Today was going to be a fun day for both of them. Suddenly a shadow fell across Maya.

"Hello, Maya."

Maya froze, afraid to move or even look in the direction of the low, mellow voice that was addressing her. It was a voice she knew very well although she hadn't heard it in a long time.

Taking a deep breath, she turned to face the young woman who was standing over her expectantly. "Hello, Paris. You look fabulous," she said as she took in the total package from flawlessly groomed hair to expensive and chic shoes. Top to bottom, Paris was looking better than Maya could ever remember seeing her.

"Look, girl, don't act like we're strangers. Stand up and give me a hug," Paris said impatiently. "We can't pretend like we barely know each other."

Maya stood and the two women embraced tightly. She was pleasantly surprised when Paris gave her an extra squeeze, clinging to her for a long moment as though she were really glad to see her, which seemed rather odd. They finally let go of each other and Paris was smiling at her with a genuine affection that was unmistakable. She was the first to speak, looking at Corey with that same affection.

"I think it's time I met this young lady, don't you?"

Maya agreed. "Corey, darling, come here and meet your Aunt Paris."

The little girl hopped out of her chair at once and went to Paris with her arms extended. Paris picked her up and hugged her closely, while Corey planted a big kiss on her cheek. "You're really my Aunt Paris?" she said. Looking at her mother, she beamed with happiness. "You said I would meet her one day and I did, Mommy. This is my real auntie!"

Maya gave a marginally good imitation of a smile. "Um, Paris, if you haven't ordered yet, maybe you could join us. I think we have a lot to talk about."

Maya looked around Ruth's loft with interest. "This is quite a place she has, isn't it? It was nice of her to invite us over," she said.

Paris had invited Ruth over to the table with Maya and Corey and the four of them had lunched together. It was Ruth's suggestion that they all come over to her place after lunch, using Kasey as an excuse. For her birthday in May, Titus had given Paris several beautiful gifts, but her very favorite was her puppy, Kasey. He was half cock-a-poo and half Pomeranian and Paris took him everywhere. He was well-behaved but mischievous and Ruth wisely surmised it was about time for him to have a walk. After Kasey danced around and greeted everyone with kisses and barks of joy, Ruth asked Maya if it was okay if she and Corey took Kasey out for a while.

"I have my cell phone right here so you can contact me any time. We won't go far, there's a little park in the back of the building. I just think maybe some privacy is in order for you ladies," she'd said.

So now it was just Paris and Maya, the two of them sitting in the living area staring at each other. Maya hadn't changed much over the five years since Paris had last seen her. She was tall, although not as tall as Paris. She was slimmer than Paris recalled her, something that wouldn't please Julian one bit. One of the things he'd loved about her was the fact that she was soft and curvy, just the way he liked a woman. Her long hair was shorter now, worn in a shoulder-length bob that looked businesslike and practical. Julian wouldn't care about that, he just loved hair, period, whether it was soft and straight, long or short, curly or nappy. As long as it was clean and fragrant, he didn't care about length. Her glasses were gone, something else that Julian always liked. There was something about a pretty girl in glasses that got to him; he said it made them look vulnerable and intelligent, two of his favorite attributes in a woman. Finally Paris spoke, figuring that one of them needed to get the conversational ball rolling.

"Well, Maya, I don't have to ask what you've been up to in the past five years. You've been raising my brother's child and keeping her existence a secret. Why did you do it, Maya? Did you hate him that much?"

Maybe it was because Paris's voice held bewilderment instead of anger. Maybe it was because she and Paris had at one time been closer than sisters. And maybe it was because Maya had been trying for years to figure out a way to bring Corey's father into her life; whatever the reason, the words just started pouring from her mouth.

"Paris, I'm not going to waste a bunch of time telling you not to hate me for what I did because I know it seems like a horrible thing to have done. All I can tell you is two things. One is that I truly tried to do the right thing from the beginning. And the other thing is that I always intended to let Julian know we have a child," she said quietly.

"You'll forgive me if I find that a little hard to swallow," Paris interjected. "But seeing as how you didn't even let him know you were pregnant, it's kind of a stretch for me to believe you intended to let him know he's a father. You know how the men in my family are about children. Julian would have been dancing in the street over that little girl," Paris said in the same puzzled tone of voice.

"At one time I would have believed that, too," Maya said sadly. "But as I told you, Paris, I did try to do the right thing. I would have never kept Corey from her family forever."

"But you left Julian without a word about being pregnant," protested Paris. "He would've never divorced you, never in a million years if he'd known you were carrying his child!"

"I didn't know I was pregnant. When I left Louisiana, I had no idea I was carrying a baby. I went home to Connecticut and I was applying for internships. I kept getting sicker and sicker and I figured it was just the stress of the divorce. It wasn't until a month after the divorce was final that I realized I was with child."

"So why didn't you tell him then? Come on, Maya, I'm trying to be fair here, but dang, you've had my brother's baby for four years and you never said a word. Nobody knew where you were or what you were doing and you claim you never intended to keep this a secret. Can you understand how hard that is for me to believe?" Paris hadn't raised her voice, but her level of frustration was beginning to show.

Just then the door opened and Kasey raced in with his lead trailing behind him, followed by Corey and

Ruth. "Hi, Mommy! We had a good time in the park. My grandma pushed me on the swings and we had fun!" Corey reported.

"Your *grandma?*" Maya said faintly.

"She's getting a little ahead of herself," Ruth said serenely. "Julian, Senior and I are engaged. So in a way, I am her grandma, or I will be, by blessing of marriage."

Maya tried changing the subject to Paris's upcoming nuptials. "And you're engaged, too. Wow, this is huge. Best wishes and all that," she said gamely. Suddenly she took a good look at her daughter, who was now seated happily in her aunt's lap. Kasey was standing on his hind legs with his feet in Corey's lap, taking advantage of the double ear-scratching he was getting. Paris and Corey could have been mother and daughter, they looked so much alike. They had the same creamy skin, the same abundant black hair, the same smile and the same mad giggle when something amused them. Corey even had a tiny beauty mark in the exact same place as Paris's, near the corner of her mouth, where it drew attention to her pretty lips.

Suddenly Maya spoke, asking Corey to tell her Aunt Paris her full name. "My name is Juliana Corinna Deveraux," she said proudly. "I was named after my daddy and you." She climbed off Paris's lap and called to Kasey. They began to play rather noisily near the kitchen while Paris let the tears roll unchecked.

"You really did mean it, didn't you?" Paris said in a near-whisper. "Whatever your reasons were, you never intended to keep her from us, did you?"

Ruth had been discreetly staying out of the way in the bedroom, but entered just in time to hand Paris a box of tissue. Maya was teary-eyed herself and turned to Paris and Ruth with a sincerity that seemed utterly believable. "I knew this day was going to come and I thought I'd be better prepared. But the fact is I'm not. I have no idea what to do next. I haven't seen your brother in a long time, but I can't believe he's changed so much that I can just stroll up to the house and say 'Oh, by the way, here's the baby I hid from you for four years.' Paris, I hate to put you in the middle of this, but you've got to help me," she entreated.

"Lord, today," was Ruth's only contribution to the conversation.

After Maya and Corey left, Ruth and Paris were left in a weird silence that was finally broken by Ruth. "Sweetie, if you're going to ask me to keep this a secret from your daddy, I don't know if it's possible. I've never lied to him yet and I don't want to start now."

"Lie to him? Oh, no, I don't want you to tell him lies, that'll only make this mess worse. What I want you to do is help me get him and Julian up here as soon as possible. This has to be dealt with quick, fast and in a hurry. Prolonging it is only going to make it worse," Paris said quickly.

Kasey barked sharply as if he agreed and both women laughed. "I swear he understands every word I say," Paris said and patted her lap so he would jump up to cuddle with her.

"I'm sure he does. That's the smartest little dog I've ever seen in my life. That's just one of the reasons I love my future son-in-law so much, he gives very good gifts."

Kasey barked again and gave her his big smile, the one that never failed to elicit an "aww" from the two ladies in his life. Paris showed all of her teeth in an identical smile. "You said *son-in-law*," she gloated.

Ruth's eyes rounded in surprise and she thought about her words for a second. "Oh, shoot. Well in a sense he will be my son-in-law, won't he? You're marrying Titus and I'm marrying your daddy, so I'll be his…" Her voice trailed off when she noticed Paris giggling like mad.

"I love doing that to you," she confessed. "You're going to be my mama-by-marriage. I don't care for that term *stepmother*. It makes you sound like a household good, like an ironing board or a ladder or something."

Before Ruth could get all gushy over this declaration, Paris went back to the job at hand. "So, mama-to-be, what the heck are we going to do about this? We need to get Daddy and Julian here pronto. Any suggestions?"

Ruth thought for a minute while Kasey jumped up next to her on the big chair and sniffed her pockets just in case she had a treat in one of them. She usually carried one or two when she took him out. Finding nothing, he sighed heavily and flopped across her lap. She rubbed his head absent-mindedly and began to speak. "There's a conference here next week. Julian was saying he wanted to come so he'd have a reason to see me that could be exempted from his taxes." She stopped talking and smiled. "Isn't that sweet? He's so adorable. And brilliant. He thinks of everything," she said in the soft tone of voice she always used when discussing her beloved.

Paris had to turn her head to keep from bursting out

into *I told you so*. Instead she cleared her throat and said it was a good thought. "That's a good reason for Julian to come up here. When he does, I'll talk to him. I won't tell him the whole story, but I'll get him to cooperate. Believe it or not, I can usually get my brothers to do anything I ask them to," she said immodestly but honestly.

Ruth knew this to be true. Paris's brothers loved her devotedly and would walk through hell for her. "Okay, well, that sounds like a plan. Or the beginnings of one. Just tell me this, sweetie. How come they got divorced in the first place? I have to tell you, Maya seems like a real keeper," she said in her frank manner.

Paris blew out a huge sigh. "Now that's one for the record books. I really don't know why they got divorced. It seemed like one day they were all blissful and the next day, she'd packed up and moved out. Nobody could really get to the bottom of it all because Julian was in such bad shape he wasn't talking. When she left him, it really tore him up," she said slowly. "Maybe if I tell you how they met, it'll help you understand the whole mess better."

Ruth curled up in the oversized armchair with Kasey beside her. "That sounds like a plan. Okay, how did they get together in the first place?"

Chapter 15

Julian Deveraux's eyes lit up when he saw his baby sister standing on the steps of the university library. She was home for the summer and rather than sit around relaxing like a normal person, she was taking classes. She was a bright and academically focused young woman of whom he was very proud, but she wasn't the reason behind the sudden light in his eyes. That look was for the young woman standing next to Paris. *Who is she? She's a cutie, whoever she is,* he thought. Like every Deveraux man in family history, Julian Deveraux had an eye for the ladies. And this one was just his taste.

She was tall, almost as tall as Paris, who was about

five-ten. She was a luscious shade of brown, like melting milk chocolate. Her skin was smooth and velvety-looking, too, and he wondered if it would taste as sweet as it looked. She was beautifully put together, with real hips and a real bosom intersected by a small waist. He loved a woman with a curvy body and hers looked perfect to him. She had long black hair that came below her shoulder blades in a long heavy braid. Her features were pretty and classic; she had a nose that was neither too wide nor too broad, a luscious-looking mouth with a Cupid's bow and thick natural eyebrows over big dreamy eyes with long lashes. And she was wearing glasses, little wire-rimmed ones that only served to draw more attention to those big eyes.

For one wild moment Julian pictured her lying next to him with her hair spread out against a crisp pillow-case and her dreamy eyes softened with contentment. For some reason she smelled like lilacs and he was about to show her more of the passion they had just shared. He had to jerk himself back into reality before the young woman thought he was deranged. He greeted Paris and asked very nicely who her friend was. Paris smiled and began the introductions.

"Maya Simmons, this is my oldest brother, Julian. Maya is from Connecticut and she's in med school. Maya, Julian goes here, too. He's just finishing law school," she said. Before either one of them could exchange a word, Paris glanced at her wristwatch and gasped. "Shoot, I'm fixin' to be late for class! Maya, don't forget you're coming over for dinner," she said over her shoulder as she darted off.

Julian could have kissed his baby sister. For one

thing, she knew just what he liked in a woman. And for another, she'd never been late for a class in her entire academic career. She was just giving them a chance to be alone, God bless her. He took another look at Maya, who was looking better every minute. She was wearing a midcalf skirt and a modest T-shirt with a white lab coat thrown over one arm and a stethoscope sticking out of the pocket. Suddenly she spoke.

"It was nice to meet you, but I have to go," she said. Her voice almost made him collapse on the spot. It was soft and well-modulated, but deeper in tone than he would have expected. That low, sultry voice was the last thing he would have expected to hear from those pretty lips and it sent a nice little shiver up his spine. He gave her his best smile, the one that had been charming females of all ages since he was in grade school.

"I'm surprised we've never run into each other before," he said.

She looked puzzled by the statement. "Why would we? It's a big campus," she pointed out. "And we're in totally different disciplines, so there's really no reason why we should." She rearranged her book bag and jacket, and again said she had to leave.

"Are you on your way to class, or maybe to clinic? I'll be more than happy to give you a lift," he offered gallantly.

"No, thank you," she said with polite disinterest.

"Well, if you don't have a class right now, maybe we could get an iced tea or a cup of coffee," he said, demonstrating the legendary Deveraux charm.

"No, thank you. Have a nice day," she said and without another glance in his direction she turned and left him standing there looking like a gawky freshman. A high school freshman at that. He couldn't stop watching her walk away, though, and was immensely cheered to note that she had a high, round booty to go with the rest of her bounty.

Paris joined him as he stood on the stairs looking at Maya's retreating figure. She'd been hiding behind a huge column to see how things progressed and she was shaking her head as she returned to his side. "What did you say to her, you oaf? Obviously you scared her off," she said with disgust.

Julian smiled down at her from his towering height. All Deveraux men were blessed in that department. "Are you kidding? I'm going to marry that young lady. She just doesn't know it yet," he said with a slow, sexy grin. "She's gorgeous, smart and she has sense enough to run from a predator. She's gonna be mine, just wait and see. C'mon, I'll buy you lunch and you can tell me everything you know about her." Without waiting for an answer, he draped his arm over her shoulders and they took off in the direction of his parked car.

Maya was so shaken by her encounter with Julian that she walked all the way back to her apartment. She usually took the bus or carpooled, but she was too rattled to do anything else but put one foot in front of the other. She lived in a big old house that had been divided into four generously sized apartments. She shared a second-floor two-bedroom with a fellow med student and on occasion there was a third or fourth person staying there on the pullout couch in the living room. When she'd reached the second floor and opened the door, she closed it immediately and leaned against it as if to catch her breath. She wasn't really out of breath; all the walking she did on campus kept her in shape, as well as her regular swimming. Maya loved the water and took the time to swim several times a week in the natatorium on campus.

No, it wasn't a lack of breath that was making her heart pound like a jackhammer; it was the encounter with the handsomest man she'd ever seen in her life. Why in the world did she have to run into someone like that? It was like being a diabetic in a pastry shop, full of delightful goodies that were all off-limits. And Julian Deveraux was definitely in that category. He should have the words *Danger, Do Not Enter* tattooed on his forehead. She was about to peel herself off the door and get something to eat before studying when her room-mate, Minoo, came into the living room.

"What in the world is wrong with you?" she asked in alarm. "Is someone after you?" Considering the fact that they lived in a fairly dicey neighborhood, it wasn't an impossibility.

Maya stood up straight and picked her book bag up from where she'd dropped it. "No, it wasn't like that at all. In fact, I almost wish it had been a purse snatcher or something because this is much worse," she mumbled as she straggled across the room to sit down at their dining room table.

Minoo's eyes grew huge. She was East Indian; petite, funny, intense and very pretty. "You're not making any sense at all. What are you talking about?"

Maya crossed her legs at the ankle and looked away from her friend. Finally she began talking and playing with the end of her braid at the same time. "You remember my friend Paris?"

"The tall girl, very pretty and nice? Yes, of course. What about her?" Minoo demanded.

Maya sighed heavily. "She introduced me to one of her brothers today. I knew she had four brothers—she talks about them all the time. But I had no idea they looked like that," she muttered. Finally meeting Minoo's worried gaze, she explained, "I met her oldest brother, Julian. In my entire life I've never been affected by a man like that. He's tall and he smells good and he has nice manners and he's just so handsome you wouldn't believe it. I've seen good-looking men before but nobody ever made me weak in the knees. I had to get away from there while I could still walk," she said, dropping her head into her hands.

Minoo's eyes filled with understanding. "Oh, now I see. Was he stuck up and rude? Sometimes really good-looking men are," she said.

Maya kicked at a table leg as she tried to explain. "No, Minoo, he wasn't like that at all. He was really polite, very pleasant, in fact. He asked me to have coffee with him, he offered me a ride to class, and he was very, very nice."

"So what's the problem? He sounds like a very nice man, what's wrong with him?" Minoo demanded.

"There's nothing wrong with him, but there's a whole lot wrong with *me*," Maya said with a wry twist to her mouth. "On my best day I couldn't hope to get a man like that interested in me and this is far from my best day. Men like that end up with tall, skinny, perfect-looking women who don't smell like disinfectant and puke by the end of the day. That's our usual perfume after a clinic day, if you recall. They don't spend every hour of the day studying and every hour of the night toiling away in the hospital on whatever rotation you get stuck with. A dumpy medical student from Connecticut is not what Mr. Julian Deveraux is looking for in his life, trust me."

Minoo's expressive face went from concerned to exasperated to compassionate as Maya let out her frustrations. When she finally wound down, Minoo got up from the table and patted her hand. "I'm making you some tea. A glass of chai is just what you need. It will help you put everything into perspective."

"There's nothing to put into perspective. I think I'm being very realistic about this. There's no point in getting all excited about a man who's way out of my league," Maya retorted bitterly.

"Honestly, Maya, I don't know how you managed to get this far in medical school with such a fragile ego. You have everything a man could possibly want, including a beautiful figure. My cousin almost lost his mind when he met you, remember? In my country, men would be crawling on their hands and knees to get to you and you somehow think that this man is out of your league?" She banged the teakettle with force as she spoke. "You are brilliant, Maya. You graduated from high school early, you got your undergraduate degree in three years instead of four and your MCAT scores are a legend on this campus. You're the one student everyone envies, the one everyone wants to emulate and you feel inadequate because you don't think you conform to some bizarre standard of Western beauty?"

Minoo continued to fuss as she prepared the fragrant,

spicy chai. "Has it ever occurred to you that everyone doesn't think the way you do? What makes you think this man is so stupid that he can't have his own standard of beauty? You might be just the kind of woman he desires—how do you know?"

The look of shock on Maya's face was so hilarious Minoo had to stop her lecture and laugh at her. She came and embraced her friend, kissing her on the cheek as she did so. "I'm sorry to be so harsh, but I can't stand to see you unhappy like this. That's why I'm glad I have an arranged marriage. I thought I would hate it, but I'm looking forward to it," she admitted.

"But you've met him, haven't you? I mean, you two already know each other and he's not horrible or anything, right?"

Minoo laughed merrily. "I have known him for a long time and he is a wonderful man. If he were someone I found absolutely horrible or vice versa, we could call it off. But lucky me, he is tall and handsome, he is also studying medicine and he has very liberal ideas about women and men and marriage. We've always liked each other very much. We didn't tell our parents that, we just let them think it was all their idea," she laughed. "But you're not fooling me. You are being very silly about this man. Just because a man is handsome, does that mean he's also mean and stupid? Of course not. You should give him a chance, Maya. If he asks you out again, you should go. I insist," she said with finality. "You will go out with him or I'll call my cousin and tell him you like him, he'll be here on the first plane to take you back to India with him."

Maya laughed uproariously at that, while Minoo

calmly served the chai in tall glasses filled with ice. "You keep laughing and you'll find yourself in New Delhi with six children and no degree. My cousin is not very liberated," she warned as they began to sip the sweet, milky tea that was both spicy and soothing.

Over the next few weeks, Julian exercised every weapon in his considerable arsenal to woo Maya. Even though she continued to blow him off, he didn't stop trying. To a Deveraux the word *no* meant try harder. He'd picked Paris's brain thoroughly for information that would make his path to Maya easier to tread, but she wasn't much help.

"Look, she's very sweet, so don't even think about messing over her. She's an only child and she's from Connecticut. Her mother and father were really strict with her and I have a feeling she hasn't dated too much. She's really, really smart, some kind of genius, actually. She's like a superhero around here. They call her the curve-buster because she routinely scores so high on all tests. They even give her some props in her clinicals and they usually treat med students like doody, you know what I mean. But Maya kind of holds her own because she's quiet and minds her own business, but she has a way with people. She doesn't act like a know-it-all, but dang, she's real close to being one," Paris had told him.

He'd held off as long as he could, but the day she attended church with Paris was his undoing. She'd worn a pink dress and she looked so pretty it was all he could do not to grab her and run out of the church with her. She was sitting in the pew the family usually occupied, with Paris on one side and his father on the other, so all he could do was try to pay attention to the service and not stare at her legs, which were stupendous. If he ever had any influence over her he'd get her to stop wearing midcalf skirts, they covered up something he considered to be a national treasure. Or maybe she should keep wearing them so no one could see those gorgeous legs except him. He was thinking about it so hard he almost missed the collection plate when it was handed to him.

He was thrilled to discover that this was the Sunday Maya was coming to dinner and he wasted no time in inviting himself along. It was okay though, since his brothers were also in attendance, the whole noisy, nosy crew of them. He quickly decided that his best course of action was to be the quiet one that day. He was the perfect gentleman, helping Paris set the table, leading the grace and refusing to rise to any of the pointed remarks his brothers threw his way. They knew that Maya was just his type and they could feel his temperature rising so it was their extreme pleasure to needle him all afternoon. He refused to go for the bait, though.

Instead of trying to sit next to Maya, he'd seated himself across from her so he had a better view of her face. He'd never seen a face he liked better. She looked like a doll with her wavy hair cascading down her back. The top was held away from her face in a big barrette, and soft, silky tendrils escaped and made her look sweetly feminine. She had a mind like a steel trap, though. She talked law with his father and impressed the hell out of his brothers, who were all aspiring lawyers like himself. She was smart, gentle and funny and before the meal had reached its conclusion, Julian knew in his heart that she was the one for him. No matter what it took, he wasn't going to rest until she was his wife.

He started slowly, sending her a card here and a plant there. He was very canny about his choice of plants rather than flowers because he was right. She didn't care for cut flowers, but she adored having green growing things around her. How he knew this he couldn't have said, but Maya just didn't seem like the dozen roses type. He stopped just short of stalking her, although he now knew her class schedule by heart and could find her on campus anytime he wanted to. They did encounter each other around the university a few times, and each time she was cordial if not warm, giving him the impression that she could at least stand the sight of him. He finally asked for her telephone number, which was a mere formality since he could have extorted it from Paris any time. He was touched to his heart when she wrote it down for him in his notebook. His slow, steady courtship now included telephone calls, which he made sure weren't too frequent and too long. But he loved talking to her so much it was like torture for him to hang up the phone. He craved the sound of her voice like a starving man craved food; it was like sustenance to his soul.

He'd worked up the nerve to ask her out a couple of times, but she'd refused both times, citing exams as the reason. He didn't harass her or beg her to go out with him because having just finished law school, he knew how very hectic her schedule was. It just didn't stop him from wanting her more and more every time he thought about her, heard her dulcet voice or, best of all, caught a glimpse of her. But good things come to those who wait and the opportunity he'd wanted so long finally fell into his lap. It was a hot night and Maya happened to be on duty in the emergency room when what looked like the remains of a gang war straggled in. It wasn't any such thing; it was just Julian and his overly spirited brothers.

Maya was shocked to find Julian in the examining room. He was sitting on the side of the bed looking like he'd been run over by a truck. One eye showed some definite bruising and a cut over the other eye was bleeding copiously, as head wounds will. His shirt was torn at the shoulder and his long legs, quite visible in shorts, had a number of scratches on them. She stared at him for a moment before speaking, and when she did, her normal doctor's demeanor was gone. "Julian, what on earth happened to you?" she gasped.

"This? Aww, this was just a family spat. My brothers and I were playing football and one thing led to another and this is the result," he said offhandedly. "Trust me, we've all looked worse than this."

She took his vital signs with trembling hands and dabbed at the cut over his eye. "You're going to need stitches, you know. I'll try to make sure it doesn't leave a scar," she murmured.

In a short time he was laying down on the narrow emergency room cot while she administered a local anesthetic under the guidance of the resident doctor. While they waited for it to take effect, the resident left to answer a page and Julian surprised her by grabbing her wrist. "You want to know what really happened, Maya? My brothers were giving me a hard time because you won't go out with me. So I let them have it. Fists were swinging, names were called, clothes were shredded and now I'm bleeding to death in your arms," he said with a pitiful sigh.

Maya had to laugh, he looked so forlorn. "You're not bleeding to death, Julian, that's kind of an overstatement," she said, giving him the first real smile he could remember.

"That's because you can't see my heart," he said softly. "It bleeds a little more every day because you don't like me."

Maya was momentarily taken aback by his words, but she recovered quickly. "I like you just fine, Julian, don't be ridiculous."

"Then why won't you go out with me? I just want to take you somewhere nice and get to know you better. Is that some kind of crime in Connecticut?"

This time she giggled, a tinkling sound that set Julian's heart dancing. "Of course it's not a crime. People are allowed to date in my home state, Julian."

"Every time you say my name I feel it," he whispered. "I feel it all over my body like a soft wind. Will you please go out with me?"

In an equally soft voice, Maya answered him. "Yes, I will. Now hold still so I can make this pretty," she crooned as she began making the tiny stitches to close the cut over his eye.

Chapter 16

Kasey was sound asleep on Ruth's lap, but Ruth was riveted by Paris's tale. "So she really wouldn't go out with him?"

"Nope. Maya wouldn't give him the time of day, honey. To an extent that might have made her more attractive to him because women used to fall all over him. From the time he was about ten years old the phone would be ringing off the hook with all these little fast-tailed girls hunting him down like crazy," she said, rolling her eyes. "If I got to the phone first I'd tell 'em to quit chasing my brother and get a life. I wasn't very popular with him for a while," she laughed. "But chicks used to jump through hoops of fire for that boy. It was ridiculous. It was disgusting! When he was a freshman in high school he went to the prom with a *senior,* can you imagine? Maya was the first woman who ever told him no."

Ruth's laughter woke Kasey, who opened one eye, yawned and went back to sleep. "So that was what got next to him, hmm? She played hard to get?"

"Oh, no, that's not what did it. He really did fall hard for her. It was like she was the one he'd been looking for all his life. He loved everything about her from the inside out. He liked her looks, that's for sure. He used to call her *Chocolat,* with the French pronunciation, because he said she was the only thing on earth that was sweeter than the finest chocolate ever made. But he also loved her brains, her ambition and drive. He was incredibly proud to be with her and he bragged on her constantly. He was crazy about her, Ruth."

"Then whatever happened to break them up must have been catastrophic. It had to be really dreadful to separate them, unless Maya didn't feel the same way about him," she said gently.

"Maya adored him. She was very quiet by nature, but with Julian she was livelier, more outgoing. They used to do things to please each other all the time. They were always surprising each other with little things like breakfast in bed, back rubs, crazy gifts, stuff like that. She talked about Julian constantly when they weren't together. He would stay up with her when she studied and pick her up every night she had to work, and make her lunch or take her out to lunch every day. She really thought Julian was the most wonderful man on earth. As soon as they saw each other their eyes would start sparkling like Christmas lights and that's no joke. There was nobody in the world for Maya but Julian, nobody," Paris said sadly.

"And you have no idea what destroyed their marriage? Julian never talked about it?"

"Absolutely not. Julian wouldn't say a word about it, but he was crushed. Frankly, he was a mess after she left. He did a lot of drinking, a lot of cursing and a lot of other antisocial things. He would hardly say a word to anyone in the family, as a matter of fact. If it hadn't been for his friend Monica he might have ended up in the psych ward and that's no joke," Paris told her.

Ruth raised an eyebrow. "Who is Monica?"

"Monica Montclair is an old friend of the family. After we moved to New Orleans, she and her family lived nearby and we got to be friends. Her mother is a real good friend of Daddy's. You met her—Charmaine Montclair, remember?"

Ruth had to struggle hard not to grimace. "Oh, yes, I remember her. So her daughter was a good friend of Julian's? And she helped him through his crisis, did she?"

Paris smiled at the suspicious tone of Ruth's voice. "Really, she did. They were always really tight and he wouldn't have made it without her. She was able to be there for him in a way no one else was, she was the only person he would talk to. He gradually came out of his funk and went back to being the Julian we all know and love, but in the past five years I haven't seen that look in his eyes, not once. I really believe a heart can break, Aunt Ruth, because she destroyed his. I didn't know what that felt like until Titus and I had that misunderstanding, but then you know what that was all about, you were there."

Ruth leaned on the back of the chair and stared at the

ceiling for a long moment. "And she kept his child away from him for four years. I'm going to have to stop dogging Sylvia about watching soap operas because this has all the earmarks of some high drama."

"Yeah, you're right. This is going to put *The Young and the Restless* to shame, honey. Somehow we have to get him up here to meet his child and hope that Chicago is still standing when he finds out the truth. And the only way we're going to do that is if we get Daddy to help," she said with a bright and hopeful look in Ruth's direction.

"And my role in this production would be what?" Ruth asked politely. "Am I supposed to get involved in this in some way?"

Paris's face split in a big grin and she started singing the old R&B classic "We Are Family," which made Ruth start laughing again. This time Kasey woke up with a little bark and glared at both women.

"Oh, you're gonna play me, huh? Do you actually think I'm going to use my feminine wiles to coerce your father into some kind of scheme? Is that what you're telling me?"

Paris jumped up from the sofa and ran over to the big chair, where she squeezed in next to Ruth and hugged her hard. "Yes, I am, Mama! You know I get to call you that after you and Daddy are married."

"Stop it! You're not going to be twisting *me* around your little finger, missy!" Ruth hugged her back with fervor and almost broke down in tears because it was true, in a very short time this would be her daughter-by-marriage and she couldn't be happier. "Just hand me my cell phone and let's get this runaway train rolling," she said, trying to blink away the moisture in her eyes. "Ewww, thank you Kasey, but that's not necessary," she squealed as Kasey helped her out by licking her face all over.

There was never a time when Mac wasn't glad to hear his beloved's voice, and this was no exception. The conversation started out especially well when Ruth purred into his ear, "What are you wearing?"

He stretched out on the bed and leaned back on the pillows with a big smile. "A towel, honey. I just got out of the shower."

"I wish I was there with you," she sighed. "You wouldn't be wearing that much."

His laughed boomed out and Bojangles came running. He seemed to have a sixth sense where Ruth was concerned and always knew when she was on the phone. "Your cat is standing on my chest now. He seems to want to have a word with you."

"Well, darlin', that's a coincidence because I need to have a word with you. Our daughter has something to tell you and I'm supposed to be setting the mood or something. You may want to get a little bit of that Napoleon brandy to sip while we chat."

Mac raised an eyebrow and tried not to laugh when Bojangles cocked his head to one side. She'd done it again, referred to Paris as "their" daughter. Whatever else was going on was secondary to the loving feeling those words gave him. "This sounds real serious, darlin'. Do I need to come up there?"

"Yes, as a matter of fact you do. And you need to bring Julian. And you need to come soon, angel."

He rose up on one elbow and his voice got deep and serious. "Honey, what's going on up there?"

"Go get the brandy and we'll tell you all about it," Ruth assured him. "It's a doozy, I'll grant you that, but nothing we can't get through together."

The conversation took a couple of hours, but the end result was the desired one. After several "Well, I'll be damned"s Mac was totally on board with the plan. "It's not going to be pretty, but it has to be done. If we only had some clear idea of why she did it, it might make it easier. But that's a piece of vital information we're not going to have when we enter this mess, which could work in our favor or blow the whole thing to pieces," he said slowly.

"What do you mean, baby?"

"One of the first things you learn in law is to never ask a question in the courtroom that you don't know the answer to and we're getting ready to go it one step further than that. We're getting ready to drop a bomb on him with no idea of what led up to this point. But he's been denied long enough, honey. It's time for my son to get to know his daughter and we'll all just have to deal with the fallout the best way we can." He was silent for a moment, and then asked the inevitable question.

"What's she like, honey? Tell me about my grandbaby."

"Julian, she's absolutely adorable. She looks just like Paris and she has a huge vocabulary and lovely manners. Maya has done a wonderful job of raising that young lady. You're going to love her. I love her already."

"And you don't mind marrying a grandpa, huh? You know this is going to make you a grandmother," he teased.

"That was the plan, baby. I may have gotten cheated out of birth children, but I'm going to have a houseful of grandbabies," she gloated. "She already calls me her grandma," she added proudly.

Mac smiled broadly as he drained the last drop of brandy from the snifter. He'd taken her advice and fortified himself for the complicated conversation. "This is going to work, honey. We're going to pray on it and somehow God is going to get us through this. I'll do my best to keep a lid on him, but I don't envy Maya, not one little bit. I loved her dearly and I'm sure whatever reasons she had for this action were good ones, at least in her head they were. But this isn't going to be easy for Julian to deal with, not by any stretch of the imagination."

"No, baby, it's not. And it's not going to be any easier for Maya. I'm just going with my feminine intuition, but I'd swear on my subscription to *Essence* that she still cares for him. In fact, I know she does. She named their baby Juliana Corinna Deveraux, for God's sake. Women don't name their children after ex-husbands unless there's a lot of love there. Something horrible happened to tear those two apart and maybe, just maybe, we'll find out what it was."

"I hope you're right, honey. Okay, we'll be there next Friday. I hope your walls are soundproof because there's bound to be a major explosion up in there when Julian finds out what she's been hiding from him," he said quietly. "I hate the idea of ambushing my son like this, but if I just tell him the news he might have a heart attack on the spot. May as well get it all over at once," he said with a deep breath. After a brief silence, his mood lightened. "By the way, darlin', what are *you* wearing?"

* * *

Maya was a wreck. The thing she'd been dreading for five years was about to happen and there was no way she could even pretend like she was ready for it. She knew the day of reckoning was inevitable, but that didn't mean she was looking forward to it. What she had done was wrong, it was stupid and selfish, but it was the only thing she could've done under the circumstances. She had to keep reminding herself of that as she brushed Corey's abundant hair. Corey was excited enough for all of them, Maya thought. She hadn't stopped talking about her daddy since the day she'd met Paris and Ruth. She'd been asking questions about her father off and on since she was old enough to realize that most of her friends had two parents and Maya had always tried to answer her questions honestly.

She had told her that her father was Julian Deveraux, that he was an attorney in New Orleans, that he was very tall and very nice and that one day he would come and get her for a visit. She'd even shown her pictures of Julian so the child would have some sense of the man who'd fathered her, and for the most part, Corey seemed satisfied. But the questions were becoming more frequent and more pointed and Maya had been running out of answers. It was only a matter of time before the father-and-daughter reunion had to take place and running into Paris was the catalyst she needed to right the terrible wrong she'd done. *So what if he wronged me? Two wrongs have never made a right, not in the history of the world,* she thought bitterly. *The minute I knew I was carrying his baby I should have gotten on a plane and gone back to Louisiana to confront him. It wouldn't have gotten my husband back, but it was the right thing to do.*

"I'm really going to see my daddy today?" Corey asked for the tenth or fiftieth time. Maya had lost track of how many times she'd heard the question that day.

"Yes, baby, you're really going to see your daddy today. And your granddaddy, too. That's why you have to sit still so I can make you look pretty, okay?"

"Does he love me?" Corey's innocent voice ripped the tear in Maya's heart even bigger.

"Yes, baby, he does. When he sees you he's going to be very happy and excited and he's going to love you more than anything." At least she knew that was the truth. Once Julian saw his little girl he was going to fall in love with her. What her ex-husband was going to do when he saw *her*, well, that was the problem. She was fairly sure he wouldn't say anything or do anything cruel in front of his father and Ruth and certainly not his daughter, but when they were alone… She abruptly stopped brushing Corey's hair, announcing that she was finished. She was fighting a sudden wave of nausea and feared another trip to the bathroom was coming, but she shook it off.

"You're all done, honey," she said, stroking her daughter's precious face.

"Do I look pretty?" Corey asked as she twirled around.

"Yes, you do. Go look in the mirror and see what you think."

They were in Ruth's master bedroom, where there was a big antique mirror leaning against the wall. Corey admired her reflection, smiling at the big pale green bow that held the ponytail at the top of her head back off her face. The rest of her hair hung in thick waves, a real novelty for the child. Her hair was usually worn in ponytails or braids, but this was a special occasion. She was wearing a pretty little dress in a matching shade of pale green. It was sleeveless with a high waist and a full skirt, and a pair of little sandals completed her ensemble. Maya's stomach turned over again as she heard the doorbell ring. Corey was chattering away about something and didn't hear it, but Maya knew her moment of reckoning was at hand. She just hoped she didn't pass out from the pressure. *But what else could I have done?*

Julian had a feeling something weird was afoot, primarily because Paris had tipped him off. Oh, not directly, she was too canny for that. If Paris had a secret, she'd never tell because she had a strong sense of honor. But she'd met Mac and Julian at O'Hare, which was a surprise to him. "What are you doing here, Coco? I thought you'd be in Atlanta getting ready for the wedding or something," he commented as he gave her a brief hug and kiss on the cheek.

"Well, I *am* getting ready for the wedding," she said. "Ruth and I found some fabulous fabric for the gown and Perry is here to take my measurements and we have to see about gowns for the attendants and stationery—" She stopped talking when Julian put his hand over her mouth.

"I'm so sorry I asked," he laughed. "You know, you could take all the money you spend on a big wedding and buy a house or something. I don't understand this need for pomp and circumstance," he joked.

She ignored him while she gave her father a tight hug and a kiss on the cheek. She whispered something in his ear and Julian saw him nod slightly. Mac announced that he was going to check on their bags and went over to the carousel that corresponded with their flight. It was then that Paris made her move. She turned to him at once, taking his hand and holding it tightly, the way she'd done when she was a little girl.

"Julian, I need you to do me a favor, okay?" she asked sweetly.

"Of course, baby sister, you know I'll do anything for you. What is it?"

"I need you to make me a promise about something. You've never broken a promise to me in my whole life, and I know you won't break it now, right?" Her eyes were huge and serious as she spoke.

"I would never break my word to you. Now what is it? Obviously, it's something really important. Talk to me, Coco, what's going on?"

Paris tightened her grip on his hand. "I want you to promise me that you're going to try to understand something that has no understanding. I need you to be the most open-minded you've ever been in your life, Julian. And I want you to promise that you won't lose your temper, no matter what happens today. Please promise me, okay?"

Julian's face had already begun to turn mottled red with rage. "Are you trying to tell me that Titus got you pregnant? Is this why the wedding was moved up from December to August?"

Paris rolled her eyes and jerked her hand away. "Julian, honestly. We moved the wedding up because since he found out his birth father is a pastor he insists that we can't…well, never mind, it's not your business," she said grumpily. "This has absolutely nothing to do with me. Just promise me, right now."

"Okay, okay. You have my word."

Maya could hear the sounds of people entering the loft. She strained to hear Ruth's gracious welcome to Julian and she could even hear the softer greeting she had for his father. In a few minutes, Ruth came into the bedroom and sat down on her king-sized panel bed with a sigh. "Paris will be in to get you in just a minute or so, and Julian, that is *my* Julian, will come in here with Corey and me." She smiled sympathetically when she saw the sheer panic on Maya's face. "Breathe, sweetie. It'll be fine, I promise you. You look beautiful, so try to relax," she counseled.

While Corey showed her outfit off to Ruth, Maya took a few deep cleansing breaths, blowing them out slowly. She was an adult, she was smart and resourceful, and she'd raised a charming and lovable child while completing a difficult internship and residency. Yes, she'd screwed up, but as far as she knew, there was no death penalty for mistakes. It was her turn to look in the mirror and she wasn't terribly reassured by what she saw. Her hair was in its usual bob cut, wavy and held back on one side with a purple comb. She, too, was wearing a sleeveless dress, but hers was a chic violet linen, one that buttoned down in the front. It had a flared skirt that ended just below her knee and with it she wore casual thong sandals with multicolored beads in shades of purple. She looked chic but if you looked closer there was nothing in her eyes but trepidation. She turned around suddenly and was about to tell Ruth to stop it, that she couldn't go through with it.

They had come up with this idea because everything else from a phone call to an e-mail to a fax just seemed too impersonal, after all the time that had passed. And knowing Julian the way they did, there was no way someone could tell him he had a child and expect him to wait around for weeks, days or even hours before he saw his offspring. His father and sister agreed this was the best way, but it felt like an ambush to Maya. It was wrong, it was unfair to spring it on him like this, and she had to stop it. But before she could open her mouth, the bedroom door opened and Paris held out her hand.

Like a robot, she walked over to Paris and took the hand she was extending, unaware that her hand was trembling. She could hear the deep, booming voice of her former father-in-law and when she heard Julian's voice answer him, her knees buckled slightly. All too quickly the two women went down the short hallway that opened into the living area. Maya thanked God that his back was to them; she didn't think she'd be able to handle it otherwise. Paris cleared her throat softly and spoke to him.

"Julian, there's someone here you haven't seen in a long time," she said gently.

He turned around and there was no sound in the cavernous room at all, none whatsoever. Everything seemed frozen, like someone had touched the pause button on a DVD. It was hard to say who was the most surprised when he finally reacted. He simply walked across the room and took her hand from his sister's grasp. Holding both of her hands in his own, he stared down at her. "Maya," he whispered, and touched his lips to hers. He wrapped his arms around her and held her closely. "It's been too long, Maya."

The relief in the room was palpable. It was as though a collective sigh rippled through the loft. The plan might have actually worked if it hadn't been for one unexpected thing. As Julian was leading Maya to the sofa to sit down, a new voice was heard.

"Is it my turn now? Do I get to meet my daddy now? I can't wait anymore," Corey announced as she appeared in the living area with Ruth on her heels.

Julian's knees seemed to give way as he collapsed onto the sofa. His face was paper-white as he stared at the child who'd just dashed into the room. Corey seemed to sense that something was amiss and turned shy, putting her index finger to the corner of her mouth. Julian rubbed his hand over his face and spoke in a quiet voice that was full of emotion. He held out his arms and said, "Yes, it is your turn, darling. Come here, Daddy can't wait anymore, either."

Chapter 17

As long as she lived, Maya would never forget the look on Julian's face when he saw his daughter for the first time. Or the absolute elation on Corey's when he held out his arms to her. She ran to him and put her little arms around his neck and hugged him tightly while he picked her up and held her as though he couldn't let go. He might have continued to hold her forever but her muffled voice protested. "I can't breathe, Daddy!"

He reluctantly released her and allowed her feet to touch the floor. She stood between his legs with a huge smile on her face and one hand on each of his knees. He returned the smile while his eyes glistened with a suspicious moisture. Maya spoke softly, saying, "Tell your daddy your name, sweetheart."

Corey went up and down on her toes as she

answered. "My name is Juliana Corinna Deveraux and I'm four," she said proudly, holding up four fingers.

Julian's throat worked furiously before he could respond. "Well, I think you should get a kiss for each year. There's one, two, three and four," he said softly, kissing her forehead, both cheeks and her chin.

"I'll be five soon," Corey informed him, holding out her arms for another kiss, which Julian gladly placed on her nose.

Maya's own throat was constricted with unshed tears and she was about to rise from the sofa to leave them alone, but Julian's strong hand clamped around her wrist to detain her.

"You're my real daddy and I'm your little girl," Corey said with a beaming smile. "I like you, you're just like Mommy said." She climbed into his lap without asking permission and leaned into the crook of his arm, smiling up at him.

Julian shot Maya a look that she couldn't interpret. "What did she say about me, sugar?"

"She said you were very nice and very tall. And handsome, too. She said you were real handsome and that you would come and see me and take me home with you for a visit. And she said I would meet my grandpa, too."

Julian's eyes crinkled in a smile. "That's your grandpa right there. Would you like to meet him?"

"Yes, I would. He's handsome, too, isn't he?" Corey said approvingly.

Maya went to get up again, so Mac could sit down, but Julian stopped her once again, his hand easily spanning her narrow wrist. Mac came over and took Corey's little hand and kissed the back of it.

"Do you have a hug for me, too? I've been waiting a long time to meet you, angel cake."

Corey held up her arms and Mac picked her up, holding her close and giving her a kiss on each cheek. "You're a beautiful little girl."

"Thank you," she said politely. "You're very pretty, too. Not as pretty as my daddy, but you look nice. You're going to marry my grandma Ruth, aren't you?"

"I sure am," Mac assured her. He carried her over to the big chair and sat down with her in his lap. Kasey was tired of being ignored and jumped up on the chair with them. He settled down for a nice head scratch while Mac and Corey got to know each other. Mac was asking her silly questions to make her laugh and Paris and Ruth sat at the dining room table wiping tears from their eyes. Maya had yet to say a word, simply because she didn't know what to say. Julian didn't seem to have any such problem, however. His hand moved from her wrist to clasp her damp, trembling hand tightly while he stared at her. In a low voice he asked her the question she'd been dreading for days.

"How could you do this to us, Maya? Did you hate me that much?" he said so quietly that no one else could hear his agonized words.

"Julian, I…I did what I thought I had to do. There wasn't any other way," she replied in an equally low voice.

"Maya, that's a load of crap and you know it. We have a lot to talk about and the sooner we get started, the better." He looked at Corey, who was talking to him.

"Daddy, you have to come to our house. You have to

see my bedroom and our plants, and my pictures. And I have a present for you, too, but I'm not supposed to tell you that," she said, covering her mouth. Her eyes bright with excitement, she moved her hand and gave him a smile so much like Paris's it was eerie. "When are you going to come see our house, Daddy?"

Julian gave Maya another unreadable look and said, "How about right now, sugar?" He slowly let go of Maya's hand and abruptly asked where her car keys were. "I'm driving."

"Look, Julian, I don't think this is a good idea," Maya said with an edge to her voice. "We can get together tomorrow and get everything ironed out, but I don't want…"

"Maya, right now I don't give a damn what you want or don't want. You don't want to argue with me right now, trust me. Now, where are your car keys?"

Ruth, Paris and Mac looked at each other with relieved expressions. "Well, at least no blood was shed," Paris said, looking around the loft for evidence of carnage. "Julian was a perfect gentleman, which is a great relief."

Ruth tsked and shook her head. "Julian is in shock, sweetie. He's just going through the motions right now. Give him a little while and he'll be able to express himself fully."

Mac was once again impressed with his fiancée's perception where his children were concerned. "I'm afraid she's right, cupcake. In a little while he's going to regain his senses and I don't think poor Maya will be seeing this gentlemanly side of him. Quite the opposite, in fact," he said with a frown.

"Then we'd better be ready to rescue her. We'll give them two hours, and then we'd better go over there so he doesn't scare the baby to death," Ruth said with brisk practicality. She put her arms around Mac's waist and smiled up at him. "So, Grandpa, what do you think of your granddaughter? Is she a peach or what?"

Mac's eyes grew unnaturally bright. "She's amazing. Maya has raised a beautiful child, a smart and sweet one. She's so much like Paris I can't believe it," he said, his voice filled with love.

"Daddy, I was nothing like Corey! I was the worst little thug in Louisiana and you know it! I wasn't even close to being that adorable," Paris protested.

Mac gave her a steady and serious look. "If that's what you believe, I didn't do a very good job as a father because that child is your very image, Paris Corinna. You were every bit as beautiful as she is and just as charming. And you still are."

Paris's mouth fell open and she stared at her father without being able to say a word. He held out his free arm, the one that wasn't wrapped around Ruth, to her and she went to him for a hug. "Daddy, that's the sweetest thing you've ever said to me," she murmured.

He kissed her on the top of her head. "Synchronize your watches, we don't want to leave them alone too long. Poor Maya looks like she's had as much as she can take today."

The drive to Maya's house actually didn't take that long. She lived in a gentrified area that wasn't too far from Ruth. To Maya the short trip seemed to last an eternity. It could have been fifteen days instead of the fifteen real minutes. She sat so close to the door, the handle was imprinted on her hip, something that seemed to amuse Julian.

"You don't have to stick to the door like that. You look like I'm about to attack you or something," he said with a mild sneer.

"How do I know what you're going to do? You seem pretty adamant about getting your own way right now," she answered back and immediately wished she hadn't.

The transformation in him was instant and anything but reassuring; his eyes, normally so kind and full of laughter, narrowed into icy pinpoints of anger. "You're absolutely correct about that, Maya. I do intend to get my own way but that doesn't include hurting you. Quit cowering over there like a cornered rat before you scare the girl."

Luckily, Corey wasn't paying attention to her parents' conversation. She was too busy conducting a travelogue from her back seat perch in her child safety seat. "Look Daddy, that's where we buy bread, and we get vegetables and fruit from Mr. Cho on the corner. That's where we get our clothes dry-cleaned, and that's where I take ballet," she informed him.

"Do you like ballet, sugar?" he asked as he looked at her animated face in the rearview mirror.

"It's okay," she answered indifferently. "I want to take tae kwon do, but Mommy said no. Tae kwon do is funner though. Brandon takes it and it's lots funner than ballet."

"Not funner, honey. It's more fun," Maya said automatically.

"If it's more fun why can't I take it instead of ballet?" Corey asked reasonably.

Julian was visibly struggling not to laugh. "Who's Brandon, sugar?"

"My boyfriend," she said casually. "Here's our house, Daddy!"

Now it was Maya who was choking back laughter at the look on Julian's face when Corey referred to her playmate as her boyfriend. She went back to her previous somber state when Julian parked the car and came around to open her door, holding out his hand to her as though they were on a date. He got Corey out of her car seat and the three of them entered the townhouse looking like a typical American family coming home from an outing. Nothing could have been further from the truth, but their look was completely deceiving. When they reached the front door, Maya's hands were shaking so hard Julian had to take the key from her and insert it into the lock. Corey took over from that point, taking her father's hand and leading him around the spacious two-story town house. Maya allowed them to take the tour alone, she needed some time to regroup and gather her thoughts.

She stood in the living room, wiping her hands down the front of her linen dress. She was pleased with their surroundings, although she wasn't particularly house-proud. She wanted Corey to grow up with nice things, but she also wanted her to be able to play freely and not have to worry about breaking things or spilling things. There was a big comfortable sofa with a matching love seat and armchair, all in navy blue. The throw pillows were brightly patterned African prints, and there were similar throws on the love seat and sofa. The floors were hardwood, but there was a big colorful area rug that tied all the colors together and added flair to the simply furnished space. The thing that made the room so eye-catching was the array of healthy green plants that abounded in all the windows and tables around the room, and also the colorful artwork on the walls. They were just prints and posters of art Maya found appealing, but the way she'd had them framed made them look rich and expensive.

After saying a quick prayer for guidance, Maya went into the kitchen. She needed to do something with her hands to keep busy. She opened the refrigerator and got out a bag of lemons. *When life gives you lemons, make lemonade,* she thought with a short laugh that bordered on the hysterical. She washed her hands well, and then washed the fruit one at a time, her mind going in circles like a caged gerbil on a wheel. Seeing Julian had a powerful effect on her. How could it not, he was the first and only man she'd ever loved. He still looked the same, if anything he looked better. Tall and dashing with café au lait skin, beautiful wavy hair and the lean, saturnine good looks he'd inherited from his father; Julian was quite a man. The tiny scar over his left eye was almost invisible, unless, like Maya, one knew it was there. He resembled his father, with his heavy moustache and lean, broad-shouldered physique, but his eyes were his own, large and clear with long curly lashes and a way of looking directly into her soul.

Maya sliced the lemons in half and used a reamer to extract the juice and seeds. She strained the liquid into a glass pitcher and added spring water and sugar, stirring until the sugar was dissolved. She cut the last lemon into thin circles and added them to the pitcher

with ice from the automatic dispenser built into the refrigerator door. After she did that, she hesitated for a
moment, and then reached into the refrigerator for a
container of raspberries, which she rinsed quickly and
patted dry. She put them on a plate and mashed them
into a pulp, reserving about half of them, and then
stirred the pulp into to the pitcher. She put ice in two
tall glasses and one old-fashioned glass, before getting
a bottle of Perrier water from the door of the refrigerator. A slight tremor ran through her body as she remembered the first time she'd made raspberry lemonade for
Julian.

It was a summer afternoon and Julian was taking her
for a drive into the country and a picnic. He was going
to bring the entire meal, but she insisted on making a
contribution. She'd made big fat oatmeal cookies with
walnuts and dried cherries and just a touch of cinnamon.
And she'd also made raspberry lemonade, something
her favorite aunt had taught her to make when she was
very small. Unfortunately, the weather didn't cooperate and it rained all afternoon. Maya could still
remember the feeling of disappointment she'd experienced. It was just their second date and she was looking
forward to spending more time with him. The first date
had gone so well she could finally admit she was en-
thralled with the handsome young lawyer and she
wanted nothing more than to see him again.

She had been standing at the window frowning at the
steady rain, oblivious to the fact that it was warm and
fragrant and refreshing. All it meant to her was that her
date had to be cancelled. When the knock came at her
door it startled her so that she jumped. She was so

caught up in her dislike of the rain she'd lost track of
time. When she opened her door she was both thrilled
and surprised to see Julian standing there with a big
wicker basket in one hand and a thriving green fern in
the other.

"Julian, what are you doing here?"

He handed her the fern and used his handkerchief to
blot away the raindrops from his forehead. "We have a
date, if I remember correctly. May I come in?"

Maya felt her cheeks grow hot from embarrassment.
She'd been so busy sulking about the weather she'd
forgotten her manners completely. "Of course, come in,
Julian. Yes, we did have a date, but as you can see—"
she waved at the open windows "—it's been called on
account of rain," she said with a wistful sigh.

"Maya, sweetheart, you must never allow the
mundane to interrupt the extraordinary," he said. "We
can go for a drive anytime, but we're having this picnic
today. You went to a lot of trouble to make sure you
were free today, and I made you a fabulous lunch and
we're going to relax and enjoy ourselves right here," he
informed her. He flashed her that gorgeous smile of his
and she just melted inside.

"Julian, your shirt's wet. Would you like something
else to put on? I have some scrubs around here that
would probably fit you," she offered shyly.

Without warning, he whipped off the damp blue Polo
shirt he was wearing and exposed his lean body. Maya
felt something she'd never experienced in her life—
desire. The sheer force of it almost made her pass out.
Julian was slender, but muscular with broad shoulders
and a perfect musculature that was enhanced by the

silky hair on his chest. Her face was flaming hot now, as were other parts of her anatomy, and she managed to squeak out a few words before fleeing to the sanctuary of her bedroom for the shirt.

"I, umm, I, ahh, I'll be right back, please make yourself at home," she gasped as she ran out of the room.

When she returned with a XX-sized scrub top in institutional-green, she was stunned to see that he'd spread a blanket on the floor and arranged their picnic in the middle. He was still shirtless and her second sighting of him was no less unsettling than the first. She tossed the shirt at him and turned her head away from the sight of his bronzed beauty. "That looks wonderful, Julian. Put that on and I'll go get the lemonade."

She had to make herself count to twenty before she could go back into the living room with the tall pitcher and the glasses of ice, each with some raspberries mixed in. She filled his glass, topping it off with sparkling water and stirring it with a long spoon before handing it to him. His eyes widened as he tasted it and he emptied the glass before handing it back to her for more.

"Sorry to be such a pig, but that's delicious. Almost as sweet as you," he told her.

Maya was so relieved that his tempting frame was completely covered that she ignored his teasing. She looked at the food arrayed on the blanket and licked her lips in anticipation. "That looks wonderful, Julian. What is it?" She indicated the large round loaf of Italian bread stuffed to bursting with wonderful fillings.

"It's my personal version of a muffuletta. Have you had a muffuletta sandwich before?"

Maya was familiar with the New Orleans favorite, a hefty po'boy-style sandwich with a special olive condiment. It was made with several kinds of olives, roasted red peppers, onions, and garlic and usually combined with cold cuts like Genoa salami, ham and the like. Julian's was made with smoked turkey and thinly sliced chicken breast and it was divine. He cut it into small wedges and fed it to her bite by bite. He'd also brought an assortment of fresh vegetables and a fruit salad, plus a brand of kettle cooked potato chips only available in Louisiana. By the time they finished eating, Maya was too stuffed to move. She was moaning with repletion and Julian looked very pleased with himself.

"Are you enjoying our picnic, baby?"

Maya nodded her head in response; she was too satisfied to speak.

"Good, because it's not over yet. I brought a couple of movies for us to watch while we make room for dessert."

He'd brought copies of *Cabin in the Sky* and *Stormy Weather* and Maya was both surprised and pleased. While she got the DVD player turned on, he quickly and efficiently cleaned up the remains of their spread, with the exception of the rest of the lemonade, which he declared the best he'd ever had. They sat next to each other on the sofa and before she knew it, they were cuddled together watching the incomparable vintage movies as if they'd been a couple for years. And later, when he'd turned to kiss her for the first time, it felt like they'd been together forever, like they'd never be apart again.

Maya had to fight hard to keep the hot tears from overflowing as she went into the freezer for some homemade cookies. She didn't get to cook often, and when she did she would power-cook, making dozens of cookies, for instance, so that when she wanted to give Corey a special treat, she could just pop them in the oven. She had just turned the oven on when Julian entered the kitchen. He didn't look any better than she felt, she noticed.

He looked almost haggard and his eyes were bleak when he asked her the same question he'd asked earlier. "How could you do this to us, Maya? How?"

She looked back at him mutely. It was a question she couldn't really answer, not now.

Chapter 18

When Julian looked at Maya, it was as though no time had passed since the last time he'd held her in his arms. She looked a little different, but she was still his *Chocolat,* his beautiful chocolate baby doll. She was too skinny and she had a becoming new hairstyle, but everything else was the same. Except, of course, for the fact that she'd borne his child and neglected to tell him about it for the past four years; that was the part he was having a little difficulty with. He fully expected the explosive temper for which he was known to have erupted by now, but for some reason, it hadn't. He was angry, of course, but he was also confused and the two elements didn't mix well in his normally logical and orderly mind.

Maya spoke first, asking where Corey was. "She's

upstairs talking to her granddaddy on the phone. She'll be down in a minute, I'm sure."

"Don't count on it. Corey can talk a person's ear off. I think you've noticed that by now." Maya gave him a weak smile and handed him a glass of lemonade.

Julian had noticed a lot of things as Corey showed him around the house. She had held his hand and showed him everything there was to see from room to room. He had to admit his heart stirred in a special way when he looked into Maya's bedroom. It was simply furnished but it looked like a magazine illustration. Maya had a knack for making discount store finds look like designer goods. He remembered the love she'd lavished on their first home and how much he loved coming home every night. The tour ended in Corey's bedroom and she was thrilled to show it off to him.

"This is my room, Daddy. I have a big-girl bed and everything," she informed him gleefully. It was a delightful-looking room, feminine and pretty in various shades of pink, pale yellow and lavender. A big Hello Kitty stuffed doll was centered on the bed, and an array of smaller stuffed toys and dolls were on the shelves and the dresser. "Come sit down, Daddy, and see my things," she cajoled. Julian was more than happy to comply; he wanted to see where his daughter was growing up. The first thing he noticed was the picture on the nightstand next to the bed. To his shock, it was a picture of him and Maya with their arms around each other, smiling for all they were worth. It had been taken on the day they eloped, the happiest day of his life.

Corey saw him looking at it and eagerly told him that she had lots more pictures. "I have a whole book,

Daddy. Here, I'll show you," she said eagerly and ran to her bookcase, where she retrieved a medium-sized pink scrapbook with her name on it in a pretty script. "Open it, Daddy. Mommy made it for me when I was little," she said excitedly as she climbed up on the bed with him. She took off her shoes and tossed them on the floor. "No shoes on the bed, Daddy. Mommy will get you for it," she warned.

"I'll try to remember," he said with a grin. "Okay, sugar, let's see what we have here," he said as she snuggled into his side as if she'd been doing it since birth. He opened the book and was stunned to see the contents. The first pages were snapshots of him. Some from childhood, some from adolescence and college and others from the blissful time he and Maya were together. And the pictures weren't just stuck on the pages, either; there were carefully handwritten stories about him and little decorative items to make each page vivid and entertaining.

"See, Daddy? That's you! And see, there's my grandpa, and my uncle Wade and my uncle Philippe and uncle Lucien. And that's my grandpa's house right there," she said, pointing at a picture that was indeed of the family home in New Orleans. "And that's my aunt Paris!"

Julian was so shaken by emotion he couldn't trust himself to speak. Maya had obviously educated their child on the facts of her family; she hadn't hidden anything from her about who her people were. She had, in fact, presented them very lovingly and with great detail. Yet she couldn't pick up a phone and say "Oh, by the way, we're having a baby"?

Corey began patting his arm. "Daddy, I have a present just for you, okay? I'm going to get it for you," she said excitedly as she climbed off the bed and scampered out of the room. Julian was glad for her departure because it gave him a chance to wipe his eyes and pinch the bridge of his nose. *She was wrong. No matter how beautiful Corey is, no matter how much she told Corey about us, Maya was wrong to do this.* It seemed as though he had to keep thinking harsh thoughts in order to remember that he was the plaintiff, not the defendant. She was the one who had a lot of explaining to do and no matter what she said, this was the most heinous thing a woman could do to a man, as far as he was concerned. *She must have really hated me to leave town knowing she was carrying our child.*

He could feel the anger rising and derived a eerie fortitude from it; it was almost like an elixir of strength flowing through his veins. Just then, Corey returned with another album. This one was purple with *Daddy* written on it in gold letters. He had to smile; it was in his fraternity colors. While Corey made herself comfortable again, he put an arm around her. "What have we got here, sugar?"

"This is *your* book, Daddy. Mommy made it for you. Open it up and see," she urged. Julian smiled indulgently at her eagerness until he turned the first page. There was Maya, wet from perspiration with tears of joy rolling down her face, holding Corey. They were still in the delivery room and although Maya would no doubt argue with him, she had never looked more beautiful to him. There were pictures of every day of Corey's first year from the moment of her birth. Her first year was captured in page after page of pictures, six to eight pictures per page. As she grew older, there were fewer pictures per year, but each year was represented. As with Corey's scrapbook, there were little notes and stories about her and all her firsts; her first word, her first steps alone, her potty training and all the funny little things she'd done and said since her birth.

The anger he was carefully nurturing was at war with the rush of emotion that was overcoming him and he was finding it hard to breathe. Thanking God for His intervention, Julian pounced on his cell phone when it began to chime. He couldn't have said what he'd have done without the distraction; probably broke down in sobs like a damned punk.

"Yeah, Judge, we're fine. We're looking at scrapbooks, actually. You coming to get me or what?"

"Is that Grandpa? Can I talk to him?" Corey asked.

"Absolutely, sugar. I'm going downstairs to talk to your mommy, okay?"

He left her sitting on the bed, propped up against the pile of ruffled pillows with her legs crossed, looking exactly the way Paris had looked at her age. He walked into the wall on his way down the stairs, but he was too full of raging emotions to notice. This must be what people feel like when they wake up from comas. Years have passed and all they remember is the day they passed out. This is crazy, this doesn't make any sense, he thought as he followed the fragrance of fresh-baked cookies to the kitchen.

And there she was, looking as pretty as a pile of ripe plums in a basket. The woman he'd fallen in love with at first sight, the woman he'd sworn to love forever, the woman who'd broken his heart in so many pieces he still hadn't found them all. She turned around when she heard him and he was savagely pleased to see that she looked nervous. She looked terrified, in fact, and he took a momentary perverse pleasure in her fear. He needed to see that; he needed any means necessary to keep the upper hand, and the notion was unsettling. He accepted the glass of raspberry lemonade she put in his hand and a jolt of memory accosted him. Their eyes met and he relived the first time he'd had the refreshing drink.

"It's still wonderful, Maya. Thank you," he said quietly. "But this doesn't change anything. You and I have a lot to talk about. How could you hate me so much that you'd keep that beautiful little girl away from me? How could you walk out on me, knowing you were carrying my child and not look back? You took something from me that I'll never get back, woman. You took the first years of my child's life, years I'm never going to have again. How in the hell could you be that cruel, Maya?" His voice was low but it resonated with pure fury. The pain was etched on his face and he was visibly controlling himself with great effort. The look on Maya's face was one of astonishment. She stared at him as though he were suddenly speaking another language.

"Julian, what are you talking about? This was your choice, too. I admit I was wrong not to pursue the matter further, but that was how you wanted it. Once you made it clear that you wanted your affair more than you wanted me and our baby, what else could I do?"

Now it was Julian's turn to look at Maya as if she were speaking Xhosa or some other foreign tongue. "Maya, don't start that crap again," he began angrily. He stopped as soon as he heard Corey coming down the stairs.

"Daddy, Grandpa said to call him back. Ooh, lemonade! And cookies! Is this a party, Mommy?"

Before Maya could answer, her pager went off. She punched a speed dial number into her cell phone and said she'd be right there. "Okay, sweets. Mommy has to go in to work. Get your shoes on and get your bag and let's roll," she said briskly.

"Hold on, Maya. Where is she going and why?" Julian demanded.

"This is my last night of being on call for a shift in the emergency room. I just finished my residency and I was hoping this wouldn't happen. Unfortunately, I just got called. There's a five-car pileup on the interstate south of here and some of the victims are being airlifted in. I'm taking her to her sitter because I can't very well leave her here, now can I?" Her resentment of his question was evident in her posture and the sharp tone of her voice.

"Well, why can't *I* stay with her?" Julian asked.

"Because I won't be back until morning and I can't ask you to babysit all night," she told him.

Now it was Julian's turn to look resentful. "I can't *babysit* my own child, but I can certainly stay with her, unless you don't trust me."

"Daddy's going to stay all night? And put me to bed and tell me a story?" Corey's elation needed no interpretation.

Julian silently dared Maya to protest. "Okay, fine," she said. "Only no more liquids before bed and make sure she's in the bed by nine at the very latest. She has all kinds of ways of circumventing bedtime," she said with the smile he remembered.

"Come kiss me good-night, sweetness. And be very, very good for Daddy, you hear me?"

Julian watched as Maya grabbed her keys and headed for the front door. "There's an extra set of keys on the hook by the refrigerator. My cell phone number is on the refrigerator door and so is the admin number for the emergency room. If you need anything or can't find something, call the admin number and they can get a message to me."

She had her hand on the doorknob when Julian caught up with her. He had Corey on his hip as though he'd been carrying her that way for years. "Wait a minute," he protested.

Maya paused and turned to look at him. "What?"

"You be safe out there. Are you sure you don't want me to drive you?"

She looked surprised at the sound of concern in his voice. "I'll be fine. Thank you for asking," she said softly. Before he realized what he was doing, he kissed her on the lips. "Take care of yourself."

Mac was relieved when his cell phone went off and he could see Julian's number on his caller ID. "Well, he's still alive, that has to be a good sign," he cracked to Ruth as he answered the phone. They talked for a few minutes and when the call was over, Ruth was waiting expectantly for a report. He looked at Ruth and rubbed the back of his ear with his forefinger before speaking. "Julian is spending the night," he said.

Ruth's eyes widened the way they did when she was

excited. Before she could let out a whoop of joy, Mac covered her mouth with his hand. "Hold on, honey. Maya got called in to work and instead of taking Corey to the sitter, Julian wanted to stay with her. He was calling me to see if I could bring him his bag and to let me know he wouldn't be back tonight."

She wouldn't be discouraged, though. "That's still a good sign—no, a *great* sign, Julian. She wouldn't let him stay there unless she still trusted him. She knows him well enough to know that he's going to take care of the baby and she's confident that he's not going to try and steal her away in the middle of the night. Believe it or not, that's progress," she said confidently.

They were still in the living room, where they had been watching *Last Holiday* with Paris. Paris agreed with Ruth completely, adding that she would be more than happy to take Julian's luggage to Maya's house. "In fact, this is a good time for me to pick his brain a little. I've had just about enough of not knowing what the heck went on between them. I love Maya and I want my sister-in-law back in the family."

The look of determination on her face was all too familiar to her father, who just shook his head. "Okay, cupcake. But you drive carefully and call me when you get there. And don't bully your brother, let him talk if he wants to, but don't interrogate him," he warned.

"Who, me? Would I do that?" she asked in a fake-innocent voice.

Ruth and Mac looked at each other and answered in one voice, "Yes!"

It took about fifteen minutes for Paris to get the gear in the car, with Mac's help. After she and Kasey were on their way, he returned to the loft with a look of utter satisfaction on his face. He went in search of Ruth, who was in the bedroom. "We're alone, honey, just the two of us, you and me. We have the whole place to ourselves and a lot of time on our hands. How do you think we should spend it?"

Ruth walked over to him with a sultry smile. "I've already started the tub and lit the candles and there's a bottle of that nonalcoholic spumante on ice. If you'll be so kind as to remove every item of your clothing and come into the bathroom with me, I'll show you how we can spend that time," she said seductively.

"That's just one of the things I love about you, honey. You can read my mind."

Julian was surprised to see his sister at Maya's door with the ever-cheerful Kasey wriggling in her arms. "We're seeking shelter," she announced.

"Why aren't you staying at the loft? I thought Ruth had two bedrooms," he said.

"She does have two bedrooms and a pullout couch. But let me ask you something, would you want to be in the next room when Daddy and Ruth are umm, getting reacquainted?" She waited for his reaction and it wasn't long in coming.

"Oh, hell no. I almost busted in on them at home," he confided, telling her about the morning he'd accidentally retrieved Ruth's bra from Bojangles.

They both started laughing, although Julian added that it made him proud. "I'm glad to know I have something to look forward to. Daddy and Ruth seem to really enjoy being in love, if you get my drift."

Paris beamed. "Isn't it wonderful? I just don't want to share that joy. The loft just isn't big enough for all of us. Now when she moves to New Orleans, it'll be different, that house is big enough for three simultaneous orgies."

Julian pretended to be appalled. "Coco, where did you learn to talk like that?"

"From you," she retorted. "Now where's my niece?" She looked around and was told that the little lady was upstairs getting ready for bed.

"Maybe you can help her, she doesn't seem to think I'm qualified to give her a bath," he added wryly.

Paris and Julian went upstairs with Kasey scampering ahead and Corey was happy to see her new auntie and her auntie's adorable dog. They had fallen in love at first sight when they met at the loft and now he was happily licking her toes. "How about I give you a nice bubbly bath and I'll tell you all about how your grandpa used to bathe me, okay?"

"Okay, Aunt Paris. Can Kasey come, too?"

"Absolutely not," Paris said firmly. "Kasey really likes water and he's been known to jump into bathtubs. He'll be right here when you get done."

Julian went downstairs and figured out how to operate Maya's stereo in about two seconds. He found a CD that had been one of their favorites when they were married and put it in. It was a kind of slow torture, but he needed to hear the soothing sounds. They both enjoyed all kinds of music, including old-school smooth jazz and in a moment, the beautiful "You Are My Starship" by Norman Connors filled the room and he stretched out on the sofa to listen, transported to another time and place.

He went back to the day he kissed her, a rainy afternoon when they shared a picnic in her living room.

After their first kiss, Julian knew Maya was a virgin. There was something innocently sweet about the way she turned her lips to his and the soft sigh of surprise that floated out of her hot, tender mouth when their tongues met for the first time that let him know she was untouched. He'd kissed her with all the gentleness he could muster, wanting to make it beautiful for her. He had put his hands on her shoulders and he could feel her trembling ever so slightly, like a flower rustling in a spring wind. It made him even gentler as he pulled her into his arms and held her close, so close that he could feel her heart pounding. Her lips were so sweet, so soft and delicate, he was afraid he might hurt her, but she'd kissed him back with a yearning desire that set him on fire.

When he was able to speak again, he whispered to her, "You've never been with a man, have you Maya?"

He would have expected her to be embarrassed by his frank question, but she didn't seem to be. "No, I haven't. I'm the only virgin in Tulane medical school, as near as I can figure," she admitted. "Probably in the whole university. That makes me pretty lame, I guess."

Julian had kissed her again, drinking in her sweetness until he was dizzy from the sensations her lips and tongue created in his body. "No, baby, that's a good thing. It's a wonderful thing. It means that you have enough self-respect and confidence to wait for the right man," he told her. She had arched her body into his and kissed him back. She might have been inexperienced but her instincts were better than any other woman he'd ever been with. "I'm the right man, Maya. I'm the only man for you," he'd whispered.

He gave a harsh laugh, stung by his own arrogance. But he'd meant every word he'd said. He *was* the only man for Maya; the one who could appreciate her intellect and encourage her ambition; the one who could love her the way she needed to be loved and introduce her to passion in the right way. He was the one who could see her beauty and sensuality, the one who could show her what it meant to be a woman with a man who loved her beyond reason. And he was also the man she'd left without a reason, the one she'd deceived for five painfully long years. He was roused from his brooding by the sound of Paris's voice from upstairs.

"Julian, there's a little girl up here who's waiting for her daddy to tell her good-night," she called.

He got off the sofa at once and went to the stairs. *Her daddy.* Fantastic as that still seemed, he and Maya had created the incredible child who was waiting for him on the stair landing. Her face was wreathed in smiles and she was wearing pink-and-white summer pajamas with little Hello Kittys all over them. She held up her arms and he swung her up to carry her into the bedroom. She smelled like the special children's bubble bath in which Paris had bathed her, and she gave him a big hug and kiss on the cheek.

"Are you ready for bed, sugar baby?"

She shook her head vigorously. "You have to braid my hair first or Mommy won't be able to comb it. I sleep like a wildcat, she says. And then you have to read me a story." Her face suddenly looked doubtful. "Can daddies braid hair?"

Julian and Paris looked at each other and laughed. He carried Corey into the bedroom as he assured her that he could. "This daddy can because I used to braid your Aunt Paris's hair when she was little. Where's your comb and brush?"

He sat her on his lap and gently took down the loose topknot Paris had arranged for her bath. He brushed it carefully and combed it through, then arranged it in two pigtails with pink ponytail holders. "There. You're all done, what do you think?"

She slid off his lap and went to inspect herself in the mirror on her closet door. "I look very nice. You did a good job, Daddy. Now we have to say our prayers and you have to read to me," she instructed him. She selected a book from the shelf, and then knelt next to the bed, looking at Julian expectantly. "You have to get down here, too, Daddy so Jesus can hear you real good."

He did so at once, trying hard to swallow the lump in his throat. He listened as Corey thanked God for her beautiful day, and for her mommy and daddy and her grandma and grandpa, for her auntie Paris and Kasey and for all her uncles. She added in the names of her boyfriend Brandon, her preschool teacher, her Sunday school teacher, the poor children all over the world, the old people in the hospitals and all the animals. Julian was beginning to wonder if the prayer would ever end when she finally said "Amen." She allowed him to tuck her into bed and then held up her book. "Now my story, Daddy."

She had chosen her favorite book, *If You Give a Mouse a Cookie,* and Julian gamely read it to her with all kinds of expression in his voice. She smiled sleepily when he was done. "You did that good, Daddy. Almost as good as Mommy. Can you cook breakfast?"

"You'll find out in the morning, sugar baby. Sleep well, Corey." He kissed her forehead and sat on the bed watching her sleep until the hot dampness in his eyes threatened to overflow. It was beyond belief that he and Maya had made this innocent miracle and even more unbelievable that he was just meeting her today. When Maya got home he had a lot of questions for her and the answers had better be good ones.

Chapter 19

Julian was finally able to tear himself away from his sleeping child and went down the stairs to find his sister. She was waiting in the kitchen, sitting at the table reading the scrapbooks and eating one of Maya's cookies. She smiled at Julian as she brushed the crumbs from her fingertips. "I forgot how well Maya can cook. I only ate one, though, I've got to fit in my wedding dress or Perry will beat my behind," she said, smoothing her hands down her waist.

"Aww, Coco, quit trippin'. You look beautiful just the way you are. Please don't turn into one of those women who count every calorie and carb that goes into their mouths. No one wants a bone but a dog," he mumbled.

Kasey barked his agreement, which made them both laugh. Julian walked over to the kitchen sink and splashed cold water on his face, drying it with paper towels from the dispenser under the cupboard. He threw the wadded up towels into the trash can, and then sat down heavily at the table across from his sister. He was touched to see a glass of ice water and two Tylenol waiting for him. Paris knew from experience that severe stress led right to a massive headache. She watched him swallow the pills while she folded her hands like a little girl. Then she waded in with both feet, which he was expecting.

"Well, big brother, I never asked you this before because you made it plain that it wasn't my business. But I don't care at this point because now your business is our business, I mean, it affects the whole family. So exactly what happened with you and Maya?" she asked bluntly.

He gave her a twisted grimace that barely passed for a smile. "How long have you been rehearsing that one, Coco?" He drained the water and went to the refrigerator for more before he sat down again and looked her full in the face. "I can't answer that because I have no freakin' idea what made her go off like that. I thought we were happy, Paris, I honestly did. I was happy, I can tell you that much. Everything I did, I did for her and she was the same way.

"We talked to each other, we listened to each other, we respected each other and God knows I supported her in everything she did. I'd help her study, I'd wait up for her on clinic nights and rub her feet when she came home. Maybe I babied her too much, but that wasn't my intention. I was just crazy about her and I wanted her to know it. I wanted her to understand that above all else I loved her and I was there for her no matter what."

Paris's face showed her concern for her brother. "But

Julian, she was happy. I knew Maya before she met you and she was just as sweet as she could be, but there was always something a little reserved about her. She was really quiet, almost repressed. She was an only child and I always had the impression that she'd been raised in a really strict environment. She was always so proper and precise, almost robotic," Paris recalled. "Well compared to me and Chastain, that is. We were like hellions next to Maya." Chastain was Paris's best friend and partner in crime back in New Orleans and it was true, they bore as much resemblance to the ladylike Maya as weeds to a prize-winning rosebush.

"But after you and Maya hooked up, she changed. She was more relaxed, more confident, and she was certainly happier. She laughed all the time and she even started cracking jokes, the raunchy ones she'd hear at the hospital. And there is no doubt in my mind that she loved you. She thought you were the best man she'd ever met and she was so proud to be with you! Sometimes when she and Chastain and I would be hanging out she'd get this dreamy look on her face and go off into her own little world and if you asked her what was on her mind she'd smile and say 'my Julian.' That's how she referred to you—'my Julian.' Now how does that kind of love turn sour? Something had to have happened to make her leave you the way she did."

Julian slammed his hand down on the table, startling Kasey, who looked at him sternly and gave a little bark. "Paris, I'm trying to tell you, I have no idea what went wrong. She suddenly came up with the harebrained idea that I was having an affair. I thought she was kidding at first, and then I realized she was serious. She kept asking me about it, accusing me of it, really, and I got tired of arguing about it. We had a couple of really big arguments, and the last one turned really ugly. I had to go out of town that week to take a deposition and when I got back on Friday with a big plant and a gold bracelet to apologize, she was gone."

He stopped talking and began rolling the glass in his palms until his grip tightened on it so hard Paris feared it would shatter and cut his hand. She reached over to take it from him, and he realized what he was doing. "Paris, you have no idea what went through my mind. I thought she'd been kidnapped until I realized that most of her things were gone. I had actually called the police to file a missing person report and then I found the letter she left me. It really wasn't a letter so much as a note saying she couldn't take it anymore, that she loved me too much to stand by while I destroyed our marriage. Can you believe it? After all we'd been to each other, after all the love we shared, she gets this nutbox notion in her head and just takes off for who knows where," he said angrily.

His voice was reaching the range of decibels familiar to anyone who knew the Deveraux men and Paris had to remind him there was a sleeping child in the house. He lowered his voice at once but continued talking. "I tried to call her at her parents' house and they claimed she wasn't there. I tried everything I knew to get in touch with her and then I got the divorce papers in the mail and that was it. If she was willing to trash everything we had over some bull—well, over some stupid, idiotic rumors and lies, so be it." His fury fairly leaped out of his eyes, tempered with a hurt look that Paris was all too familiar with. "What really hurts is that she knew she was pregnant when she left. She left Louisiana carrying my baby and she never said a word to me. How could she be that selfish, Paris? How could any woman be that cruel?"

Paris raised her hands in supplication. "Wait a minute, Julian. Maya didn't know she was carrying Corey until after the divorce was final. She was back home in Connecticut applying for internships and she started getting sicker and sicker, which she attributed to nerves. She was three months pregnant before she knew she was having your baby."

Julian looked surprised to hear that, but not mollified in the least. "She still should have contacted me. For her to have kept this to herself for all these years, it was just wrong, Paris, and there's no way in hell I could ever forgive her for it."

Paris sighed and looked again at the two scrapbooks, so lovingly prepared with such amazing detail. "None of this adds up, Julian. Where did she get the idea you were cheating on her?"

Julian started to bellow his answer and Paris pointed to the ceiling to remind him once again they weren't alone in the house. With great effort he forced himself to speak quietly. "I have no freakin' idea where she got that from. I never looked at another woman after I met her. She was convinced, Coco, she was completely fixated on the idea. If I was five minutes late coming home, if I had to go out of town for a day, if I went to get some beignets on Saturday morning, she was convinced I was seeing this nonexistent mistress. And the worst part is she was convinced I was having an affair with Monica, of all people."

Paris's eyes widened in shock. "Monica Montclair? Did you explain that Monica was like the last person on earth you'd be sleeping with? I mean, y'all were always close friends, but an affair?"

"Coco, I tried and tried to explain to her. I even offered to have Monica come over and explain to her that we were nothing but good friends. She went wild. That was the night we had the worst argument I've ever had with another human being. It was awful. We said some terrible things to each other. Then I went to Nashville the next day and when I came back two days later, she was gone."

"Well, Julian, I have to ask you why you didn't go after her. You could have found her easily enough. You could have hired somebody like Titus and he'd have tracked her down in a day." Her fiancé, Titus Argonne, owned a private investigations firm that could and did handle any kind of case from missing children to international industrial espionage.

"I didn't want to find her," he said bleakly. "If she hated me that damn much, fine, let her go with God, that was my attitude. If she despised me so much and just turn her back on me for no good reason, I was better off without her. After several weeks of almost continual inebriation and self-pity, that was the conclusion to which I came," he said with a bitter laugh.

Paris turned the scrapbooks around so they faced him. With one hand on each one she looked at her brother and said, "Julian, I don't know what made her act the way she did. I don't know why she got the idea that you were cheating on her and why she felt so desperate that she had to run out on you and file for divorce, but I can tell you one thing—she didn't hate you. If she hated you, she wouldn't have given birth to Corey. Having a baby and trying to complete an internship and residency is too hard for me to even imagine and she could have taken the easy way out," Paris said in a quiet, penetrating voice.

"And she named her after us, which is again, not a sign of hatred. But most of all, Julian, take another look at these scrapbooks. If she hated you so much, she would have never taken the time and trouble to put these together so painstakingly. These were made with love, Julian, a lot of it. And not just love for Corey. Every single page shows how much she cares for you."

For a brief moment, Julian's face softened and he reached for the purple book with his name on it. "*Nothing* about this adds up, Coco. But before I leave here, I'm getting some answers and for her sake they'd better be good ones."

Paris eventually went upstairs. She had decided to sleep with Corey so that Julian could have the guest room. Kasey settled down on the floor at the foot of the bed and in a short time they were both sound asleep. Julian finally stopped studying the scrapbooks. They were beautiful and, as Paris said, they had been created with a lot of love. Who the love was for he couldn't say; he had to assume it was Maya's love for Corey that had led to their creation. In any case, he could feel his headache coming back. He decided to take a quick shower and go to bed. He was going to need a clear head in the morning because there were a lot of things to be discussed and a lot of decisions to be made. He'd need his wits about him tomorrow and he was never at his best without at least a few hours sleep.

He showered rapidly but thoroughly, using some of the bath gel he found in the shelf unit that was hanging around the showerhead. He wished he hadn't because it smelled so much like Maya. He lathered his long, lean body over and over again, thinking about Maya the whole time. Baths and showers had come to mean something very special and erotic in their household. He had to choke back a laugh as he remembered Corey's comment about baths earlier. He had told her he was going to give her a bath and she'd looked surprised. "But daddies don't give baths, only mommies do," she'd told him. "Boys can't give girls baths, Daddy."

As he rinsed the fragrant suds from his body he was once again in a time and place when everything was beautiful with him and Maya. He toweled himself dry and wrapped the towel around his waist, then went into Maya's bedroom and sat down on the side of her bed. He was remembering the first time they'd made love and how delighted she was to discover the joys of bathing together.

After he knew she was a virgin, Julian did everything in his power to keep his hands off her. He wanted to take it slow and easy with Maya because she deserved to be treated with tenderness. He was determined not to rush her into anything she wasn't emotionally prepared to handle, but it was harder and harder to resist her alluring femininity. They would kiss good-night and still be kissing an hour later. Julian would go home so frustrated and overheated he thought he would explode, but it never occurred to him to stop seeing her. The worst part for him was the fact that Maya was a willing participant; she was more than willing to give him everything because, as she told him one afternoon, she wanted him to be her first lover.

They had been sitting on the sofa in his apartment with the French doors open to allow in the soft summer breeze. The music was soft and inviting, there were scented candles and she was straddling him, her blouse open so he could see her round, smooth breasts ensconced in a pretty pale blue bra. He was holding onto her hips and his self-control was leaving the building; she was so sexy and tempting he wanted nothing more than to bury himself in her for hours and hours, but he was trying hard to resist. She wasn't making it easy for him, though.

"Julian," she purred as she kissed him gently. "I'm not a child, you know. I'm a fully grown adult and I know what I want. And what I want is for us to be lovers. I don't think my being a virgin should matter to you. I want you to be the first man to make love to me."

Julian could still remember the primal fury that had overtaken him at her words. He'd reacted with that same fury, he recalled. It was a wonder he hadn't scared her to death on the spot. He had set her aside on the sofa, getting up so he could pace around like an angry lion. "What do you mean, the *first* man to make love to you? Are you planning to have a lot of lovers, Maya? Because that ain't gonna happen, not as long as I'm alive. You're my woman, and I'm your man and that's the end of it. You and I are getting married tomorrow and that's going to be the end of this discussion. First man, my ass," he'd roared. "I'm your only man, *Chocolat,* and you'd better get used to the idea."

Instead of being terrified like most women might have been, Maya had laughed at him. She got into a kneeling position on the sofa and looked at him with love shining out of her eyes. "So is this a proposal? Because I haven't exactly heard the right words. And it seems to me there should be some going down on one knee and a ring or something," she'd teased him.

Julian had stopping pacing at once and looked at her, her hair mussed and her deliciously rounded body showing just enough for him to have what was beginning to feel like a permanent erection. She looked so adorable he couldn't remember why he'd gotten so angry. He went back to the sofa, where she wrapped her arms around his neck and her legs around his waist and they were once again tangled up in each other, kissing madly.

"I didn't intend to propose like that, Maya. I meant to take you someplace beautiful and do it the way you're supposed to with champagne and roses and a great big ring, but I can't wait. I love you, I love you more than anything or anyone in the world and I always will. Will you please, please put me out of my misery and marry me?"

"Well, I don't know," she mused. "You're really cute and you're gainfully employed and you kiss real nice, so maybe," she giggled. "You have a terrible temper but we'll probably have some cute babies, so I guess it'll be okay." The giggles turned into full-out laughter as Julian began tickling her.

"Say you love me," he demanded. "I poured my heart out to you and you're making fun of me. Say it!"

"I do love you, Julian," she said, smiling into his eyes. "You're the kindest, sweetest, most thoughtful man in the whole world and I love you. I love you," she whispered. "I'll always love you. You're my Prince Charming, didn't you know that?"

"Yeah, I figured I was, but I like to hear it," he growled as he began kissing her neck.

He stretched out on the bed, crossing his arms behind his head. They had indeed gotten married the next day. In Louisiana the normal seventy-two-hour waiting period after the issuance of a marriage license could be waived by a city judge, and since Julian was an attorney, albeit a new one, he had the advantage of knowing several judges who looked upon him kindly since his father was a superior court judge. It was a tiny wedding, with only Minoo and Wade as witnesses. Julian had picked Wade because he was the most close-mouthed of all the Deverauxes. They planned on having a big ceremony later, with all their family and friends in attendance, but for now, this would suffice. They were man and wife and that's all that mattered.

He wore a nice navy suit, and she had on a pretty white dress. Her hair was pulled off her face with gardenias and she carried a small bouquet of gardenias and ivy. To this day the fragrance of gardenias had a powerful effect on Julian; whenever he smelled them he thought about his wedding day. And that always made him think of his wedding night, the most perfect, most passionate night in his memory.

He had taken Maya to a beautiful private guesthouse that was normally booked months in advance. It just so happened that there was a cancellation and since he'd known the owner for years, it was a simple matter for him to take advantage of the facility. When he drove into the circular drive in front of the house, he stopped the car in front of the door and turned to Maya, looking serious and very loving. "This is it, Mrs. Deveraux. This is the beginning of the rest of our lives," he'd told her.

She returned his look with the sweetest smile he'd ever seen and she took his hand. "Let's get started, Mr. Deveraux."

He'd insisted on carrying her across the threshold in the traditional manner and was pleased that she didn't offer up a protest; she went along with it willingly and kissed his neck and ear while she told him how much she loved him. When he finally set her on her feet in the small foyer they were both dizzy and yearning for each other. They walked through the perfectly furnished love nest and were delighted by the ambiance. There were fresh flowers and lush green plants everywhere among the highly polished antique furniture and an abundance of candles in heavy glass holders. French doors on either side of a fireplace led out to a private walled garden that had a big double hammock with a canopy. There was a big fishpond with koi swimming around and it looked like the perfect place for a tryst, with big oak and magnolia trees creating a private oasis safe from prying eyes.

Everything was in shades of blue from the walls, which were covered with pale blue watered silk wallpaper, to the deep blue damask sofas and chairs. Julian didn't know damask from burlap, but Maya supplied him with details. All he was really interested in was the bedroom, all done in ivory and gold. The bed was a reproduction of an antique, a huge four-poster with a canopy and sheer curtains. Maya told him it was a reproduction because it was king-sized and real period beds weren't that big. Julian knew that Maya was talking so much because she was nervous. Despite her eagerness to share herself with him and despite the fact that they were now man and wife, she was as nervous as any other bride. Julian took her face in both hands and kissed her tenderly.

"Come on, *Chocolat,* let's take a bath together," he said in the softest voice he could manage.

"A bath? You mean at the same time? We can't do that," she whispered.

"Oh, but we can. You're my wife and I'm your husband and we can do anything we want," he told her, kissing the end of her nose.

Their clothes had already been unpacked and put away by the highly efficient staff, so all they had to do was relax. Rather, Maya relaxed in the garden with a glass of champagne while Julian ran the bath and lit the candles. When everything was ready he came out to the garden to get her and once again carried her into the guesthouse. This time, though, he carried her into the bathroom. He set her down carefully, like the precious work of art she was. Maya looked around the big room with the huge claw-footed tub and the scented candles burning on the vanity and the shelves on the walls. The tub was full of steamy fragrant bubbles and the candles shed a warm amber glow on everything. She looked like a doll in her wedding ensemble, standing perfectly still with a look of wonder on her face. "Now what do we do?" she asked in a near whisper.

He turned her around so he could access the zipper on her dress. "We get undressed and we get in. Then I'll show you everything you need to know." He didn't want to admit it, but his hands were shaking a little as he unzipped her dress and helped her out of it. He removed her slip, her bra, pantyhose and her little bikini panties and when he looked at her lush dark beauty for the first time he felt a stab of desire so deep it was like a knife piercing his heart. He was about to help her into the tub when she shook her head. "Now it's your turn," she told him.

She watched him get out of his shirt, his pants and his briefs, as he had already removed his shoes and socks. She looked her fill at him, especially at the huge throbbing erection that was all too evident. Now she allowed him to lift her into the tub and she sighed with pleasure as the hot scented water surrounded her body. He stepped in behind her and pulled her against him so her back was resting on his chest. Picking up one of the thick washcloths on the stool next to the tub, he dipped it in the water and squeezed it over her breasts while she made a sound of contentment. "See? I told you we could do this," he murmured in her ear.

She leaned forward a little, just enough to scoop her hair up and twist it into a knot, which she anchored with the hairpin holding the gardenia. Then she leaned into him again, this time arching her back so that her darkly desirable nipples could be seen over the bubbles.

Julian took his time with her, using the scented bath gel and his hands to massage every inch of her body, starting with her neck and shoulders, then her arms and hands. He lingered over her breasts, massaging them in circles while he manipulated her nipples until she moaned his name aloud. He caressed her stomach, her hips and her thighs, stopping only to gently massage the area between her legs, which she parted at once to allow him easier access. When he gently touched her for the first time in the center of her womanhood, her nipples grew even more distended and she moved against his erection, sliding her wet body up and down against him. He told her to turn around and she did. She put her hands on his shoulders and leaned over to kiss him, her breasts rubbing against his chest for the first time.

"Julian, this is wonderful," she sighed. "I love this. Is this what making love is like?"

He was massaging her back with his sudsy hands, stroking her sensitive rib cage and sliding his hands down around her rounded derriere. She had applied bath gel to him and was soaping his broad shoulders and chest when she asked the question. He pulled her even closer, so she could feel the strength of his desire for her. Her eyes widened and closed and she moved against him, gasping when she felt his tip about to enter her. "Yes, baby, this is all about making love. But we're not going to do it in here, not tonight."

She moved again, her hips circling in a method as old as time, seeking that which would bring her the ultimate fulfillment. "If we're not, we'd better get out of here," she moaned. And in minutes they were wrapped in towels and holding each other in the middle of the huge bed with the feather mattress. Julian had used the handheld shower to rinse them off as quickly as humanly possible and carried her off to bed, where he intended to show her just what being his wife meant.

At some point during his reminiscing, Julian had drifted into a sound sleep, still clad in only a towel, still lying on Maya's bed. It was scent memory that roused him from his slumber. It was gardenias, the sweet, cloying scent that brought him back to consciousness. He opened his eyes slowly and thought he was still dreaming because in the dim light from the hallway he saw a sight he hadn't seen for five years; he saw Maya dripping wet with only a towel wrapped around her. He was jarred back into full alertness now because he had a problem. How was he going to let her know he was in the room without scaring her half to death?

Chapter 20

Maya's eyes opened slowly. She fully expected this to be the worst morning of her life, seeing as how the previous night proved to be one of the worst in recent history. The emergency room had been a horrible mess of bleeding and severely injured people, all of whom needed drastic measures to save their lives. She stopped counting the number of patients she was dealing with and went on emotional autopilot. Triage the ones who had to go to the operating room, tend to those who could be treated and released and work miracles on those who couldn't. What a wonderful night to end her tenure as a resident at Cook County Hospital. She dragged herself home at six in the morning when things were once again quiet and still in the emergency room, and as soon she pulled up in the driveway she had to fight an urge to put her head down on the steering wheel and sleep. She managed to come in the front door making a minimum amount of noise, and kicked her shoes off at once, frowning at the blood that had gotten on them. Making a mental note to throw them in the washer, she went wearily up the stairs.

Her first stop was Corey's room, where she raised an eyebrow. Kasey, the little dog belonging to Paris, was at the foot of the bed wagging his tail at her and Paris was clinging to the side of the double bed for all she was worth. That was because Corey was doing her usual number of spreading out all over the bed; sleeping with Corey was like sleeping with an electrified octopus. She pulled the child over to one side of the bed so that Paris would have more room. Kissing her on the forehead she whispered, "Mommy's here," even though Corey wouldn't hear the words. She reached down to pat Kasey and got a wet kiss on the hand. Yawning widely, she almost staggered into the bathroom and stripped off her clothes so she could shower away the disinfectant smell that would always be associated with the ER in her head.

When she was finished scrubbing away the stench in clouds of scented bubbles, she rinsed her body and wrapped herself in a towel. She entered her darkened bedroom and went to the dresser to take out a fresh summer nightie. She didn't turn on the light; the dim light from the hall was sufficient and she didn't want to wake anyone. Corey slept like a log, but she certainly didn't want to wake Julian, whom she assumed was in the guest room, or Paris, who might be her only ally come morning. She walked over to the bed to sit down so she could put on lotion, only to come in contact with Julian's body. Julian's naked body at that. Before she could open her mouth he had clamped his hand over it, whispering urgently, "It's me, Maya, don't scream."

She promptly bit his hand, making him stifle a shout. She jumped up from her awkward position and turned on the bedside light. She clutched the towel, which had naturally started to fall off, and glared at him, baring her teeth in a vicious snarl. "*Scream?* You'd better hope I don't shoot you! What the hell are you doing in my bed, you dolt? Why do you think I have a guest room? It's for *guests,* which, until this moment, you were. Now you're an intruder and I should call the cops on you. Get out of here!" she whispered fiercely.

He didn't move at once, which made her even madder. "Stop staring at me and get out of my room before I do something we'll both regret," she warned him.

He finally found his voice and in a maddeningly calm tone said, "You already have, Maya. You kept my child from me. I can't think of anything worse than that."

Unaware that the shifting towel was exposing most of her breasts, Maya clenched her teeth in pure rage. "Oh, no you don't. That's a conversation for the morning when we're both fully dressed and you're not in my bedroom, much less my bed. And if you don't think I can do worse, use your imagination. Now get the hell out of here, Julian. Don't make me say it again."

When he'd finally left, saying they'd talk in the morning, she'd put on her gown and tossed the bedcovers back, swearing under her breath. She'd learned some very colorful language over the years while she was becoming a doctor. And even though the words weren't a part of her normal vocabulary, she knew what they meant and how to use them. The nerve of that big ape, coming into her bedroom, sprawling out on her bed and worse yet, he was watching her parade around half-naked! She got in the bed, trying to ignore the fact that she could still detect Julian's scent on the pillow shams and trying very hard to forget that she'd seen his body.

She tossed restlessly, remembering with exact detail how his shoulders looked. They had always been one of her favorite parts of his anatomy. When she was held in his warm embrace with her hands caressing those broad shoulders she felt so safe and secure there was nothing in the world that could touch her. When he was dressed for the office, before he put on his suit coat, she loved the way he filled out his shirt, the way his lean muscles tapered into his slim waist. And when she re-membered how she saw him naked for the first time…she had to turn her head into the pillow to keep from moaning out loud. The first time she'd seen him without clothes was their wedding night, the night she found out what it meant to be a woman in love with a man who loved her back. Hot tears made an unwelcome appearance and she fought them as long as she could, but they leaked out anyway. It happened every time she remembered the magical night in the guest house. As though she had no will of her own, her thoughts went back to that beautiful time that they would never share again….

The bedroom of the guesthouse was lovely, filled with antique reproductions and smelling like flowers from the bowls of potpourri and the scented candles that were burning all around. The mattress was incredible, pouffy and soft but with an underlying firmness. There was a featherbed on top of the mattress and it was amazing to lie on, but that was all due to Julian. They had taken a bubble bath together and his hands had caressed her all over, bringing her to the brink of indescribable release over and over, but he wouldn't let her go into that sexual abyss. Their first time, he insisted, should be in bed. And when he brought her to their marriage bed, it was with such tenderness that she knew he cherished her. She could look into his beautiful eyes and see nothing but love and what she saw in his eyes made her want to weep. He'd handed her a flute of champagne and saluted her with the one in his hand.

"To my only love, my *Chocolat,* my wife," he murmured.

"I'll always love you, Julian. You're everything to me," she whispered. They each took a sip of the cold, bubbly libation and he took the flutes and put them on the bedside table. He reached for her and she went into his arms without hesitation. Their mouths met eagerly and their champagne-flavored tongues met, deepening the kiss and exciting her to an even higher level of desire. He took the gardenia out of her hair and loosened it from the loose updo, spreading it out on the pillow.

"That's how I pictured you," he told her. "The first time I met you, I could see you in a big soft bed with your hair all over the pillow."

His hands were exploring her breasts while he looked at her the way no man ever had and no other man ever would. She wanted to speak but he put his mouth on her breasts, licking and sucking her sensitive nipple as though it were a gourmet chocolate. While she was abandoning herself to that exquisite sensation, his hand was traveling down her body, stroking her stomach and farther down to the triangle of silky curls that defined her womanhood. She moved urgently, opening her thighs so that he could touch her where he wanted, as his caress drew a fire out of her she didn't know she possessed. When both her breasts had been treated to his exquisite loving, he began to apply the same sweet torture to her body, slowly licking every inch of her, lavishing a long languorous kill on her navel, all the while fondling and manipulating her tender folds until her breathing was coming in small, soft pants.

"Julian," she breathed. "Julian, Julian…ohhh," she cried as his mouth found the very core of her yearning. She wasn't prepared for the force of the orgasm that shook her body, but she welcomed it, moving her hips and crying her husband's name. He loved her fiercely yet tenderly, his lips and tongue making a feast of her, swallowing her honeyed nectar as though it were the essence of life to him. When he was finally finished he licked his way up to her mouth and another banquet ensued as they kissed long and hard. His hands slid down her curves to her hips, where he held her firmly but gently as he began to ease into the opening he'd so lovingly prepared. Her eyes were locked on his but she couldn't keep them open as she felt his length become one with her for the first time. It was slow and easy at first, the hard thickness of his desire opening her, expanding her in a way she'd never experienced. What should have been painful was pure pleasure and she wrapped her legs around his waist to accommodate him, urging him with quick movements of her sweat dampened hips to push harder. She clung to his shoulders as he pumped into her, and a sudden brief pain signaled the end of her innocence and the beginning of real passion.

She could only hold onto his shoulders, tightening her legs around him as they continued to mate, harder and faster until a shattering explosion rocked them both into their own private galaxy. He cried her name hoarsely while she moaned and bit into his shoulder. Even though they both climaxed in a thunderous, heated release, they couldn't stop. It went on and on until Julian finally pulled away and reversed their positions so she was lying on top of him. They were both sweaty and breathless and the musky aroma of their love drifted through the room with the scent from the candles. Maya was crying by now, her tears dripping down his neck.

"Did I hurt you, baby? I didn't mean to, but I couldn't stop. Are you okay, sweetheart?"

"I'm happy, Julian. I'm so happy that you love me. I had no idea it would be like this." She wiped the tears away and snuggled even closer. "We belong to each other, Julian, and we're never, ever going to be apart."

He wrapped his arms around her even tighter. "No, *Chocolat,* never. We'll always be together, baby, I promise you."

That damned dream. It was the main reason she woke up in such a foul mood. Whenever she thought about their wedding night she would dream about it in such detail that she would wake up tingling all over. It hurt so badly to relive that night when she and Julian were madly in love and their whole lives were ahead of them. It was painful enough when she was alone, but with him in her house it hurt so bad to think about it she wanted to lock herself in the bathroom and cry. Thank God she didn't have time for that foolishness; she had a child to take care of. She threw back the sheet that covered her and got up. Prudently putting on a robe, she first went to check on Corey, who was usually wide awake by now. Her bed was empty, although neatly made up. She could hear Paris and Corey chatting away about something downstairs, so she hurried to get dressed and join them.

After she washed up and dressed in a cool-looking sundress with a fun pattern of tropical fish on it, she went downstairs expecting to find Corey and Paris in the kitchen. Instead, there was Julian, standing in front of the stove making breakfast. She frowned at the sight of him, but she was going to handle her business this morning and Julian Deveraux wasn't going to rattle her, not today.

"Where's my daughter?" The edge in her voice had the same effect as flinging down a gauntlet. To her surprise, Julian didn't take the bait. He turned around and gave her a perfectly civil reply.

"Our daughter is accompanying her aunt while she walks the dog. I didn't think you'd mind if she went out for a little while. Good morning to you, too," he added.

"Good morning," she said, a little embarrassed that she had to be prompted to show her normal good manners. The appetizing aroma of whatever he was cooking finally got to Maya and she had to comment. "That smells good."

"I'm making you breakfast. Banana pancakes and turkey bacon with scrambled eggs, orange juice and coffee. Have a seat."

She sat down automatically even as she protested that she couldn't eat that much. He turned around and gave her the smile that could still make her knees knock. "You need to eat that much. You're looking a little skinny."

He set a plate in front of her and her eyes lit up with pleasure. Julian used to cook breakfast for her all the time when they were married and he could make pancakes like no one else in this world. She thanked him before bowing her head to say grace. While she put her napkin in her lap she asked how Corey had liked her breakfast. He sat down across from her and poured her coffee from the carafe in his hand.

"Corey was most impressed that her daddy could cook," he said with a proud smile. "She said I could cook almost as good as her mommy, which I gathered was high praise."

Maya's eyes closed as she took her first bite of the golden brown pancake. "These taste just like I remember them. They're delicious, Julian, thank you."

She ate in silence for a few minutes, trying to ignore Julian's close scrutiny. She really didn't have much of a choice in the matter because he chose that moment to start speaking.

"Maya, I've been trying to make sense of this and you're going to have to help me out here. I've been trying to figure out why you kept our child a secret from me for four years and I can't come up with any kind of answer that makes sense. If you just hated me, that would be one thing, but I don't think you do. You named her after me, Maya. You made those beautiful scrapbooks and told her all about me and my family. You've done an amazing job of raising her by yourself, but what I don't understand is why you did it? Why in the hell couldn't you pick up a phone and tell me you were carrying our child? What did I do that was so horrible that you couldn't even let me know I was a father?" Julian didn't raise his voice, which in a way was worse than yelling.

Maya stared at him and put her fork down. "I should have been more persistent, I guess. I should have done it through the court system, I should have tried harder to make you a part of Corey's life and I'll always regret that I didn't. You'll never know how guilty I feel about that," she said passionately. "But Julian, what I don't understand is why you keep acting as though I never tried to contact you. I tried calling you when I found out I was pregnant. I wrote you when I found out your phone number had been changed. And I got your answer, that you had no interest in me or my child and that a clean break was best. You didn't even offer child support and I wasn't about to ask you for it. So why do you keep acting like you didn't have any part in this?" Maya wasn't as successful in keeping her voice level and it had gotten louder and more strident with anger as she spoke. Julian didn't seem to notice that, he was too focused on what she was saying.

"Maya, what are you talking about? You never contacted me and I certainly never gave you an answer of any kind. Do you honestly think I could ignore my own child? How could you think that I would let you have our child alone and raise it without me? You don't know me at all, do you, Maya?"

Maya was staring at him, vainly trying to make sense of what he was saying. "All I know is that you promised to love me forever but you left me for Monica. Monica became more important to you than me or our marriage and that's what made me leave. And I still have the letters, Julian. I have the letters you sent me when I wrote to you about my pregnancy and about Corey's birth. As to your question, no, Julian, I don't know you at all. The man I married, the man I *loved,* is gone and all that's left is you," she said hotly, not caring at all that his face paled and his eyes looked unnaturally black and full of pain.

"I have no idea what you're talking about, Maya. Hell, I don't even know why you still believe that Monica and I were having an affair. No matter how many times I told you it wasn't true, you insisted it was. I kept telling you it wasn't true and you kept at me like some kind of prosecutor, you just kept nagging me and blaming me and you wouldn't listen to a word I had to say. I was never unfaithful to you, Maya. Not in thought, not in concept and certainly not in deed. There was never any other woman in my life, Maya, never. And especially not Monica. I could never understand where you got that crazy idea from." He was on his feet now, pacing back and forth with his hands in his pockets, looking as confused as she felt.

She had to suppress a strange urge to comfort him. This wasn't the time to get weak, everything had to come out now or they'd never get these things said. "You wait right here, Julian. I've got the letters and I'll show them to you," she said as she rose from the breakfast table and walked over to the doorway to go to the living room. She went to a credenza, opened the bottom drawer and took out an envelope. She went back into the kitchen and tossed it to him. "I didn't make it up, Julian," she said wearily. "It wasn't like I suddenly woke up and said, 'Hey, my husband is sleeping around on me!'" she said bitterly. "Someone I trusted, someone *you* trusted, came to me and told me what was going on, Julian. I didn't ask for the information, they volunteered it.

"And it wasn't just words—there were pictures, dates, places, all kinds of details. I asked you about it because I wanted you to tell me it wasn't true. I wanted you to deny it, but you wouldn't. You just kept saying it wasn't possible and that I was crazy. That I was being paranoid and neurotic, remember? You would never defend yourself or explain your actions. All you would do is look at me like I was dirt on the floor and say it wasn't possible. Why wasn't it possible, Julian? Men stray all the time, so why was it just so impossible that you did the same thing?"

Julian had stopped pacing and was reading the two letters rapidly. They were written on a computer and there was no signature. They read exactly the way she'd told him, brief perfunctory letters that dismissed her as though she were nothing. He couldn't believe that she accepted the callous words as coming from him. He threw the letters on the floor and grabbed her upper arms. "Why wouldn't I cheat on you? Because I loved you, damn it! Because you were the only woman I wanted, the only one I needed. I didn't want anyone else but you, Maya. There was no one else in the world but you. And whoever told you otherwise was a liar, a sick and twisted liar. Who told you all those lies, Maya?"

She stared at him for a long moment, looking into his eyes as though they held the key to her salvation. In a voice barely above a whisper she told him the name and was shocked when all the color left his face.

"Maya, I don't know how things got this messed up, but we're going to fix this. We're going to get to the bottom of this and put it behind us," he said in something like his normal tone of voice.

Maya wanted to believe him with all her heart, but too much had happened; there was too much betrayal and bad feelings to just wish it all away. "Julian, that's a nice notion, but it's not going to happen. I'll never stop regretting that I didn't push harder to make Corey a part of your life and you can have regular visitation. I'm never going to try to keep you two apart, I promise that. But as for the rest of it, that ship sailed a long time ago, and I think we both know it. We're divorced now, or did you forget that?"

To her utter surprise Julian relaxed his grip on her arms, and began stroking them softly, his hands moving up and down in a comforting rhythm. "Uhh, there's something I've been meaning to tell you, Maya. About the divorce, that is. We're not. Divorced, I mean. We're actually still man and wife."

Chapter 21

"What?" Maya was shaking her head like there was water in her ear. "I'm sorry, I didn't hear you right. What did you say?"

"I said we're still married, Maya," Julian said quietly. "Didn't you notice you never got the papers back? Didn't that lawyer of yours ever mention the fact that I never responded? How could you not know the divorce wasn't final?"

Maya shook his hands off her arms and started walking back and forth, not looking at him. "This is impossible. It's impossible," she mumbled. "I went back to Connecticut after I left Louisiana, basically because I couldn't think of anywhere else to go. My parents weren't surprised to see me, at least my mother wasn't. She's always told me I couldn't hold on to you. She said a woman like me was just setting herself up by getting involved with a man like you because I wasn't going to be enough for you. Nice, huh? Lots of support there," she said with a nasty little laugh.

"I went to Daddy's lawyer and he drew up the papers. I can't remember what happened next because Daddy got sick. He had prostate cancer and he'd apparently had it for some time. All I could do was stand back and watch, basically. I went from doctor's office to doctor's office, I begged him to take his medications, but they made him sick. I begged him to eat, but he couldn't. I spent hours and hours in the hospital watching him get sicker and sicker. And oh, by the way, I had figured out I was pregnant by then and I also spent a lot of time throwing up. It was a fun time for me, Julian, just a real party. So, no, I didn't really notice that I didn't get some final divorce papers in the mail.

"I was too busy dealing with hospice care, because my mother couldn't handle it. I was too busy making funeral arrangements, because my mother had taken to her bed. I was too busy trying to get through probate and get rid of the house because my mother couldn't stand the thought of living there anymore. And then I was too busy having a baby to worry about it anymore. After I got those letters from you I just didn't give a damn. I didn't care what happened to you anymore, Julian, I was finished. I'd had all I could take from you and I had someone who needed me. I had my baby and she was all that mattered." She raked her fingers through her hair, disheveling it completely. Her pacing finally stopped at the counter by the sink. Slowly she turned around and looked at him with utter hatred in her eyes.

"And now you have the gall to tell me we're not divorced? And you somehow think we can make this all better?" Of its own volition, as though she had no control over its movement, her hand reached into a bowl of very ripe tomatoes and she picked up the biggest one and threw it at him, scoring a direct hit in the middle of his chest. "You idiot!" was all she said as she hurled another, this one hitting him in the forehead. "You *threw the papers away?* What kind of moronic sub-species did you come from, you selfish pretty boy? You manipulative jerk, how dare you?" With every question another tomato missile was hurled and most of them met their mark, although the walls and floor weren't immune to their red, ripe juiciness. Julian's best defense was to try to stay out of her way and she had great aim, thanks to years of softball during her med school days. Throwing something was a great way to let off steam.

How long it would have gone on was anyone's guess but Corey and Paris returned with Kasey and the three of them stood in the doorway in total amazement. Corey was the first one to speak and she sounded stunned as only a small child could. "Mommy, you and Daddy made a *big* mess," she said in a voice hushed with wonder.

One week later, Maya was in the last place she ever expected to be—New Orleans. Once she and Julian had talked, after cleaning up the tomatoes, he insisted the only way they could get everything out in the open was to go back where it all began. Maya had no choice but to go along with him because she, too, wanted to know once and for all where the truth lay. Corey was simply thrilled to be going anywhere with her daddy and her grandpa. She had decided they were the most wonderful men on the planet and she was absolutely on her head with excitement about going to "*N'awlins*." Julian had taught her to say it the way the locals did and she used it as often as possible. Maya was happy the child was so ecstatic, but she was just confused. She was thrilled that Ruth was going, too; she needed to have her stabilizing influence. Paris was back in Atlanta, working on the wedding and her television show, so she was only a phone call away. But Ruth was under the same roof and it made Maya very, very happy.

Maya and Corey were staying in Mac's big house, while Julian stayed in his town house, which wasn't far from his father's home. It was probably a good thing, too, because as angry as Maya was when she found out they weren't divorced, it was nothing compared to Mac's reaction. When Julian admitted to his father that he had tossed the divorce papers out, Mac had turned a deep red and asked his son if he'd been brain-damaged in an accident about which Mac knew nothing.

"Son, what in the hell were you thinking? Are you crazy or did you think the judicial system was somehow going to make an exception for you because you look good or something? Why in the hell did you spend all that time and money going to law school if you were going to behave like the worst jack leg con artist in Louisiana? Do you understand that you have placed your entire law career in jeopardy, you idiot? If Maya decides to file a complaint with the bar association, something I strongly urge her to do, your ass will be hung out to dry and I'll let it twist in the damned wind," Mac had roared.

Maya got all this information secondhand as she wasn't present when Julian told his father what he'd done. She actually felt sorry for him when he related the very colorful way in which his father had reacted. They had been sitting in Corey's bedroom while Maya packed her things. Corey was out with Ruth for a ladies day with her friends Capiz and Sylvia. Paris, declaring that her work here was done, had already left for Atlanta. Julian was watching the neat, precise way she was putting things away in the suitcase while he talked to her.

"Man, I haven't seen Pop that mad since we burned down the garage," he said, shaking his head. At Maya's quizzical look he assured her she didn't want to know the details. "This was before we moved to New Orleans, while we were still in Lafayette. Just say it was a bad idea cooked up by me and my brothers and let it go. The judge was about to explode back then and he wasn't too much better this time. He couldn't decide whether he wanted to have me committed or medicated," he said, tossing Hello Kitty up and down while he unburdened himself.

Maya finished counting out underwear and socks for Corey, then turned her attention to the dresser drawers. "Julian, you have to admit it wasn't like you to do that. You're one of the most responsible people I've ever met in my life. Why *did* you just throw the papers out instead of signing them?"

Julian stopped tossing the toy and got up from the bed, walking around the room until he came to the big rocking chair where Maya had sung Corey to sleep on countless nights. He sat down and looked out the window for a while before answering. "I had a lot of reasons, Maya. None of them made sense, but I had my reasons. The biggest one was that I wasn't letting you go. If you thought you could just walk out of my life and send me some damned papers in the mail and that would be the end of our marriage you were gonna have another thing coming because I wasn't about to let you go that easily. Oh, *hell,* no. The other reason, well, that was simple. I was drunk," he said in a flat voice devoid of any inflection. "I was sloppy, pitiful, falling-down drunk. I got drunk the day I found your note and I stayed that way for about three weeks."

Maya covered her mouth with her hand and turned away from him. It was too unbelievable, too painful to hear. She heard the rocking chair give its familiar creak as he left his seat and came to her, putting his hands on her shoulders. "Don't do that, sweetheart. I was pretty pathetic for a while, but I got over it. Believe it or not, Monica helped me." She stiffened when she heard the name and he turned her around to face him. "I keep telling you, she's really a good friend. You never had to worry about anything between the two of us. When we get home, you'll see," he promised. "The truth will all come out, trust me."

Maya's shoulders relaxed and she allowed him to comfort her, but she had to ask him another question. "But if it was all lies, why didn't you come after me? You had to know where I was, Julian."

He tipped her chin up so he could look her directly in the eyes. "Pride, for one thing. I was tired of defending myself for something I hadn't done and if you had that little trust in me, I wasn't going to beg you," he said softly. "The other reason was fear, pure and simple. I didn't want to see the look in your eyes when you told me you didn't love me anymore. I couldn't have taken it, Maya—it would have killed me for sure."

He pulled her closer to him and held her tenderly. "I wish I had come after you. I'm so sorry I wasn't with you when your father died. I should have known about it. Maya, you shouldn't have had to deal with all of that. You should have had your husband with you. I know how close you were to your dad and I'm really sorry he's gone."

Maya expelled a long shaky breath into his shoulder. "Julian, please stop apologizing for that. That's the fourth time you've told me how sorry you are and I believe you, honey, I really do. Corey and I are okay, we really are. Mom is happy in her high-rise in Atlantic City. She lives very well because Daddy knew how to invest his money. She and I aren't any closer than we ever were, but I've been very lucky. I have the most beautiful little girl in the whole wide world and I have you to thank for her. Every time I look at her I remember how much you loved me, once upon a time," she said softly.

"What do you mean, 'once'?" he replied as his lips began to close on hers.

They were about to kiss when Corey came home and interrupted the magic moment. They really hadn't had any time alone since then, what with packing and traveling; now they were all in New Orleans and it was almost time for what Julian called "the moment of truth." Maya wished he wouldn't use that phrase because it sounded so melodramatic. But if it was going to put an end to all the misunderstandings and lies that had destroyed their lives she was all for it. That didn't

mean she was ready for it, though. Julian had gone to
the office to take care of some business, and he would
be back soon so that they could confront the culprit
together. Maya was a mass of nerves. She wasn't ready
to handle this, but Julian insisted it had to be done and
the sooner the better. She needed to talk to someone and
only one person would do. *Ruth.*

Mac was at his office and Ruth and Corey were in the
solarium looking at bridal books. Ruth wasn't sure how
big a wedding she and Mac wanted to have, but she liked
looking at the different ideas presented in the books.
When Maya went to find her, she and Corey were
drinking lemonade and deciding which dresses they
liked best. Ruth looked up with a big smile for Maya and
invited her to sit down. She accepted, sitting down close
to the older woman and opening her arms wide for
Corey, who never missed an opportunity for a hug. It
was about time for lunch and Mac had called earlier to
say he was bringing it home and for them not to lift a
finger. Maya held Corey on her lap and listened to her
talk about being a flower girl. Paris had asked the child
to be in her upcoming wedding and Corey was so
pleased that it was—after her father, her grandfather and
Bojangles the cat—her main topic of conversation.
Maya really wanted to talk to Ruth, but not where Corey
could hear. Luckily Mac came in the side entrance and
Corey ran off to greet him, leaving the two women
alone.

Ruth reached over and took Maya's hand, which was
ice-cold. "You're nervous, aren't you?"

Maya nodded vigorously. "I really am. So much has

happened so fast, you know? Just a few weeks ago I knew who I was and what I was doing. I was a divorced single mother about to complete her residency and go into practice at a pediatric clinic not too far from the house. My daughter was healthy and thriving and everything was safe and secure. I knew that one day I'd have to contact her father and let the two of them meet, if that's what he wanted, but all of this—" she waved her free hand vaguely "—this was just not in the plan.

"I wasn't expecting all this, Ruth. I thought I had all the answers and I'd done the best things I could do given the circumstances. But hearing Julian's side of the story…I never thought, I mean I never considered the fact that someone was lying to me."

Ruth squeezed her hand gently. "It's understandable, sweetie. If someone you trust and admire, someone you care for tells you some very credible sounding lies, why wouldn't you believe them? And you were much younger at the time, too. Don't be so hard on yourself."

Maya tried to smile and failed miserably. "When my parents met Julian after we eloped, my father was very pleased with my choice. He told me that Julian really loved me, he could see it in the way he looked at me, the way he talked to me and about me, and he said it was obvious that this was the right man for me. He said that Julian would love me and take care of me forever. My daddy was happy for us, he really was.

"My mother wasn't though. She pulled me to one side and told me that I had ruined my life. She said I had no chance of holding onto a man like Julian and I needed to get ready for a lifetime of heartache just like she'd had. She told me my father had been cheating on her for years with anything in a skirt and that I was due for more of the same. I remember her very words: 'All God gave you was a brain. You don't have the looks or the personality to keep a man interested in you. You should have never gotten married because all you're going to get is pain.' Can you imagine a mother saying that? And I found out later it was a lie, the part about Daddy cheating on her.

"When he was in the very last stages we talked a lot and he told me how Mother used to accuse him of cheating. He said he never had, but she seemed to want to believe it. He told me that if I ever had another chance to get back with Julian I should grab it and run because the love we had was worth keeping." She looked lost for a moment and then she looked resolute.

"Ruth, I swear I have no idea what to do next. I just don't know. I can't separate Corey and her daddy. That would be cruel and unusual, not to mention impossible. But what do I do? How do I deal with the fact that I'm still legally married to Julian? What am I supposed to do, just leave everything I've built in Chicago behind and start over here?"

She was pleasantly surprised when Ruth laughed softly. "Join the club, sweetie. That's just what I'm doing, remember? It wasn't an easy decision, but…oh, let me stop lying. I love being with my Julian more than anything Chicago has to offer so I'm very happy to be moving here. But let's not jump the gun. My best advice to you is to take it one day at a time. First, you and Julian have to do your thing this afternoon. Concentrate on that, Maya, think about getting to the heart of the wound between you and Julian. And once that's over you can concentrate on tonight."

Maya made a face. She'd forgotten, or tried to forget that Julian's brothers were coming over that evening. They wanted to meet their niece and they were going to do the cooking. "Ruth, I don't know which I fear most, to be honest with you. I'm dreading this afternoon, but I know I'm not ready for tonight. What are they going to think about this mess? They probably all hate me and I can't blame them."

"One step at a time, Maya, just one. Julian won't be leaving your side, remember that."

As if he'd heard the whole conversation, Julian walked into the solarium looking like the warm, protective man she remembered. He held out his hand to her and said, "It's time, Maya. Let's get this over with."

When she put her hand into his, all she felt was comfort.

Chapter 22

Maya had no idea that she was holding Julian's hand in a death grip. Their fingers had been entwined since they left the house. She had been virtually silent on the short ride to their destination and now that they were standing at the door, she could feel the last vestiges of her courage deserting her. Until Julian let go of her hand and put his arm around her waist. He kissed her hair and the soft skin of her forehead, telling her without words that everything was going to be all right. He rang the bell and in a few moments, the door opened. He was standing in such a way that Maya couldn't be seen, which is what he wanted. The woman in the doorway beamed happily and greeted him affectionately.

"Julian, honey it's been too long! How have you been? Come on in," she said merrily.

"Hello, Aunt Charmaine. It has been a long time. You remember Maya, don't you?"

It was then that he moved so Maya could be seen all too clearly by the older woman. Her mouth dropped open in shock and her complexion turned the color of congealed rice just before she passed out cold. It was at that exact moment that Maya knew beyond a shadow of a doubt that everything Julian had told her was true.

After a period of chaos in which the woman was revived, propped up on a sofa next to her bewildered husband and Julian and Maya were seated on a settee in the living room, the truth finally came out. Julian opened his mouth to start talking, but Maya wanted the floor.

"Mrs. Montclair, you lied to me. You lied to me about the most precious thing in my life, my husband. I was young and stupid because I listened to those lies, but it was because I was a little insecure and because I trusted you," she said in a cold, level voice. "Why wouldn't I trust you? Julian and his brothers call you Aunt Charmaine. You were so nice to me when Julian and I eloped. You made me feel welcome, like part of the family. You took me shopping, you introduced me to your book club, and you treated me like I'd want an aunt to treat me. You were one of the people I felt closest to here in New Orleans. You knew I was shy and gawky and you kept telling me how pretty I was and you helped me look my best." Her voice was as cold as ice now, with real disdain creeping in.

"So when you came to me in tears and told me that your daughter Monica was having an affair with my husband, why wouldn't I believe you? Especially since I didn't go for the bait the first time."

Charmaine actually shrank into her seat when Maya stood up and walked toward her. "I didn't believe you at first, remember? I said you were wrong—there was no way Julian would ever cheat on me, not with Monica, not with anyone. But you kept it up, didn't you? You had hotel receipts, you had pictures, you had all kinds of things to back up your story and you wept bitter tears every time because you didn't want her father to know what she'd done. You do remember telling me those things, don't you? You finally got me to believe your lies and I started in on Julian," she said hotly, her eyes beginning to flash with real anger.

"I accused him, I nagged him, and I confronted him until he must have thought I was crazy. And when I couldn't stand it anymore I left town, like an idiot. What a fool I was! I'm smart enough to be a damned doctor, but I'm way too stupid to be a wife because I let you and your vicious, pointless lies destroy my marriage. Well, that's my bad, because I was a big enough sap to fall for it," she said in low, dangerous tones.

"But when I found out I was pregnant, I called you," she spat, pointing her finger in the woman's face. "I called you, because Julian's number was disconnected and I was too embarrassed to call his father or his brothers. I told you I was going to write to him and you told me not to because he and Monica were in Jamaica together. But I wrote him anyway. Too bad for you I keep copies of everything because I have copies of all the letters I sent him. And I have copies of the letters he supposedly sent to me. He's seen them, by the way, and he says he didn't write them. I have a pretty good idea who did, though. Wanna take a guess?"

By now Charmaine was weeping loudly and it was not a pretty sight. Her auburn hair, which was normally styled perfectly, was a mess from her running her hands through it. Her mascara was streaming down her face and it was mottled with red from her sniveling. Her poor husband was completely mystified by the goings-on and said so. He was the head deacon of the biggest A.M.E. church in New Orleans, as well as the owner of the biggest mortuary in the city. The Montclairs were an old and socially prominent family and the kind of thing that Maya was describing couldn't have happened, never in a million years.

Alden Montclair sprang to his wife's defense. "Now look here, it was a shame that you two young people couldn't keep your marriage together. Charmaine and I spent time in prayer over that because we thought you were going to make a go of it, we really did. But where you got the idea that my wife had anything to do with this is beyond me," he said forcefully. He was about to address Maya when the glint in her eyes convinced him it would be better to talk to Julian.

"Julian, your family and mine have been close since you first moved to New Orleans. How could you possibly believe something like that about Charmaine? She's never showed you anything but love and affection, son, and for you to believe what this woman is saying is beyond my comprehension."

Julian spoke for the first time and he left no doubt as to his loyalties. "Think twice, Uncle Alden. That woman is my wife and I won't tolerate her being disrespected by you or anyone else."

"I'd take his advice if I were you." All heads turned

towards the new voice in the room. There in the doorway stood the center of the controversy, Monica Montclair. "It just so happens that Maya is telling the truth. And more importantly, I know why you did it, Mother."

Monica was tall, slender and very attractive, wearing the kind of sleek designer outfit that Maya had always envied. She was staring at her mother with a look of angry disdain and her mother looked back with absolute horror on her face. She attempted to faint again, but Monica dared her to try it.

"Cut it out, Mother. You should be ashamed of yourself for what you did to Julian and Maya. And if you don't cut out the histrionics, I'll go to church on Sunday morning and tell the whole church what you did and why."

Charmaine stifled a theatrical moan when she saw the glint in her daughter's eye. "I was just trying to protect you, Monica. I wanted you to have a normal life and I thought you could do that with Julian. You always said he was the only man you'd ever marry, so I thought if I could get Maya to go away, you could be with him and…and…"

"And I wouldn't be gay anymore. Well, Mother, here's the news flash: The fact is I'm a lesbian. The only reason I used to say I'd marry Julian is because he's always known that I'm gay and he accepts me just the way I am. I knew I was an embarrassment to you, but I had no idea how far you'd go to 'cure' me. You destroyed their marriage, Mother, just so you could save face. I just hope they have the grace to forgive you someday for what you did. I'm not sure that I can," she said with a steely edge to her voice.

Her father had taken his arm from around his wife and drawn away from her, staring as though he'd never seen the woman beside him before. "Charmaine, we have a lot of talking to do. But before we can do that you need to beg their pardon, no, their forgiveness for what you did." He shook his head and continued to look at her like she was a stranger. "I never thought the day would come when I'd be ashamed of anything you did, but that day is here," he said sadly.

When Maya and Julian returned to his father's house, the cookout was in full swing and Corey had made slaves of all her uncles. She was sitting on Philippe's lap and Lucien was trying to get her to commit to something. "Come on, darling, who's the cutest, me or your Uncle Phil?"

Corey looked from one to the other and said with utter sincerity, "My daddy."

This made Wade, who was manning the grill, burst into laughter. "She's got you there. She's a smart little cookie, like me," he said proudly.

Maya was hesitant about stepping into the yard until Lucien spotted her. "Maya! Come here, baby, and let us look at you. It's been way too long, sister-in-law. How have you been?" He didn't wait for an answer; he just swung her up into his arms while Philippe and Wade came over to add their hugs to the melee.

She was in a mild state of shock when all the hugs and kisses were over and the Deveraux men were surrounding her with smiles on their handsome faces. She had been expecting the worst, but she'd gotten the best reception she could have possibly had. Corey tugged at her hand and roused her back to the here and now. "Mommy, come see what my uncles brought me," she said happily. "It's in the house." Maya went with her gladly; she needed time to put everything together.

As soon as the ladies went into the house, Julian's brothers converged on him. They all sat around the round wrought-iron table with the glass top and waited for an update. Wade, the most thoughtful, had something to say first. "Julian, she's a beauty. It's like she's a clone of Paris or something. And she already knew who we were," he marveled. "She knew who we were before Pop introduced us. She could even tell Phil and Lucien apart, man. Even I can't do that sometimes," he joked.

Julian waited until the conversation died down before telling his brothers what had transpired at the Montclairs. "Maya told Charmaine off for old and new and Alden got his back up until Monica showed up. She was the reason Charmaine told all those lies to Maya. It was because she wanted to break us up so Monica would marry me," he said, shaking his head.

Philippe and Lucien looked at each other before speaking as one person. "Hasn't anybody told her that Monica is a lesbian?"

Julian threw his hands up. "That was the whole point! Charmaine had always had a feeling that something 'wasn't right' about Monica and this was a last-ditch attempt to get her hitched before her 'shameful secret' was exposed. Monica used to joke that the only man she would ever marry was me, but her mother didn't know that she said that because I knew she was gay and I didn't care. And that's why when Maya came to me saying I was having an affair with Monica it was so absurd to me."

Wade muttered something truly vulgar under his breath which Julian nobly ignored. Then he asked what Maya had done when Monica walked in. "Did she freak out or anything?"

"Not at all. I think she realized once and for all that I'd been telling the truth all along when Charmaine passed out. As soon as she laid eyes on Maya she fell out like a dead woman," he said with a short laugh. "Man, Maya was on fire! I've never seen her worked up like that before. My girl has a serious temper," he said proudly.

Lucien grinned. "Yeah, we heard all about the tomatoes, bro. Corey is quite the little informant. You might want to remember that going forward," he said with a gleeful grin.

Wade, always the most practical of the brothers, asked the most practical question. "So what happens now? What's going to happen with you and Maya?"

All eyes turned to Julian, waiting for his answer, but at the moment, he didn't have one. Maya was standing in the doorway and he went to join her.

Much later that night, Ruth was snug against Mac's side as they lay in his big bed. "It's been quite a day," she murmured. She was stroking his chest, her hand brushing the thick, silky hair. She nestled into his neck and inhaled, loving the clean scent of his skin. "I love the way you smell," she murmured.

Mac turned so that his leg was curved over her,

drawing her closer. "I love you, honey. Are you sure about moving here? I told you I can move to Chicago. I can retire from the bench and set up a practice in Illinois. Or I can retire altogether—I don't plan to work forever. I don't want to uproot you and drag you off to Louisiana, away from all your friends," he said softly, moaning a little because her roaming hand had made its way to a very sensitive spot.

Ruth smiled in the darkness of the room, although she knew he couldn't see her expression. "Listen, big daddy, I've never done anything in my life I didn't want to do. I love you, love you like crazy. I love this house, I love this city, I love our sons and our daughter and I especially love our granddaughter. I'm not doing anything so spectacular in Chicago that I can't come here," she murmured as she turned into his body, rolling so that she was on top of him. Her naked body moved sensuously on his, making his growing erection harder and thicker as she opened her thighs to feel more of him.

"I can't wait until we're man and wife," she confessed. "I want to see my things mixed in with your things, I want to see my clothes hanging in the closet with yours, and I want to go to church with you on Sundays, especially since that Montclair woman had to confess her sins. I'm really looking forward to seeing her pious butt every Sunday morning," she said with a wicked chuckle. She stopped talking when Mac turned on the bedside lamp. "Why'd you do that, Julian?" She blinked and hid her face in his shoulder against the unexpected light.

"Two reasons," he told her. "One, so I could find

those damned condoms, and the other is so I can look at you. I love to look at you, honey, especially when you're wearing what you're wearing."

"I'm not wearing anything, Julian. In case you hadn't noticed, I don't have on a single stitch," she laughed.

"My point exactly. Let's make love, baby."

Ruth moved so that she was kneeling over him, kissing his neck, then his shoulders and moving down his chest. She took the condom from his hand and slid it under the pillow. "You won't need that for a while," she said softly.

Chapter 23

It was hard to say who was having the best time at Paris's wedding, but Kasey and Corey were having a ball. The reception was outdoors so Kasey was naturally in attendance, wearing a dressy collar that was made like a bow tie. He was quite proud of it, too. All afternoon he would obligingly stop and hold his head back to show it off when asked. And Corey was absolutely beside herself with joy. When they got to Atlanta she was amazed to meet all the Deveraux children and even more amazed that they were related to her. She had turned to her mother with stars in her eyes and exclaimed, "I knew I had uncles but I didn't know I had so many cousins! We have a big family now, Mommy!"

Maya was trying to avoid tears, but hearing those words from her daughter made the guilt she was feeling

rise up like a tidal wave. All the time she'd wasted
keeping Corey away from her father and her father's
family seemed selfish in the extreme now. She'd ruined
three lives because she was too cowardly and too naive
to face down the woman's lies and now she didn't know
what to do next. When she saw Julian standing up with
the rest of his brothers and cousins in the wedding, she
felt lost and melancholy, even though the sight of Corey
and all her little cousins in their beautiful dresses with
the wreaths of flowers in their hair was a joyous experience. Paris had talked to her about it, but like everyone
else, she seemed to think there was nothing about the
situation that was so unusual it couldn't be fixed.

"Maya, honey, Julian is still in love with you and
you're still in love with him, so what's the big deal?
You're still married and you have the greatest little girl
in the world and there's no reason for you not to be
together, so what's the problem?"

The problem was that Julian was acting like everything was fine with him the way it was. True, everyone
had been caught up in the wedding preparations, what
with showers and bachelor parties and bridesmaid's
parties and traveling to Atlanta, but she thought that at
some point they'd sit down and have a conversation. She
had no idea what was on his mind, but it didn't seem
like he was terribly interested in putting their marriage
back on track. But he was interested in making up for
lost time with Corey, and that was just fine with her. She
was watching the two of them on the dance floor, with
Corey standing on her father's feet as Julian danced her
around the floor. It was like watching one of those
sappily sweet camera commercials or something and it

was completely adorable. When the number was over, Corey ran off to play with her cousins and Maya had to duck her head to avoid crying in earnest.

Everything was so beautiful, the wedding had been perfect and the reception was so well-planned and executed. She wondered idly what it would have been like to have a real wedding instead of eloping the way she and Julian had. Lost in thought, she wasn't aware of Julian's presence until he touched her, putting his hand on her bare shoulder.

"Hello, *Chocolat.* You look gorgeous. You look like you should be the bride," he told her. "We should have had a big wedding, Maya. You would've looked so beautiful walking down the aisle," he said in the sexy voice that drove her crazy.

Now she really had to work to keep the tears down. "Thank you," she murmured.

Suddenly he leaned over to whisper in her ear. "Corey is going home with Malcolm and Selena, if that's okay with you. Their girls are having a slumber party with all the cousins and they're begging for Corey to come, too."

Maya was touched and said of course, it was fine with her.

"Good. Now will you come with me? Please?" Julian asked.

With wonder and hope in her eyes, Maya said she would. He took her hand and held it the rest of the evening.

After the reception began winding down, after the bouquet had been tossed and caught by Ruth and the garter by Mac, Julian made his move. He grabbed Maya by the hand and said they were getting out of there. He took her to their daughter first, so she could say good-night. Corey held up her arms for a kiss and Maya stooped down to give her a tight hug and a big kiss.

"Mommy, I love you. I'm having so much fun. I *like* having a big family," she said. "Can we stay in N'awlins forever?"

Maya's could feel her eyes tear up and she darted a look at Julian, who didn't seem to have heard the remark because he was busy getting his own hugs from his little girl. When her cousins Amariee, Jilleyin and Jasmine had come to get Corey, Julian took Maya's hand again and they headed out. They went quickly to a limousine that was waiting at the entrance to the venue where the reception was being held and in minutes they were on their way. Maya looked out the tinted window of the luxury car and asked where they were going.

"Do you trust me, Maya?" Julian asked.

"Yes, I do. Of course I do," Maya said in surprise.

"Then relax and enjoy the ride, sweetness."

Maya surprised him by taking at his word. She went into his arms willingly and eagerly, holding onto him while he made her comfortable in his lap. She put her face in the crook of his neck and nestled into him with a soft little sigh. They didn't really talk; they just held each other until they reached their destination, the Atlanta W Hotel.

As with all W hotels, check-in was quick and effi-cient. They were taken to their suite, where to Maya's shock there was an array of surprises just for her. There were two bottles of nonalcoholic passion fruit spumante chilling in a big ice bucket on a stand, a room service cart with a delicious-looking array of hors d'oeuvres, and pastries and a box of Belgian chocolates. There was also a delicate, very expensive-looking peignoir with a matching gown arranged on the bed. Maya walked around looking at everything like a child in a toy store until Julian reached for her. "Do you like this, Maya? I wanted to surprise you."

Maya's arms went around his neck and she stood on tiptoe to reach his lips. "I am surprised, Julian. Very surprised," she whispered as their lips connected. The kiss was long and tender, but the passion that had always flowed between them was still there. Julian gripped her waist and lifted her up so their faces were on the same level and her shoes slipped off her feet one at a time. He gradually lowered her to the floor with excruciating care, so slowly that she could feel his arousal and it gave her a thrill she hadn't felt since the last time she was in his arms.

"Wow," she whispered.

Julian took her by the hand and led her over to the sofa. She was about to sit down when he surprised her again by turning her around and looking at her as though he'd never seen her before. "I can't get over how pretty you look. You look like a page out of *Vogue* or *Essence* or something, Maya. So beautiful," he said reverently.

She put both hands to her cheeks, which were pleasantly warm from his compliments. Her dress was quite lovely; it was a strapless pale pink silk organza with an empire waist, and a full skirt that flirted around her knees to show off her long, shapely legs. Her shoes, before they'd slipped off in the wake of their kiss, were delicate mules in a soft pink with a tiny flower on the toe. Her hair was in a loose updo with curling tendrils that caressed her neck and face and her only jewelry was a pair of diamond studs and a thin gold chain with a perfect diamond in its center. Both of them had been a gift from Julian on their first Valentine's Day together and the sight of them against her baby-soft dark skin made him smile.

"You look very handsome, too," she told him. "There's something about a beautiful man in a tailored tuxedo that makes women melt."

"Don't do that," he said in mock-alarm. "Not unless you do it on me. Come here, baby."

He sat down on the sofa and pulled her into his lap. He looked at her with eyes made hot with desire before cupping her face and taking her mouth in a long, hot kiss. This one was slow and thorough, their tongues and lips coming alive with remembered bliss. Julian tasted Maya's sweetness and moaned with pleasure as they kissed longer and harder. They kissed for a long time, their hands caressing each other's faces, the fragrance of Maya's light perfume surrounding them and creating an intimate cocoon from which neither of them wanted to escape.

"Maya, I love you," he breathed. "I've been in love with you since the day we met and I'll love you until the day I die. The only person I could love as much as I love you is our baby and I have to tell you, Maya, I'm greedy. I want another one, baby. I want as many as you'll have because they'll all be as beautiful and incredible as you are. I'll move to Chicago if you want me to, I don't care where we live, but you have to give us another chance.

Can you do that, sweetheart? Can you give us a chance to be a family, you and Corey and me?"

He was kissing and licking her neck while he made his impassioned plea and she was giggling and moaning with pleasure while he talked. "Julian, umm, that feels so good!" she sighed. "Julian, I have a job," she said. "Ooh, do that again," she pleaded shamelessly.

"I know you have a job, baby, that's why I'll move to Chicago," he told her as he plundered her collarbone, licking down into her cleavage.

She moaned again, trembling a little when he hit a particularly sensitive spot. "No, Julian, I got a job in New Orleans. I don't want to leave Louisiana, I love it there because you and your family are there and our baby loves it there. I want us to be a family right there where it all began. We made our baby in New Orleans, what better place to raise her?"

Julian was stunned into silence by her admission, but not for long. "*Chocolat,* I want to get married again. I want us to have a real wedding this time, can we do that? I bought you a ring and everything."

Maya's eyes lit up with surprise. "I still have my plain gold band, Julian. I wear it every day," she confessed.

"Well, I always wanted to get you a beautiful engagement ring and I never got around to it. I never found anything special enough for you but now I think I have. I had this made for you," he said as he took a small box out of his pocket.

She opened it with shaking fingers and went completely still when she saw what it contained. The ring was a big oval diamond, about four carats. It was set in eighteen-carat gold and there were three smaller stones on each side of the main stone. The main stone was brilliantly faceted and had a soft pink cast, while the smaller stones were pale green and lavender. She held out her hand so Julian could put it on her and she wanted to weep with joy.

"Those are all diamonds, but they're different colors. Kind of like you, they're precious and rare and unusual. I hope you like it," he said in a low, compelling voice. "I hope you love me as much as I love you."

"I love you more than you'll ever know because you gave me our baby and you never stopped loving me. I know that now. I'm so sorry I didn't have enough faith in you."

"You were tricked, baby, you were deceived in the worst possible way. Forget it—that was our past. This is our future right here. But I have to ask you one favor," he cautioned her. "There is one thing I'd like you to do."

"Anything at all, sweetheart. What is it?"

"Take a bath with me."

They smiled ravishing smiles at each other and Maya jumped off his lap. "I'll race you to the bathroom," she called over her shoulder.

Chapter 24

The plan was for Ruth, Maya and Corey to come back to New Orleans with Mac and Julian, but the weather didn't want to cooperate. A huge tropical storm named Katrina was making its way across the Gulf of Mexico and it looked like it was headed right for Louisiana. The Deveraux men weren't taking any chances; they insisted that their women stay put in Atlanta until the weather improved. Ruth, ever-practical, didn't mind too much because she decided to go back to Chicago to start the process of packing up her beloved loft.

"I need to get started on this, Julian. I know we haven't set an exact date yet, but there's no point in waiting until the last minute. I can put my time to good use until the big, bad storm goes away."

She and Mac were in their own suite in Bennie and

Clay's guesthouse. The couple had bought the house next door to them and converted it into five separate suites for guests with a large central kitchen, great room and home theater. They loved to entertain and since they both came from big families, there were usually guests around, especially for an event like Paris's wedding. Ruth was sitting on the long sofa in the living area of the suite and Mac was stretched out with his head in her lap. "Fine, honey. I think it's a good idea to get started on the packing. I'll come up and help you when I can. But don't take this storm lightly, baby. Tropical storms pick up energy when they're over open water and by the time they hit land they become hurricanes. This one could be a category three or four and they're no joke, believe me."

"I always do, darling." Ruth was massaging Mac's temples and just enjoying the feel of him and the sight of him in her lap. He was so darned good-looking and so darned sweet Ruth still wasn't sure she deserved him. Before she could stop herself she'd told him those very words, which caused him to open his eyes and give her a stern look.

"How many times do I have to tell you, I'm the lucky one in this partnership, honey. And by the way, I want us married before too much longer. How about we just elope in a month or so? Do you want a big wedding?"

"Nope, I just want you. I love you, Julian, and all I want is to be with you."

A statement that sweet couldn't go unrewarded and a couple of hours later, she was still naked and tingling from his reaction. "Okay. As soon as that storm is over, we're eloping, Julian. We can go to

Hawaii and get married there, then come home and have a big party."

He agreed, rubbing his big hand in slow circles on her bared behind. "And a long honeymoon, just the two of us."

Corey didn't mind staying in Atlanta because she had lots of cousins with whom to play. She was also enthusiastic about the idea of all of them living together in N'awlins. But she did have one request as far as any future babies were concerned. "I want two," she said, holding up two fingers. "Two just alike, like Malcolm and Marty and Bella and Kate and all those other twos. Can we have two, please?"

Julian and Maya had burst out laughing, which died away when they realized there was a good possibility that they could have twins. Multiple births were quite usual in the Deveraux family. "Well, we'll do our best, sugar baby. We'll just have to work extra hard at it, won't we?" He gave his beloved a wicked grin, which she was reluctant to return.

When Corey scampered off to play with Bella and Kate, Maya confessed that she didn't want to stay in Atlanta. "I want to go home with you," she said firmly. "I have a ton of things to do before I go back to Chicago to get the place packed up, get our things shipped and get the place up for sale. I don't want to be away from you that long and I don't want to be here twiddling my thumbs. My new job doesn't start for a month and I want to…" Her voice trailed away and she looked away from him in frustration.

"You want to stay busy," he supplied. "I understand," he said soothingly.

"I want to be with you, Julian. For some reason the idea of being away from you even for a couple of days is bothering me. I just have a bad feeling or something. We've been apart for so long it's like staying apart is a bad omen. I love you, Julian, and I want to spend as much time with you as I can. I don't want to miss you again, it hurt too badly the last time," she confessed.

Julian enfolded her in his arms and held her tightly. "Let's go make love, baby. Let's go make some memories to tide you over until you're back home in my arms."

Maya smiled at her man and agreed that it sounded like a perfect plan to her. "In fact," she whispered, "I may or may not have on underwear because I was hoping you'd suggest this."

Julian grabbed her by the hand and they took off for the guesthouse, sprinting along as if they were in a track meet. In a very few minutes he was delighted to find that she really wasn't wearing any panties. She didn't have time to take off the wide-legged shorts she was wearing, he just unzipped them and before she knew what he was about to do he lifted her up with one strong arm while he unzipped his own shorts. She wrapped her legs around his waist and they made hot, energetic love right there against the door. He pumped into her over and over, while she dug her fingers into his shoulder and cried out his name. They came together in a shattering release that went on for so long she almost passed out, but Julian wasn't having it. He continued to move inside her, loving the primal moans that came from deep in her throat.

He walked them to the bedroom, stopping every few feet when the friction brought them yet another climax. When they finally reached the bed, they feverishly stripped off the rest of their clothes and began all over again, indulging in every erotic fantasy they'd nurtured during their long years apart. After a long while, when they finally came up for air, Julian looked down at Maya and smiled.

"If we keep this up, we should be able to give Corey that set of twins with no problem at all."

Maya gave him a sleepy and sexy smile in return. "I never doubted you for a minute."

It was the very end of August, the 28th, to be exact, and Ruth was hard at work deciding what she would take to New Orleans and what she would donate to charity. Capiz, Kimmi and Sylvia were helping her and the result was more like a party than a work detail. Capiz was urging her to have a sale and Kimmi was angling for freebies.

"Come on now, Ruth. I know you're not gonna go off to the swamps and not leave me a treasured memento of our friendship," she whined. "I'm like the daughter you never wanted and you're gonna leave me empty-handed?"

Ruth laughed at the hurt expression on Kimmi's face. "I think there're two big jars of Vaseline in the hall closet, how about them?"

Kimmi looked outraged and Ruth laughed even harder. "Sweetie, I promise you I'll be leaving you with plenty of stuff. But you need to quit calling my new home a swamp. Louisiana is a beautiful place, especially New Orleans. It has a unique charm that's different from anyplace you've ever been. It's mesmerizing, it really is. If you behave yourself you can come visit me whenever you like, you'll love it down there."

Now it was Capiz's turn to laugh. "You sound like a flyer from the board of tourism or something. But you're right, I've been to N'awlins several times and every time I found something else to love about the city. However, I personally think it's your Julian who's all uniquely charming and mesmerizing, what do you think, Kimmi?"

Just then, Sylvia's voice was heard. She was in the living room watching The Weather Channel while the other women were in the bedroom and she sounded odd. "Ruth, get in here, you need to see this. That storm is worse than anybody expected."

It was late in Atlanta, too late for Maya to be awake, but she'd gotten to be obsessed with the coverage of the tropical storm that was now named Hurricane Katrina. It was approaching Louisiana with the fury of a runaway train and it was bound for New Orleans. When the family and friends who'd been staying with Bennie and Clay left after the wedding, Maya and Corey moved to the main house. It just seemed silly for the two of them to occupy the huge guesthouse all alone when they could be in the main house with everyone else. Right now, Maya was thrilled with the arrangement because she needed the company. She needed to be around other people in the worst way because the fears she had regarding Julian's safety were almost overwhelming her. She was in the family room staring at the television, but late as it was, she had company, of sorts. Patrick, the Deveraux's golden retriever, was lying at her feet, Kasey, who was visiting while Paris was on her honeymoon, was on her lap and Della, the family cat, was curled up on her shoulder. She wasn't alone, but it felt like she was.

Bennie Deveraux came downstairs and turned on the kitchen lights, making the animals run to see if there was going to be a snack of some kind offered to them. Bennie didn't often feed them between meals, but they lived in hope, especially Patrick. She soon joined Maya, offering her a mug of chamomile tea with vanilla and honey added.

"Here, sweetie, I know you're frazzled and this might help," she said sympathetically as she sat down next to her.

Maya thanked her, glancing at her tummy. "How many months are you?"

Bennie beamed. "Just two. You can't even see the bump yet, but I know it's there. People must think Clay and I are crazy for having another one, but we've agreed this one will be our last. Six children are enough for anyone."

"Six or seven. You might have twins again," Maya teased her. Bennie just laughed and said the more the merrier.

"Corey is quite taken with all the twins in the family. She's put in an order for a set of her own."

Bennie put her hand on Maya's arm. "This is the first time I've had a chance to tell you how happy I am that you and Julian are together again. You were such a lovely couple and this is the first time I've seen Julian really happy since you two were separated. You belong together, sweetie, and we're so happy to have you back in the family. And Corey! What a little treasure she is. You did a beautiful job of raising her, Maya, she's just adorable."

"Sometimes I think we raised each other. She's so smart it's almost scary sometimes. She's in love with her daddy and her grandpa. And her uncles and her cousins and her grandma Ruth. You know she started calling Ruth *grandma* the first day she met her," she told Bennie. "I know she's your aunt, but I have to tell you she's closer to me than my own mother. She feels me more, she understands me. I have a feeling we're going to be very close, I really do."

"That's because Aunt Ruth is a very special woman and because she loves you. I'm so glad she and the judge are getting married. They both deserve all the happiness in the world."

Another special report came across the screen that was already broadcasting hurricane news. Both women watched transfixed by what they were seeing and hearing. Maya tried calling Julian but the call wouldn't go through due to the weather. She tried his cell, his house phone and then she tried his father's cell and house phone, all with the same results. She turned to Bennie, her eyes full of fear. "I can't reach them, Bennie. I'm scared, I really am. This is going to be worse than anybody imagined and I don't think anyone is prepared for it."

In New Orleans, the Deveraux men were gathered in Mac's kitchen. The storm was raging but the worst was yet to come. They were well-equipped with a generator and bottled water and other necessities, but it didn't lessen their concern for their fellow residents. They were very lucky because they all lived in the higher areas of town, but there was going to be flooding in some other areas. New Orleans lay below sea level. It was bowl-shaped; to be more accurate, the communities were a series of shallow bowls connected by and surrounded by water. Levees were the only thing that kept Lake Pontchartrain and the other lakes out of the city. In a storm like this one, flooding was inevitable and something the city was used to. But this had all the earmarks of being something else, something capable of destruction on a level no one could imagine.

By the morning of August 29th at approximately 6:10 a.m., Katrina reached land and the destruction began. The waters had started flowing into the city and they wouldn't stop for three days. When the surge levels were finally reached, the water continued to flow into the city until the grotesquely swollen Lake Pontchartrain waters reached the same level as the flood waters that had overtaken the city. Only then was its hunger appeased and it stopped, hovering over the drowned areas like a lion crouching over its prey.

Chapter 25

For the first few days after the disaster, chaos ruled the Crescent City, as New Orleans was also known. No one could have anticipated that much water, that fast. Everyone was braced against the hurricane, but Katrina wasn't the real culprit. It was the many breaches in the levee system that allowed the water to rush in and fill the city, leaving a desolate, flooded ruin where magnolias had bloomed and the hospitality was second to none in the world. Everyone tried to fight panic and despair as survival became the main motivation for life.

Mac was lucky, as were his sons. They all lived in the Garden District, one of the higher lying areas of town. They were even able to offer shelter to friends who'd lost everything. In a painful irony, the Montclairs fell into that category. Their house filled with water so fast that like many others, they had to take refuge on the roof of their home to await rescue. And in another act of supreme irony, it was Julian who ended up rescuing them. When it became apparent that only a massive effort from outside Louisiana was needed to help get the survivors to shelter, The Deveraux Group in Atlanta went into action.

They had private planes and helicopters and they had good people trained as pilots. They had hundreds of employees, many of whom volunteered to go be of service any way they could. They even had boats; Martin Deveraux had a houseboat, his twin brother had a speedboat and they had friend who practically lived on the water. Soon a small but highly skilled and motivated armada was on its way to New Orleans with supplies and clothing. It was but small comfort to Maya, who by now was about to lose her mind.

She was trying hard not to let Corey see how frightened she was, but it was a losing battle. What she wanted to do and needed to do was see Julian. She needed to see her husband, her father-in-law and brothers-in-law with her own eyes to make sure they were all well and safe. She begged Clay and Martin to take her with them, but they refused on no uncertain terms.

"Baby girl, we love you like a sister and there is no way in hell we'd take our sister into that mess. They're trying to get people out, not in. Hang in there, we'll bring him to you," Martin promised.

"But I'm a doctor," she protested. "I can be of help down there, Martin. Clay, make him listen to me! I need to be there, I can help," she pleaded.

Clay crossed his arms and looked down at her with love and compassion. "I'm sorry, baby, but this is how it has to be. If Julian brought my wife into a mess like this I'd put his body in a shallow grave and I know he'd do the same to me. Martin is right, honey, they don't want people coming in—they're trying to get people out of there. We'll bring him and the judge and the boys here, I promise you we will."

Not being able to contact Julian was driving her mad with anxiety and she was on the verge of imploding when her cell phone rang. It was Ruth, who had a cryptic message for her. "Get ready to leave. I know a guy who owes me one."

Mac and Julian were walking into the Superdome, where survivors were being housed, to see what assistance they could offer. Lucien and Philippe were doing the same thing at the Morial Convention Center and Wade was in a boat with some of his fishing buddies trying to rescue as many people from rooftops as they could. It was hard to say who was the most stunned when a National Guardsman approached them and told Mac there was a lady here who'd been looking for him. Mac and Julian followed the young man curiously and stopped dead in their tracks when they saw his Ruth dressed in fatigues and boots tending to the wounded. Julian had to rub his eyes when he saw Maya nearby in nondescript blue scrubs doing the same thing. Both men spoke at the same time, with the same slightly profane sentiments. "What the f—?"

Ruth looked up to see Mac headed her way with a look that was part shock, part anger and all love. She had just enough time to give Maya a heads-up before she was caught up in his arms where she belonged. After their kiss, which earned applause from their audience, Mac took her by the shoulders and gave her a little shake. "How in the hell did you get here?"

Ruth shrugged and tried not to look too pleased with herself. "I know a man who has a helicopter, that's all. There he is," she said and pointed to the man of the hour, Major Russell Honore, the man credited with bringing some kind of order to an impossible situation. Before Mac could start in on her, she put her hand over his mouth. "Look, darling, you have to understand that I'm in this for the long haul. I'm not the one to cower at home and wait for things to fix themselves. I told you I'd get on your nerves from time to time and this is one of those times. But Julian, I'm an RN and a retired soldier. How could I sit in safety when these people need so much help? I'd be a pretty piss-poor specimen of a woman if I did that, Besides…"

By now Mac had enough talk, he needed to hold her and kiss her again. Maya ripped off her latex gloves and looked at Julian with a sheepish smile. "What she said," she demurred. And received the same treatment her future mother-in-law was getting. Much later, when they were preparing to leave for the day, Mac told Ruth that the Montclairs were staying at the house.

"The Montclairs? That pompous deacon and his lying wife, the one that made all the trouble for Julian and Maya? Oh, good," she said with an evil grin. "I've been wanting to have a little girl talk with Charmaine Montclair and this will be a perfect opportunity."

Mac looked truly alarmed and had to step fast to

keep up with Ruth as she headed for the exit. "Honey, don't be too hard on her, they've had a real hard time. They lost their house and their business, now you aren't going to shoot her or anything, are you? You got a gun, honey?"

Maya and Julian were laughing helplessly as they followed them out of the arena. This was going to be a very interesting night.

Within the next few days everyone was back in Atlanta because New Orleans had been evacuated. Benny and Clay's main house and guest house were full of relatives and friends of the family, and so were the homes of all the other Deverauxes in Atlanta. Paris and her husband Titus were still moving into their new house, but even they had Philippe and Lucien staying with them. Mac finally told Ruth what was on his mind, and that was the fact that he felt it was a bad time to get married. "So much is up in the air right now, honey, I think we should wait. I can't bring you to New Orleans in the condition it's in now, so it's better that we postpone the marriage until…ouch!" He couldn't believe it, but Ruth had sucker punched him!

"What was that for?" he asked indignantly.

"For trying to do my thinking for me," she retorted. "We are too getting married and as soon as possible. Don't you remember the story of Ruth in the Bible? You're stuck with me, big daddy, for better or worse, for richer or poorer, in famine or in flood. I'm yours. You're mine. Get over it. Postpone my ass, you act like we're kids or something. Time's a-wastin', Julian, and we're not going to waste another second, got it?"

"Oh yeah, my darling honey girl, I got it for sure."

His arms around her and his lips on hers were all the assurance she would ever need.

Epilogue

"Are you ready, Ruth?" Sylvia looked at her friend in the mirror. They were in the guesthouse at Bennie and Clay's, preparing to go down to the pavilion that was between the two houses for the outdoor wedding that was to begin in a few minutes. Before Ruth could answer, Kimmi spoke up.

"She's ready all right. She's about to float out of here, can't you tell?" Her voice was at odds with her flippant words. There was a distinct hint of emotion that sounded suspiciously like tears. Capiz looked astounded as she watched the young woman.

"Kimmi, are you about to cry? You'd better buck up, girl, I don't think that mascara is waterproof," she teased.

The women were all gathered around Ruth, who was smiling with happiness. For an impromptu wedding, it had all the hallmarks of a traditional ceremony. Her best friends were there, thanks to the Deveraux Group corporate jet. Paris was there with Titus, and Corey was looking like a doll, dressed as her flower girl. Ruth had planned on having Paris and Corey as her only attendants, but Kimmi wasn't having it. She swore that if Ruth didn't include her in the festivities she would stand up when the minister asked if there was anyone objected to the wedding.

"I'll stand up and say you're my long-lost mother and you left me in a Jewel supermarket when I was six days old," she threatened.

Ruth had finally given in and the small intimate wedding they'd planned became a little bigger with the addition of Kimmi. Sylvia, Capiz and Cherelle all came early and helped get things set up, although Bennie's sisters-in-law had also lent their considerable talents and the result was beautiful. Paris and Kimmi were wearing simple georgette dresses in pale green, which complemented Ruth's ivory Tracy Reese gown with a pattern of delicate flowers on it. It was sleeveless, to show off her toned arms, and it dipped deep in the back to display her toned back. Her hair was in its usual chic style with the addition of a couple of small green tourmaline drops with the diamond bows that Mac had picked out on their first trip to New York. She looked composed and serene and very happy, something that everyone in the room could see.

"Grandma, you look very pretty," Corey praised.

"Thank you, sweetheart, and so do you. Your dress is just beautiful and you look like a little doll," Ruth said affectionately.

The child did look lovely; wearing a dress that picked up the colors of Ruth's dress and the lilac-colored frock Maya was wearing for her ceremony. When it became apparent that there was no way they could all get married in New Orleans due to the destruction, both couples had opted for a simple ceremony to be followed by a week-long honeymoon. When things gradually started escalating, as they often did in the Deveraux family, they decided to have a double wedding in Atlanta. Maya's attendants were Monica and her college roommate Minoo, who were wearing dresses in a darker shade of lilac than Maya's. Corey was flower girl for both weddings and she was giddy with happiness at the prospect of being in her mommy and daddy's re-marriage.

Outside, the two Julians were waiting patiently at the podium where the minister stood to unite the two couples. They were both attired in hansomely tailored suits with shirts coordinated to match their bride's dresses. Julian, Sr. looked around the pavilion and smiled.

"If I ever decide to invade another country, I want those women on my team," he laughed quietly. "I still can't believe they got all this accomplished in two weeks. Just think what they could do with more time and money," he marveled.

The pavilion was tented in white and there was an abundance of flowers in various shades of purple and green everywhere, thanks to Blossoms by Betty. There were rented chairs arranged on either side of a central aisle, and there were plenty of them because all the De-verauxes and Cochrans were in attendance. Julian, Jr. surveyed the spectacle and had to agree with this father.

"If someone told me two months ago that I'd remarry Maya, I'd have said they were nuts, If they had told me that I was a father and that New Orleans would be nearly destroyed by a flood, I wouldn't have believed that either, but the way this wedding has turned out has surpassed all of that. Remind me to never bet against a woman for any reason because they're the most incredible creatures on the planet. This is amazing, Pop."

The music began and all the conversation halted as the bridesmaids began their walk down the aisle. They were followed by Corey with her basket of flowers, sprinkling them down the white runner on which the brides would walk. Ruth came first, escorted by her oldest nephew, Andrew Cochran. Then came Maya on Clay Deveraux's arm. They were each handed over to the man who would love them without reservation for the rest of their lives, and the wedding began.

Ruth turned to her Julian and Maya turned to hers and both women had to blink hard to keep the moisture in their eyes from turning to real tears of joy. Kimmi had no such composure, her tears flowed freely and without reservation and she dabbed at them with a big linen handkerchief that Sylvia had thoughtfully provided for her.

Mac looked down at Ruth with his heart in his eyes and whispered something only she could hear. "I'll never stop thanking God for you, Ruth. I'm going to spend the rest of my life making you as happy as you make me."

Maya looked up at Julian and didn't hear the soft "ooh" that came from the family and friends as Julian reached over to dab a tear from her eye. "I love you," she whispered. "I'm so happy that we're back together, Julian."

He broke convention by taking one of her hands and putting a kiss on the back. "We're never going to be apart again, Maya. I never stopped loving you and I never will."

He was about to lean down and kiss her when a discreet cough from the minister made him pay attention.

"Well, I don't think our couple can wait any longer so I'd better get on with this. What God has joined together let no man lay usunder. I present you Mr. and Mrs. Julian Deveraux, senior and junior. You may now salute your brides," he added, although it was a moot point. Both men had already claimed their brides in long sweet kisses as a shower of confetti fell over them and four doves were released overhead. It was time for a lifetime of loving to begin.

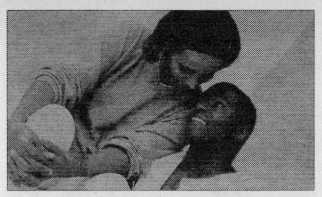

Celebrate Valentine's Day with this collection of heart-stirring stories...

Love in Bloom

"These three authors have banded together to create some excellent reading."
—*Romantic Times BOOKreviews*

FRANCINE CRAFT,
LINDA HUDSON-SMITH,
JANICE SIMS

Three beloved Arabesque authors bring romance alive in these captivating Valentine tales of first love, second chances and promises fulfilled.

Available the first week of January wherever books are sold.

ARABESQUE®

www.kimanipress.com

KPLIB0620107

To realize true love, sometimes you have to weather the storm.

Bestselling author

Melanie Schuster

Before the Storm

When Maya Simpson married Julian Deveraux,
the eldest son of the powerful Deveraux clan,
she thought they would be together forever.
But when overwhelming social pressures convinced
her of her husband's infidelity, she filed for divorce
and left—unaware that she was pregnant.

Now, four years later, they meet once again. Will their
reunion bring the family together or tear them apart?

"Schuster's superb storytelling ability is
exhibited in fine fashion."
—*Romantic Times BOOKreviews* on
UNTIL THE END OF TIME

**BEFORE THE STORM will be available the first week
of January wherever books are sold.**

KIMANI PRESS™
www.kimanipress.com   KPMS0020107

An emotional story about experiencing love
the second time around...

Sweet Memphis Crush

BRIDGET ANDERSON

Desperate to save her fourteen-year-old brother
from addiction, Jodie Dickerson moves back to
Memphis, Tennessee—just a stone's throw from her
dysfunctional family. She soon runs into sports-show
host William Duncan—the same gorgeous guy she
fell for years ago, right before he crashed a car that
killed Jodie's older brother. Can Jodie ever find
forgiveness so she and Will can realize their love?

"Anderson's wonderfully written romance is one
that readers are certain to appreciate and enjoy."
—*Booklist*

**Available the first week of January
wherever books are sold.**

ARABESQUE®

www.kimanipress.com

USA TODAY bestselling author

BRENDA JACKSON

The third title in the Forged of Steele miniseries...

Beyond Temptation

Sexy millionaire Morgan Steele will settle for nothing
less than the perfect woman. And when his arrogant
eyes settle on sultry Lena Spears, he believes he's
found her. There's only one problem—the lady in
question seems totally immune to his charm!

Only a special woman can win
the heart of a brother—
Forged of Steele

**Available the first week of January
wherever books are sold.**

KIMANI™
ROMANCE

A brand-new story of love
and drama from…

national bestselling author

MARCIA
KING-GAMBLE

All
ABOUT
ME

Big-boned beauty Chere Adams
plunges into an extreme makeover
to capture the eye of fitness fanatic
Quentin Abraham—but the more
she changes, the less he seems to
notice her. Is it possible Quentin's
more interested in the old Chere?

*Available the first week of January
wherever books are sold.*

KIMANI™
ROMANCE

KPMKG0010107

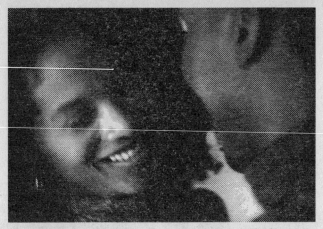
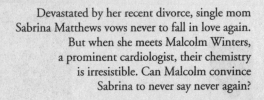